Supernatural Kid on the Block

Melissa Hosack

Whimsical Publications, LLC

Florida

Supernatural Kid on the Block is a work of fiction. Names, characters, and incidents are the products of the author's imagination and are either fictitious or are used fictitiously. Any resemblance to actual events or persons, living or dead, is entirely coincidental.

If you purchased this book without a cover, you should be aware that this book may have been stolen property and reported as "unsold and destroyed" to the publisher. In such case, neither the publisher nor the author has received payment for this "stripped book."

To purchase the authorized electronic edition of *Supernatural Kid on the Block*, visit
www.whimsicalpublications.com

Cover art by Traci Markou
Editing by Brieanna Robertson

Published in the United States by
Whimsical Publications, LLC
Florida

ISBN-13: 978-1-936167-98-2

Printed in the United States of America

At that moment, Kristie stepped into the doorway. "Cam..." Her voice trailed off and she stared at Camden in absolute horror. She spun quickly on her heels to block the sight of someone approaching behind her. "Maybe we should give him a little space. He looks really sick." As she said this, she swung the door shut behind her back, effectively hiding him from view.

Her voice faded to mumbling and Camden returned to his problems. The bathroom was on fire and he had claws, not hands. That made extinguishing the blaze difficult.

An idea popped into his head and he spun toward the shower. As he spun, there was a loud crash behind him. The contents of the bathroom counter hit the floor and scattered across the tile. His tail twitched in irritation at the inconvenient placement of toiletries.

That action took a moment to make its way into his mind. His *tail*? Camden froze, afraid to even glance over his shoulder. He didn't need to, though. He could feel it swishing through the air at his back, flicking almost as a cat's would.

He pushed that thought down, deep down. Right now, he had to worry about not burning the house down. He could freak out over his massive tail later.

Lunging forward, he latched onto the detachable shower-head and pulled it toward him. He fumbled with it, trying to clasp it between clawed hands. When he finally got a good grip, he aimed it toward the burning curtains.

Pushing the button that would release a jet of water, he gave a moan of disappointment when he realized he would first need to turn on the faucet. It had taken him this long to grab the stupid showerhead. He couldn't afford the time it would take him to twist the knob that would get the water flowing.

He closed his eyes with a groan at the solution that entered his mind. "I can't believe I'm doing this," he grumbled. Taking a deep breath, he swung his tail around. He curved the end of it around the faucet handle and twisted.

The sound of the water spraying through the showerhead invaded his ears, and his eyes flew open. It had worked, but at what cost to his fragile sanity? He'd used his tail to turn on the shower. It was just one more thing to suppress. There seemed to be more and more of that every day.

Swallowing thickly, he trained his attention on the fire.

He blasted the flames with the chilly water, frantically shaking the hose to give himself more slack.

Above the sink was a smoke detector. Even though he was doing a good job of putting out the inferno, the smoke still reached the detector. It started to screech, the sound nearly deafening him.

As the fire stuttered out completely, Camden could hear raised voices coming from the hallway. It was probably asking too much for the Taylors to ignore the alarm.

With a sigh, he reached a hand over and shut off the water. He jumped in surprise when he noticed that he did indeed have hands again. That was one good thing. Though the situation right now looked bleak.

The fire alarm had stopped ringing, but there was no hiding the singed curtains. There was also water all over the floor. He caught a glimpse of himself in the mirror and groaned. His tail had ripped out the backside of his pants and boxers. Why was his ass always hanging out recently?

He was debating climbing out the bathroom window as a means of escape when the door flew open.

The entire Taylor family stood in the hallway, and not one of them looked pleased. Kristie was biting her bottom lip in concern, but the second she saw the curtains, her hands rose to cover her mouth.

"Oh dear," Alice whispered, her eyes widening in horror. "What..." She trailed off at a loss for words.

It was Dale who finally spoke. "You were in here smoking pot, weren't you?"

Camden's eyes widened and he shook his head vehemently. "No! I...I wasn't."

"Then how the hell did you catch the curtains on fire if you weren't smoking?" Kristie's father bellowed.

Oh, Camden had been smoking all right. Just not in the sense they were thinking. There was nothing he could do to explain himself either. They'd never believe him. So he just stood there, unable to say anything in his own defense.

Dale's angry gaze flashed to Kristie. "You brought a damn pothead into our home!"

Acknowledgements

I would like to thank all of the fans of Deadly Encounters of the Supernatural Kind who encouraged me to get Camden's story finished. They were right. He needed his own tale (or should I say tail) told. I hope it was worth the wait!

I would also like to thank the wonderful people at Whimsical for allowing this sequel to happen. A special thank you goes to my family for putting up with all my long hours in front of a computer monitor while I read and double read and triple read every little line until I had it to my liking.

Thanks to Adam for helping create the character of Therius. His character is demanding his own book right now. I think I'm going to have to write that next.

A very special thank you goes to my father, Michael Brougher, for the fun artwork he did of Camden and Kristie. I love it! I hope everyone else enjoys it as well.

And for fun – Thanks to Beau for not killing Camden right away when he realized something funny was going on.

That would have been a real bummer.

Supernatural Kid On The Block

Book Two In The Supernatural Series

Artwork by Michael Brougher,
Melissa Hosack's father

Chapter 1

"Cam?" a soft, feminine voice asked into the early morning quiet. "Cammy?" A pause. "Camden?" There was another brief silence before the voice persisted. "Hello?"

Camden Harrison made a groggy sound in the back of his throat as he was pulled from a very interesting dream in which he was Godzilla, and his best friend Bradley was yelling at him for scaring Brett Favre.

"Are you awake?" the voice inquired.

He peeked one eye open to find his girlfriend, Kristie Taylor, kneeling next to him on the bed with a hopeful expression on her face.

Upon seeing his opened eye, she inched closer. "Cammy, I want waffles." Her lip was jutted out into a pout, and her eyes were downright pleading.

At the mention of food, his stomach gave a demanding rumble, and sleep was instantly forgotten. "Mmm, waffles," he mumbled.

"You'll make some then?" Kristie asked, her tone optimistic.

"There's not much to make when all I do is shove them in the toaster, but sure. Waffles sound great." With a tired grunt, he sat up and rubbed at his eyes.

"I love waffles," she gushed, rubbing her stomach and bouncing on her knees in excitement. "Love, love, love waffles. I could eat waffles, like, every day."

Camden chuckled in amusement. "So I'm taking it you like waffles?" A thought occurred to him, and he added, "I bought a container of strawberries because you eat those things like they're going out of style. If you want, I can cut some up, and you can pile them on top of your waffles, maybe sprinkle some sugar on there. That sounds—" His sentence was interrupted when Kristie's mouth was suddenly crushed to his. He made a sound of surprise as she threw herself at him, but didn't hesitate in responding.

"I love you, Camden Harrison," she mumbled against his lips.

"Because I'm making waffles?" he asked when she pulled back.

She nodded, climbing over him to straddle his lap. "Yes, because you're making me waffles. Also, because you bought strawberries for me." Pressing on his chest, she forced him to lie back down. She then leaned over and kissed him fiercely with his face trapped between her hands. "You don't treat me like some silly one-night stand."

"You sound as if you expect it."

"Old patterns and all that," she explained. Sitting back, she looked down at him. "Just because I have breast implants, that doesn't mean I'm slutty," she chastised, her comment not directed at him, but at the male population as a whole.

"I never assumed you were," Camden was quick to assure. "I'm not with you because you have breast implants. I'm with you because you know all my deep, dark secrets." He was only teasing, but the statement about him having secrets was true. Some crazy things had happened to him in the past two months. For instance, being brought back from the Ever After following his grisly death. Only a handful of people knew about that, and the woman straddling him was one of them.

"You *don't* think of me as a one-night stand, and that's one of the reasons why I like you," Kristie reasoned, interrupting his thoughts. Leaning down, she pressed her body against his and kissed him slowly. Her tongue flicked out to caress his bottom lip, causing him to groan. Suddenly, she pulled back again. "Do you even know why I have implants?"

Camden grimaced at the question. Asking his girlfriend why she thought silicone boobs were the way to go for her wasn't something he'd planned on doing. It just wasn't polite. "I figured that was your own business. You like them, and that's all that matters. I also figured that since you had them, I might as well appreciate them, too." As if to prove his point, he cupped one of the extra plump globes through her pajama top.

Kristie chuckled, nuzzling her face into his neck. "You are too much, Cammy." Though she knew she didn't have to explain herself to him, she continued with her justification. Now that the topic was out in the open, she seemed to want to illuminate him on the subject. "I used to be a gymnast. My dad made a lot of money, and that provided my mother with time to obsess over her every whim. She wanted me to be a gymnast, and she really pushed the issue. She wanted me to be the best, Olympic quality, you know? I was good, but I wasn't *that* good. She pushed me anyway. No fast food, no brownies, no waffles." She stressed the horror of her last word with a crinkle of her bunny-like nose. "I'm sure you've seen gymnasts on television. They look half-starved, and none of them even need a training bra." She rolled her eyes. "At sixteen, I rebelled. I refused to do it anymore. I was happy just to be your average cheerleader. As a gift for my seventeenth birthday, my dad bought me implants so I could look like a quote unquote real girl."

"Thank him for me," Camden said, stroking his fingers along the soft mound of flesh hidden just behind her nightie.

She laughed, sliding her hands along his bare chest. "I doubt he'd appreciate your approval." Her hands moved down to the waistband of his baggy, flannel pajama bottoms. "I do, though."

Camden's eyes nearly crossed when she slid her hand inside his pants and wrapped her fingers around him. He'd been with other women before, but none of them even held a candle to Kristie. She was in a completely different league than the average woman. She looked like a supermodel with her long legs and luscious, waist-length blonde hair. She was a cheerleader, for goodness sake. She was bendy and sexy...and way out of his league. He knew with his shaggy hair and gangly build, he wasn't the type who attracted cheerleaders.

Cheerleaders went after football players, guys with muscles. Cheerleaders liked jocks, though this cheerleader claimed she preferred vampire hunters to the athletically inclined. Lucky him.

Her hand tightened around him in an attempt to bring his attention back to what she was doing. "You're thinking too much," she warned.

Camden nodded, trying to push his doubts to the back of his mind. It had been nearly two months since he'd first hooked up with Kristie, since he'd been murdered and then resurrected. He should be getting used to the fact that his life was returning to relative normalcy...if you discounted the fact that the cheerleading captain of his University spent more nights in his bed than her own. For someone like him, that was most definitely not normal...not that he was complaining.

His lips curled into a devilish grin. "Maybe if you were wearing a little less, I wouldn't be able to think of anything else but you."

Grinning in return, Kristie removed her hand from his pants so she could pull her silk nightgown over her head. "Better?" she purred.

"Immensely. I can't even remember my own name, much less what I'd been worrying about." Though he might not be the toughest or the strongest guy on campus, every testosterone driven inch of his body took notice of Kristie in nothing but a skimpy pair of panties.

"Good," she said huskily. "I don't want you thinking too hard right now." To prove this point, she wiggled on his lap. "I want you to concentrate on some slow, good morning sex."

He groaned, unable to stop himself when she nibbled on his chin.

She giggled at his response and kissed a path to his ear. "I want you inside of me," she whispered as her teeth grazed along his earlobe. "Within the next thirty seconds."

He was happy to oblige. While she stripped out of her panties with a sexy shimmy, he frantically tugged his sweats off. He was much less refined than her with his yanking, but then again, he never would be mistaken for someone with any poise or grace in the calmest of situations.

When he flopped back into place, she was on top of him in an instant, leaping like a lioness on her prey. Before he could even prepare himself, she was guiding him into her body.

Camden shivered, sensations zipping down his spine as she caught him by surprise with his sudden entrance into her warm body.

Kristie giggled with her lips against his. She was lying flat against his chest, her arms stretched up around his head. "You're much more sensitive in the morning, aren't you?" she asked, rotating her hips forward ever so gently.

His only response was a groan. He honestly thought he might die from pleasure.

"That's answer enough," she chirped. Seemingly wanting to send him to an early, tortured grave, she began moving. She rocked on top of him in a sensual, deliberately slow tempo. Her rhythm was agonizingly unhurried, but just fast enough to get his breath coming in shallow bursts.

"I think you might drive me insane," Camden accused, "but don't stop."

With a laugh of delight, she continued with her casual pace and effectively drew him over the line of desperation. He grabbed her backside in an attempt to pull her roughly down onto him, but she resisted. She moved at her own excruciatingly slow tempo.

Camden's eyes practically rolled back in his head. He and Kristie were usually rough and fast. Her restraint and withheld vigor felt more erotic than anything he'd ever experienced in his life.

Then suddenly, she was whimpering in his ear, her breathing ragged and his name on her lips.

Camden's body quivered. He felt her spasm around him as a soft squeak escaped her lips.

That did him in. This time when she did her slow descent onto him, he held her there. He kept himself buried fully inside of her as they both climaxed. He buried his face in her neck, her hair.

They stayed that way for a long while, shivering with pleasure. Finally, Camden mumbled into her hair. "Waffles?"

She gave a groan of delight. "Mmm, waffles. I don't think there's anything better in the morning than sex followed by waffles." She climbed out of bed, reached into her overnight bag for clean undergarments, and gingerly stepped into a pair of boyshorts from Victoria's Secret.

Camden struggled less gracefully back into his pajama bottoms, blowing straggly hair out of his eyes. He studied Kristie as she slunk her silk nightgown back over her head. He loved the way she looked in the mornings with her hair all tousled from sleep.

Catching him staring, she made her way over to his side and wrapped her arms around his waist. "I like you, Cam," she confessed, kissing his chin. "You treat me good."

Camden blushed and stammered over his reply. "I...er...gug...waffles," he finally said lamely.

She didn't seem to care that he was verbally challenged. She just turned and skipped into the kitchen of his small, newly acquired off-campus apartment. She hopped up and sat on the counter, her bare feet swinging merrily in the air.

Tossing a smile in her direction, he grabbed a package of frozen waffles from his tiny freezer and broke them apart by smacking them against the countertop. Once he'd pried a few loose, he popped them into the toaster.

He was just reaching toward the stack of paper plates when his eyes caught an almost pleading look on Kristie's face. He was suddenly on guard, knowing her expression couldn't mean anything good for him.

"Cam," she wheedled, proving his hunch correct. She grabbed the drawstring of his pants and pulled him to her. "How much to do like me?" she asked, wrapping her legs around his waist.

"A ton," he responded, a little warily due to her tone. He knew that tone. With women, it was never good. They usually wanted something, something big. "You know that," he pointed out gently.

Kristie nuzzled into his neck, tickling his skin with her hair. "Enough to do me a really big favor?"

He'd been right. "Would this favor be of the sexual persuasion or perhaps entail slicing up your fruit for the waffles?" Though he asked, Camden could tell by the expression on her face it would be nothing so simple.

"No." She nibbled on his jaw in an apparent attempt to weaken his resolve. "Thanksgiving is in a couple days..."

Camden's eyebrows drew together in puzzlement, and he slowly nodded his head. "Yeah..." Thanksgiving was a mere two days away. He and Kristie had finished with their classes on Friday. They weren't due back until Monday, which still left them with a long weekend of freedom.

"My mother has been insisting I bring home the guy I've fallen head over heels for. She's eager to meet you." Though her statement was complimentary, her tone was concerned.

"You want me to go home with you for the holiday?" He was unable to keep his response from sounding astounded. Out of all the things she could have asked him, he'd expected this the least.

"I...I guess so." Catching her lackluster answer, she was quick to add, "Of course I do."

"You don't sound so sure...or happy about the idea of taking me home."

"I am happy. I want to introduce you to my family." Her voice was strained and the statement came off as the lie it was.

"You're embarrassed of me," he said dully. And why wouldn't she be? She was perfect in every way possible, and he was...well, Camden.

"No!" Kristie cried, blue eyes widening in horror. "I'm not embarrassed of you!" She wrapped her arms tightly around his neck. "I'm crazy about you! I just worry..." She trailed off with a grimace. "My parents are kind of snobby. I'm afraid they'll be mean to you. I don't want you to get the impression I'm as snooty as they are." She frowned. "I'm afraid they'll scare you off."

His heart melting, Camden leaned in and kissed her pouting lips. "You're worried about me being scared away. That's funny." His supermodel girlfriend was feeling insecure. It was cute really. "You're crazy if you think they can scare me away." He kissed her again. "Give them a call. Tell them we'll be there tomorrow."

Kristie gave a squeal of absolute delight. "Are you serious? You'll go?"

Camden bobbed his head, pleased to see the joy on her face. "I'll go."

She wrapped her tiny body around his, squeezing tightly. "You're the best!"

He chuckled, patting her head in affection. "Just keep that in mind when your parents tell you how much they hate me."

"That will only make you all the more appealing."

The waffles popped up, and Camden extracted himself from her arms with a laugh. "Good to know." Grabbing the paper plates, he tossed two waffles onto each one. He turned toward the fridge to grab her fruit and the syrup, but froze suddenly in his tracks when a wave of heat washed over him.

Kristie frowned in mild concern at his abrupt stiffness.

"You okay?"

He had no clue how to describe what was wrong with him, but there was something most decidedly wrong. It had started as a warm flush he'd brushed off as the effect Kristie had on his body, but it only continued to get worse. In the mere instant it took him to turn toward the fridge, it felt as if his body was on fire. He licked his lips in an attempt to get words past them. "I..." He trailed off as his vision swam.

"Cammy?" Real worry flickered across Kristie's face.

His green eyes lifted to hers. "I..." And then his chest felt as if it exploded. Pain raced through his body, and his vision went black.

Chapter 2

Camden awoke to three faces peering over him.

The first belonged to Kristie.

The second was his best friend, Bradley Hildebrand. She'd been like a sister to him ever since they'd been in diapers. Right now, her blue eyes were pinched with concern, and she nervously played with a lock of her mahogany-colored hair.

The third face belonged to Bradley's boyfriend, Beauregard Channing. All the problems of their recent misadventures could be linked to Beau. It wasn't exactly Beau's fault, but having a vampire boyfriend who worked as an assassin definitely complicated one's life...and the life of that person's best friend. Beau's expression was more curious than concerned. He was staring down at Camden with something close to suspicion.

"How are you feeling?" Bradley asked, her tone worried.

"Worse than when I was brought back from the dead," Camden grumbled. He struggled to sit up and was surprised to find himself in a bed rather than on his kitchen floor. "Where am I?"

Bradley went to answer, but Kristie cut her off, throwing herself dramatically to the mattress next to him. "At the hospital!" she cried with dismay. "I was so afraid you were dead again. I called nine-one-one and had them bring you an ambulance right away."

Beau frowned as if in disapproval, something Camden didn't miss.

"You're fine, though," Kristie assured. "The doctors said all your vitals are good."

Bradley shot a quick glance to Beau, who nodded. Quickly returning her gaze to her best friend, she asked, "What happened?"

Camden didn't like the look that passed between them. It was like they knew something he didn't, and they weren't going to share. It wasn't a rarity for him to be clueless about things going on around him, so he squelched down his apprehension and informed them of his horrific morning. "I felt hot, *really* hot. Then my chest started feeling weird, and then..." He trailed off, shaking his head. "Nothing. I don't remember anything after that." He paused, his eyes locking onto hers. "Why?"

"No reason," Bradley was quick to squeak. "You're my best friend. Aren't I allowed to worry about you?"

Camden couldn't shake his suspicion of her behavior, but he kept it to himself. It was probably just his misgivings about Beau's intentions rubbing off on his view of his best friend by association. Bradley was a sweetheart. Beau was the vampire who came attached with death and violence.

"Besides possible heart failure," Bradley said, interrupting his thoughts and effectively changing the topic, "what's new with you?"

Camden sent Bradley a grin of affection. The two of them were in almost all of the same classes. They saw each other for dinner at least twice a week. He'd gone two days without talking to her, and she was wondering what was new. "Besides possible heart failure? Not much. I'm going to Kristie's parents' house for Thanksgiving," he offered. "Tell your brother thanks for the invite, but I'll be otherwise engaged."

He and Bradley had spent their fair share of holidays together. Their parents were practically attached at the hips. This year the adults had decided to skip Thanksgiving and go on a cruise to the Bahamas. They'd extended the vacation to Camden and Bradley, but both declined. Bradley didn't think all the Caribbean sun would be good for Beau's vampire skin, and Camden didn't want to see his own scrawny, pale ass in a pair of swimming trunks. It would be too embarrassing. Instead, Bradley's brother Adrian, who had chosen to stay home as well, had offered to host the holiday.

"Ooh!" Bradley squealed, thankfully not feeling shunned

by his sudden change of plans. "You're meeting the parents! Sounds like you two are getting serious." She leaned back in her chair, settling in for some gossip. "Dish," she ordered. She wiggled the fingers of her right hand, and a small fireball appeared out of thin air to rest on her palm. The flames licked and danced across her skin, but they didn't hurt her. The moment Bradley had realized she was a witch and could produce all sorts of fun things on a whim, she'd never looked back. He was still trying to wrap his head around the fact that the peppy girl next door could produce flames out of mid-air.

"Bella," Beau said with soft affection, "the hospital does not allow you to smoke. I'm sure they would frown upon fireballs."

"Oops," Bradley said, making a cute, guilty expression. "I didn't think about that." With a wave of her fingers, the fire disappeared.

The look Beau shot her was one of total adoration. That was one of the main reasons Camden put up with Beau's vampire ways. Oddly, Beau seemed to truly love Bradley. The other reason was that Camden wouldn't be able to make Beau do a single thing he didn't want to even if he tried his hardest. Beau could kick his ass *without* the use of his supernatural powers. As long as he continued to make Bradley happy, Camden wouldn't worry about an imaginary fight in which he would lose terribly. Instead, he responded to Bradley's comment. "This woman cried genuine tears over my dead body." He gave Kristie's shoulder a squeeze. "How could I not get serious?"

Bradley's blue gaze shifted to Kristie. "You must be excited for Camden to finally meet your parents."

"Not really," piped the blonde, shrugging slim shoulders.

Bradley's eyes widened in surprise. "Oh," she said, obviously at a loss for words.

Deciding it would be humorous to leave Bradley in the dark, Camden didn't offer an explanation. He instead turned the conversation to her. "You're calling me serious. What about you? You've spent the last two days moving in with fang face."

Beau frowned at the jab, but Bradley continued on eagerly, the insult not even registering. "You should see how much stuff he has! And it's all so expensive. I'm afraid I'm going to break something that's worth more than my life."

"Nothing is worth more than your life, Bella," Beau said darkly.

Bradley pursed her lips in a mock kiss to her boyfriend. "Love that man," she commented. Then to Camden, she said, "Anyway, I felt totally useless, because he moved around all my furniture with his sexy super strength while I just stood there twiddling my thumbs."

"You did more than just twiddle your thumbs," Beau said, voice going husky.

"Hey! Whoa!" Camden interjected, his eyebrows drawing together in displeasure. "Remember when we first met and you were talking about Bradley's breasts to me, and I told you that she's like my sister? Remember I didn't want to talk about my sister's breasts?" On Beau's nod, he said, "I definitely don't want to hear you imply you're having sex with her."

"There was no implication," Beau said simply. "We've had sex many times."

While Camden glared at Beau, Bradley asked with a laugh, "When did you two have a conversation about my breasts?"

"Oh, way in the beginning," Camden informed her. "Back when you were still insisting you hated his guts."

Bradley turned to Beau with a little glare, but her lip was twitching with a smirk. "You had a conversation about my breasts, did you?"

"Yes. Your breasts enamored me, and I'd never even seen them outside of clothing at that point. That's how wonderful they are."

"Gag me," Camden offered.

Beau did something much worse. He continued speaking. "Don't act like you're above such conversations. I remember you talking about *her* breasts half the night," Beau said with a nod in Kristie's direction.

Her eyes widened in surprise, then flicked to Camden in confusion. "But we didn't even know each other back then."

"He knew *of* you," Beau informed her. "In a stalker-ish sort of way."

Camden felt his face flame up, but this time it wasn't possible heart failure. It was embarrassment. "Guys," he begged softly, but no one seemed to be paying him any attention.

"Really?" Kristie asked, shifting so she could see Beau

better.

"Oh yeah," Bradley was eager to reveal. "He had it pretty bad. A day didn't go by when he wasn't telling me how perfect you were." She grinned wickedly and mimicked Camden's voice. "That woman will one day bear my children."

Kristie's eyebrows rose in disbelief. "That's adorable!" She spun back to look up at Camden. "So you had the hots for me all that time?"

Camden glared at his supposed best friend. "Yeah. I suppose I did." His dirty look lowered to Kristie. "Too bad it took my death for you to notice I was alive...or had been."

Kristie waved off his grumpy comment. "Well, then I'm glad you died." Realizing how that sounded, she added, "And were brought back of course." She put a hand to her heart and sighed dramatically. "You took a bullet and had your neck viciously snapped to protect me. That was the most romantic act I've ever seen."

Camden winced, and he swore his neck started aching at the memory. "Sorry, Kris, but that's something I'm not going to be doing again. At least I hope not."

"You shouldn't have done it the first time," Bradley scolded, sounding more like his mother than his best friend.

"Speaking of which," Beau cut in with his cool, distant tone, "has anything odd been happening, aside from this morning? Are you noticing any side effects as a result of your death?"

"No. Things have been perfectly fine." Camden's eyes narrowed in suspicion. "Should I be?" His mind went back to the shared look between Bradley and Beau when he'd first woken up. They were definitely hiding something.

"Of course not," Beau was quick to assure. "You're back. Good as new. Like Bradley said earlier, we're just concerned."

"You?" Camden scoffed. "Concerned?"

Beau's lips tugged into a mocking grin. "Perhaps *concerned* was not the word choice I was going for. Curious is more accurate. Seeing as how none of us have ever been dead, I wanted to collect some information on the subject."

"Never been dead? You *are* dead," Camden reminded him.

"Undead," Beau corrected. "There's a big difference." He leaned back in his chair and casually crossed a foot over his knee. "So...no headaches? Nausea? Diarrhea? Problems performing...sexually?"

"No!" Camden cried, his face flushing beet red. "Shit. No." He shot a glance at Kristie. At least he hoped there weren't any problems. She'd never complained, but perhaps she was just sparing his feelings.

After an awkward silence, she cried. "Oh! You're all wait-ing for me." She bobbed her head in agreement to Camden's protests. "Mmm-hmm. No problems. Daily orgasms. Mucho bedroom fun."

Beau's lip curled in disgust. "Good to know."

Not sensing the vampire's sarcasm, Kristie flashed him a bright smile. "Glad I could help."

Beau slid gracefully to his feet. "On that note, I'm going home." He took Bradley's hand and helped her to her feet. "If he's getting flustered over insults to his sexual perfor-mance, he's fine."

"And I'm ready to go hide when the subject of Camden's sex life is the topic of conversation," Bradley stated. She made her way to the side of Camden's hospital bed that wasn't oc-cupied by Kristie. "Take care of yourself, Camden. I don't want to find myself standing over your dead body again."

Camden embraced her as she bent down for a hug. "Morbid thought, but point taken."

She pulled back and ruffled his messy hair. "Love you."

"I'm a loveable guy."

Bradley's palm was suddenly in his face, playfully shoving him away. "Whatever."

Camden chuckled, watching as she and Beau swept out of the room. "Whatever squared."

As soon as they were out of sight, Kristie let out a loud sigh. "You're lucky I'm not the jealous type." She slid down in the bed, curling against him and wrapping an arm around his waist.

Camden shifted so he could put his arm around her shoulder. "No need to be jealous. It's been made perfectly clear that I've had a thing for you for forever."

She chuckled, obviously amused by his embarrassment. "It's kind of nice knowing my hero had a secret crush on me. If you hadn't, I might not be alive right now." She rolled over, half draping her body across his. "That makes me very," she kissed him, "very," another kiss, "very grateful." She moved even further onto him until she was straddling his waist. She then ran her hands down his chest, nails grazing his hospital gown. "It makes me want you." Leaning over him, she pressed a kiss against his neck. "You think you're up to it? Healthwise?"

Camden gave a soft yelp when her hands slid below his waist to do a little naughty touching. "Right now?" he squeaked. "Here?"

Kristie's lips curved into a wicked grin. "Why not?"

He closed his eyes, reveling in the feel of her hand as it stroked him in places that weren't very appropriate when someone could walk in at any second. He was just on the verge of agreeing to her ludicrous idea when she gasped and sprang off of him. His eyes shot open. He expected to see a nurse, but there was no one in the room but the two of them. "Kris?" he asked in confusion.

"Bradley forgot her purse." She bent over and picked up the small handbag from the floor. "Should I call their place and leave a message for her?"

Camden groaned and leaned his head back against his pillow. "Damn." He counted to ten, silently instructing his nether region to calm down. "Nah, I'll take it to her. I need the exercise. Besides, there are probably some important things in there, like witch items and stakes. Maybe sunblock for Beau."

"Beau wears sunblock?" Kristie asked in awe.

"That was a joke." Groaning, he forced himself out of bed. He took the purse from her hands and started toward the door. "They can't have gotten far."

"Camden," Kristie said anxiously, "do you want me to go? Your legs may still be weak from..." She trailed off and bit her lip, obviously not wanting to talk about his earlier experience. "I don't want you to overdo it."

"I'll be fine." Waving off his girlfriend's warning that he should be taking it easy, he shuffled down the hallway. When he came to the turn at the corner that would take him to the elevator, he hesitated upon hearing Bradley's angered voice around the bend.

"I don't like this, Beau," she hissed. "I don't like it one bit!"

"Of course you don't like it," the vampire came back. "You think I do?"

"I'm supposed to be his best friend!" Bradley cried, her voice full of pain. "I feel like I'm spying on him."

"You *are* spying on him," Beau reminded her.

Camden's heart plummeted. Wait! *He* was her best friend. That meant Bradley was spying on *him*! Originally, he hadn't turned the corner because he didn't want to interrupt them if they were having an argument. Hearing this was much more alarming than some run-of-the-mill fight.

"This is all my fault!" Bradley wailed. "I did this to him! I'm the one to blame for making his insides catch fire."

"Bella," Beau soothed, "if you wouldn't have brought him back from the dead, he would be just that, dead. You can't blame yourself for this."

Camden desperately wanted to rush around the corner and ask what Bradley was blaming herself for, but he didn't dare.

"We just need to continue to keep an eye on things," Beau said reasonably. "Whenever this thing manifests itself, we'll take care of it."

"Take care of it?" Bradley asked, fear in her voice.

"Whenever we figure out what type of monster he's turning into, we'll deal with it accordingly."

Camden felt as if a wrecking ball had just been slammed into his stomach. "Monster?" he repeated silently. His chest tightened up, and he feared he might be having a panic attack. This is what they'd been hiding from him. When Bradley resurrected him, apparently he hadn't returned completely human. His pain earlier had been a side effect...but of what?

Bradley's panicked voice brought him back to their conversation. "You can't kill him! I don't care what he does. He's my best friend."

"And if he turns into a hell spawn and goes on a killing spree, what then?"

"I don't know," came Bradley's shaky, whispered reply.

"Just leave it in my hands, little Bella," Beau murmured, and Camden heard shuffling as Beau pulled her into a hug. "I will do what I can, and if faced with the indisputable evidence of his genetics being altered, I will deal with him accordingly. Do not fret."

Don't fret? Camden thought in horror. They were discussing his possible murder, and Beau was telling her not to fret? *He* thought he might go into cardiac arrest.

Trying to keep himself under control, he took a few deep

breaths. Panicking was not going to help. What he needed to do was get himself under control and play dumb. He had to act like nothing was wrong. He would plaster a smile on his face and keep his mouth shut. If his organs started failing, he'd smile and bear it. At least that way he'd have a chance at survival. If Beau ever decided he needed to be taken out of the picture, he would be dead nearly the instant the vampire made the decision. Beau didn't tend to second guess himself.

With that sobering thought in mind, he forced his lips to curve into a grin. He loped around the corner, gangly limbs swinging. "There you are!" he cried as if just realizing Beau and Bradley were there. "I'm glad I caught you."

Bradley jumped in surprise, her expression quickly turning to guilt. She inched away from Beau as if her subconscious wanted to put distance between her and his scheme.

Good, Camden thought. She should feel guilty. Twenty years of friendship, and she was helping to plot his death? He fought to keep those emotions off his face. "You forgot your purse," he informed her with a lopsided grin.

"Oh," Bradley said in surprise. "How careless of me."

The look she got from Beau was not pleased. "Yes," he drawled. "How careless." His calculating blue eyes slid over Camden. "You must be feeling well. You're up and out of bed already."

Camden beamed. "Yep! I feel pretty good. Totally healthy in fact. Perfect."

"Quite the recovery," Beau came back with a frown. "You bounced back quicker than what seems humanly possible. Lucky guy."

Camden blanched, realizing his desperation to appear normal came off more incriminating than helpful. "Well, I don't feel *perfect*. Perfect might not have been the most accurate word out there." He chuckled, trying to sound lighthearted, but it came across strained. "In fact, I think I need to lie back down. I'm not feeling as cured as I first thought."

"Mmm-hmm," Beau murmured, not sounding quite convinced.

Camden inched backwards, looking to escape to the safety of his room. "Well, I should get back. Need to keep my strength up."

Bradley had the decency to look genuinely concerned.

"Take care of yourself," she advised.

With a brisk nod, Camden turned and retreated. He practically raced back to his room. When he got safely inside with the door shut behind him, he leaned the front of his body against the door. With his forehead resting against the wood, he tried to convince his heart to beat at a normal rate.

Soft giggling sounded behind him. "Cammy," Kristie laughed, "you walked out of here in your hospital gown. As much as I personally love to see your bare backside, you probably shouldn't show it to everyone in the hospital."

His cheeks flamed in embarrassment. Not only had he run like a coward, he'd done it with his ass hanging out for the world to see. He spun around, gripping his gown closed behind him.

"Oh poo," Kristie griped. "I like seeing your sexy..." She trailed off, her expression becoming one of concern. "What's wrong?"

Camden grimaced. Sometimes he hated being so transparent to her. Kristie was the one person who somehow managed to see through his goofy exterior. Maybe it was because she was the only person actually paying close attention. A frown tugging at his lips, he trudged over to the bed and sank down on the corner. "Beau's going to kill me," he said, voice dull.

Her eyes widened in horror, but her expression quickly turned doubtful. "You must be mistaken."

He shook his head. "No. I'm not. I heard him and Bradley discussing it in the hallway. Apparently, when Bradley brought me back to life, she brought back an inhuman version of me or something. My chest pains seem to be a side effect of that. They think I'm going to go crazy and go on some massive killing spree." A thought occurred to him, and his green eyes widened in alarm. "It's probably not safe for you to be near me. You—"

Kristie slapped the back of his head. "I don't even want to hear that garbage," she threatened. "Even if Bradley somehow did mess things up and turn you into a biological anomaly, you aren't going to hurt me. You would never go on any killing sprees either. You're a sweet guy regardless of the fact that Beau thinks you might be a demon or something now. I trust you." Leaning over, she gave him a quick kiss. "Whatever this is...we'll deal with it, and if Beau even thinks about laying a hand on you, I'll stake him myself."

"Really?" he asked, hope in his voice.

"Really...except perhaps the staking part. Beau looks like a pretty strong guy. If he thinks about it, I will give him a stern talking to, though. Okay?"

Camden chuckled, unable to help himself. "I'm sure that will cause him to think twice." His eyes searched her face, looking for any hint of fear. "You're really okay with the fact that I might not be human anymore?"

"I am," she assured. "Besides, I think you'd look cute with horns."

He rolled his eyes, but her statement brought a smile to his face. "Good thing I've got all this hair. The horns will barely be noticeable."

"See?" Kristie asked optimistically. "I told you it wouldn't be that bad."

Laughing, Camden pulled her to sit on his lap. "You sure know how to make a guy feel good."

Chapter 3

As Kristie pulled her shiny new Jetta up her parents' driveway, Camden was in the passenger seat trying not to hyperventilate. In a mere few minutes, he would be meeting her parents. He wasn't the type of guy girls felt proud to bring home to meet Mom and Dad. He was the type of guy girls slept with when they were really drunk, the kind you had a fun romp with but would never see on a repeated basis.

"They are going to love you," Kristie said in reassurance, as if sensing his concerns. "If they don't..." She shot him a teasing grin. "I'll let you unleash your inner demon on them."

Camden grinned weakly, the expression closer to a grimace than a smile. The odds of her parents loving him were next to zero. He was always too awkward and uncertain of himself to make a good impression on adults. The only reason Bradley's parents liked him was because they'd known him since he was in diapers.

While he stewed over this, Kristie parked the car and hopped out. She bounded up the steps to a giant wraparound porch and knocked excitedly on the door.

Camden followed at a much more subdued pace, feeling as if he was a lamb being led to a slaughter. He ran his hands nervously through his messy hair, trying unsuccessfully to tame it. Too soon for his opinion, the door swung open.

A middle-aged woman stood in the doorway of the house. She had blue eyes that looked strikingly familiar to Kristie's and fluffy, chin-length blonde hair.

"Mom!" Kristie cried. She shoved her purse behind her at

Camden and threw herself into the woman's arms.

Camden stood back and let them have their reunion, clutching Kristie's purse as if it was a lifeline.

Just then, as he was holding the purse tightly to his chest, a male that he placed near their age stepped into the doorway.

From the descriptions given to him by his girlfriend, Camden assumed this was her brother. She'd said she had a brother who was a year younger than them just starting his second year of college.

Despite being older, Camden took a weary step backwards. He pinned the guy in front of him immediately as a jock. He looked as if he could bench-press a truck. The two of them were about the same height, but Kristie's brother was wider, like a linebacker. They both had blond hair, but where Camden's was dirty blond and scraggly, the other guy's was spiked and sun-bleached. His arms rippled with muscles, and his skin was nicely tanned, unlike Camden's pale complexion.

Kristie's imposing brother crossed his arms over his broad chest and eyed Camden critically. After a moment, his face filled with disdain, and he commented, "Nice purse."

Camden looked down at the pink Dolce and Gabbana bag in his arms and flushed. "Well...um..."

Kristie saved him from having to say anything. "Oakley!" she squealed. She threw herself into the arms of the blond menace and hugged him tightly.

Oakley wrapped her in a bear hug that looked almost painful, lifting her feet off the ground.

Oakley? Camden mouthed in horror. Damn. Even the dude's name was cooler than his. The name fit perfectly with the guy in front of him. Oakley and Kristie could be twins. They were both blond and looked like they belonged on a beach. It was almost irritating how perfect they were.

Kristie suddenly pulled back from her brother and grabbed Camden's arm. "Cammy, this is my mother." She turned him toward the woman who had opened the door.

"Nice to meet you, Mrs. Taylor," Camden said politely, offering a hand.

Mrs. Taylor managed to look flustered and delighted all at the same time. "Oh, call me Alice." She slid her hand into his for the most dainty handshake he'd ever experienced.

"And this is my brother, Oakley," Kristie continued, motioning toward the blond who'd attempted to crush her ribs.

Camden motioned to shake Oakley's hand, but Kristie's brother purposefully crossed his arms over his chest once again. Camden let his hand fall limply against his side, feeling the heat of embarrassment flush his face. He doubted there was anyone in the world more awkward than him.

"Mom, Oakley, this is Camden," Kristie introduced, pride on her face.

"This is the guy who fought off cult members to keep you alive?" Oakley asked skeptically.

Cult members was what the official police report said about the night he'd been killed. The general public wasn't ready to handle the news of a vampire assault. Cults seemed easier to handle.

"This is the man who took a bullet for me," Kristie agreed. She shot her brother a warning glance at his less than welcoming greeting.

Alice Taylor looked just as skeptical, but she forced a warm smile across her lips. "What a brave thing to do," she commended.

Kristie beamed up at him with pride. "I wouldn't be alive right now if it wasn't for him."

The group fell into silence as the Taylor family eyed Camden with doubt, trying to find the hero in him that Kristie saw. Their faces were full of reservation and, for Oakley, cynicism.

Kristie was the one to finally break the silence. "Where's Daddy? And Ward?" She peered around her mother into the living room.

"There's a hockey game on," Alice explained, rolling her eyes. "Your father is so glued to the television I doubt he even heard the doorbell. Ward, too." She tsked in disapproval before sliding her eyes to the car her daughter had arrived in. "Let's get you guys situated, and then we can have dinner. The game should be over by then." Her eyes snapped authoritatively to her son. "Oakley, be a dear and bring their bags in."

Oakley's eyes drifted to Camden's nearly empty hands with a sneer. "Sure. I'll get everything." With one last dirty look, he jogged off to the car, mumbling something about missing even more of the hockey game.

"Isn't he such a sweetheart?" Alice cooed.

It was Camden's turn to look skeptical. He was starting to get the notion that Oakley wasn't thrilled with his sister bringing home a boyfriend. Not that Camden could blame him. He knew he didn't fit into the picture the Taylor family made. So far, they all had supermodel good looks and perfect bodies. He resembled something closer to a wet noodle.

Seeing the near panicked look on his face, Kristie slid her arm into his. "He's just behaving like a brother," she assured him. "You act just as grouchy and protective around Bradley half the time."

He nodded, taking a deep breath to calm his nerves.

"Let me give you the tour," Kristie offered in an obvious attempt to distract him.

Her mother clapped her hands in delight. "That's an excellent idea. You can show him around while I finish dinner. I'm sure you want to show your little friend where you grew up." Pulling her daughter in for an impromptu hug, Alice whispered, "It's so good to have you home, honey." When she pulled back, she gave Camden an uncertain look. Without another word, she turned and bustled back into the house.

Camden watched her go with a sinking feeling of dread. His girlfriend's mother had just referred to him as a friend. It appeared she was trying to convince herself there wasn't anything romantic happening between him and her daughter. Apparently, he hadn't passed her initial exam. There was a tug on his hand, and he lowered his eyes to Kristie's upturned face.

"I love you," she reminded him encouragingly, her tone conveying gratitude.

He couldn't stop the grin that spread across his lips. "You just love that I'm man enough to hold your purse in front of your mother."

She grinned in absolute delight, melting the giant block of ice that seemed to be forming in his chest. "Guilty as charged."

While she was beaming up at him, and Camden was starting to feel a little more at ease, Oakley came back through with their bags. When he moved past them, his shoulder slammed roughly into Camden's. "Oops," he said evenly, his voice not holding even the slightest bit of remorse. Without another word, he continued on into the house.

Camden's eyes followed him, and he frowned. It didn't

look like he'd made a good first impression on anyone in the Taylor family.

Kristie didn't appear to notice her brother's hostile passing. She was too distracted with showing Camden around her childhood home. She once again looped her arm through his, staring up at him with excitement in her blue eyes. "I want to show you my tree house first. I spent the majority of my childhood in that thing."

Forgetting all about Oakley, Camden couldn't keep the grin off his face. "A tree house? Really? I didn't picture you as a tree climber. I pegged you as having a tea set and plastic high heels."

Kristie laughed in absolute delight. "Wait until you see this thing," she said cryptically. She tugged on his hand, pulling him in the direction of the expansive back yard. "I can't wait to see the look on your face when you get inside."

Camden chuckled as he was dragged along. "I've never seen someone so excited over a tree house before."

"That's because you've never seen one like this," she countered. Dropping his hand, she raced the remaining distance to the base of a large oak tree. There was a ladder hanging down to nearly touch the ground. Stepping gingerly onto the bottom rung, she tested its durability. When it held, she began eagerly climbing. "Come on, Cammy!" she called over her shoulder.

Shaking his head in amusement, Camden followed her up the wobbly ladder. Once his head was high enough to see into the wooden structure, his jaw dropped in awe, and he halted his climbing.

This had to be the most elaborately done tree house he'd ever seen in his life, and it had obviously been made for a girl. Pink covered almost every available surface. The floor was covered in cotton candy pink throw rugs. The frilly, lacy curtains were pink as well. There was a row of porcelain dolls on a wooden shelf against one wall. On another wall was a glass case filled with Barbie dolls. All of them wore frilly dresses and spiked high heels. Against the back wall was a pink toy box with *Kristie* written across the lid in hot pink letters. Whoever had built this house had actually wallpapered it. Pink. Of course pink. There was an air mattress draped in pink sheets and even pinker throw pillows. It was the ultimate girl's clubhouse. It was apparent that someone, probably her father judging by how close they were, was keeping it in good shape for her. There wasn't an ounce of dust or leaves to be found. Everything looked polished and perfect. Even the dolls sparkled as if protected from the outside elements.

With a laugh, Kristie reached down and tugged him to finish the rest of the climb inside. "I told you it was impressive." Once she had him standing next to her, she turned and admired the small room that had obviously been all hers growing up. "From that window, you can even see into enemy territory," she bragged in a chipper voice as she pointed toward one of the curtain-covered windows.

"Enemy territory?" Camden asked in surprise. "The Barbie clubhouse had enemies?"

Kristie bobbed her head in affirmation. "Barbie clubhouse went to war on multiple occasions." Her gaze lifted to Camden's in mock seriousness. "I will never forget the battle of the action figures."

"Battle of the action figures, huh?" he asked with a grin of amusement. He was seeing a side of his girlfriend he'd never even dreamt existed, and he was finding he liked it.

"Very serious week," she affirmed. "There was a hostage negotiation going on. The trade was the Mario Brothers for the Pink Power Ranger and Strawberry Shortcake."

"Sounds dangerous."

She grinned and bobbed her head in confirmation. "It was very dangerous. Luigi lost a leg, and Strawberry Shortcake suffered a horrific haircut. From there on out, she looked like a lesbian." She moseyed over to the window and ran a hand fondly along the sill. "At least all of the hostages made it out alive that time, which is more than can be said for Mrs. Potato Head the following week. My father was finding her mangled parts in the yard for over a month."

Camden chuckled and joined her at the window. He slid his arms around her, bracing his hands on the windowsill. "Show me this hostile territory."

Kristie nodded her head toward a Maple across the yard, which held a second tree house. "That there is boys only. I didn't have clearance to go in on a rescue extraction for Mrs. Potato Head."

Camden pressed a kiss to the top of her head. "Poor thing." A thought occurred to him, and he chuckled. "I'm in girls only territory. Should I be worried?"

Kristie spun in his arms to face him. "You are the first hostile I've ever permitted entrance." She stood on tiptoes to kiss his chin. "For you, I think I can make an exception."

With a grin, Camden lowered his lips to hers. "I'm here to negotiate a truce."

Chapter 4

Camden shifted nervously in his seat at the dining room table at the sound of approaching male voices. Everyone was gathering for dinner, which meant he was about to meet Kristie's father. Seeing how his first encounter with the members of her family he'd already met hadn't been the smoothest, he was terrified of making another bad impression.

The Taylor's lavish home was already making Camden feel inferior. He knew he was going to feel downright pathetic when Kristie's father entered the room. With him sitting down, Kristie's father would be looming over him. If he stood when Mr. Taylor entered the room, he would feel as if he was posturing. Yet, if he didn't stand, it might look disrespectful. Either way, he felt like he was destined to look like a fool. He decided it was best to just follow Kristie's lead. He would stay in his chair until she got to *her* feet.

Camden's tension eased somewhat when Kristie's father entered the room. He wasn't as imposing as Camden had pictured.

Mr. Taylor wasn't short, but he didn't reach six feet either. He was thin, his build closer to his daughter's than his burly son's. His dark hair was combed back from his forehead, and like everyone else in the family, his eyes were blue. He entered the room with a pleasant grin on his face, the first Camden had seen directed at him that wasn't forced since his arrival.

At his side was a teenage boy. The Taylor family must have had something in the drinking water, because they were breeding giants. The teen, which Camden was assuming to be Ward, looked about four or five years younger than Oakley. Camden placed him at about fifteen or sixteen. Ward appeared to be an inch or two above six feet. His hair was dark like his father's but longer. It nearly touched his shoulders. His blue eyes looked startling against all that black hair. Like his brother, his muscles bulged beneath his t-shirt. These boys had hit the gym with a serious vengeance.

"Daddy!" Kristie cried. "Ward!"

Her father gave a warm smile. "Kristie! Hey, baby girl." His eyes crinkled in a friendly manner at the corners. "Sorry I didn't see you in."

She waved him off. "The game was on. Don't even worry about it. I was getting settled in and freshening up anyway."

Ward smiled at his sister as he slid into the seat next to her at the table. "We won," he informed her.

"Of course we did," she replied with confidence. "You wouldn't be smiling if we lost. You'd be pouting like a baby." With a laugh, she nudged his arm. "I can't believe hockey takes precedence over seeing your sister," she teased. "You're lucky I was too busy showing Camden around, or I would have come in there and started a brawl."

Ward rolled his eyes with a wide grin. "Please," he snorted sarcastically. "I'm not afraid of a sissy girl."

While brother and sister bantered, Mr. Taylor's eyes slid to Camden. "You must be Camden." He held his hand out in greeting. "I'm Dale." He studied Camden for a moment before adding, "It's nice to actually get to meet you instead of just hearing stories." As Camden shook his hand, he continued, "I'm relieved to see that you're human."

Camden inhaled sharply at Dale's last comment, his breath stinging his throat. "What?" he asked apprehensively, his eyes flicking to Kristie, who was too busy teasing her brother to notice his panic, before returning to her father.

"The way Kristie talks about you, I was starting to believe you were a Greek god or something. It's nice to know you're actually one of us normal people."

Realizing Kristie's father couldn't possibly know he'd recently been resurrected from the dead, Camden gave a weak smile. "I'm definitely nowhere close to being a Greek god. They have more muscles."

"You can say that again," Oakley, in all his blond perfection, mumbled under his breath.

Alice chuckled, though it sounded forced. "What a comedian."

Camden was uncertain of whether she was referring to him or her son.

Before he could ask her to clarify, not that he actually would, Alice Taylor sprang to her feet. "Let me go grab dinner. We're having duck a L'orange for the main course alongside cognac shrimp with beurre blanc sauce." She clapped her hands together in delight. "Ooh! And for dessert I've prepared banana tarte tartin with homemade French rum sauce. It is absolutely divine."

Camden's jaw nearly hit the table. He wasn't even certain what half of that was.

"Mom's a gourmet chef," Kristie explained as Alice bustled out of the room. "She took a bunch of classes at the local university." She patted his hand comfortingly. "It's all good. Don't worry."

Camden nodded nervously. He'd recognized the words duck, shrimp, and banana, but surely the three of those things wouldn't be together, right? She wouldn't be serving a banana, duck, and shrimp meatloaf. He sure hoped not. He wasn't a big fan of meatloaf to begin with.

Alice returned with a tray resting on her palm. "I made red pepper gougers as an appetizer. Eat up," she chirped as she set them on the table. "I'll be right back with the duck."

Camden turned to Kristie with a laugh of disbelief. "Wow. That's some fancy sounding food."

"Perhaps," Oakley said with a disdainful snicker, "for a hick."

Kristie's pretty blue eyes narrowed. "If it wasn't for Mom, you wouldn't know the first thing about French cuisine." She popped one of the small appetizers into her mouth. "So don't be so prissy."

Oakley glared at Camden as if the insult had come from him.

Trying his best to avoid conflict, Camden grabbed one of the pepper bites and popped it into his mouth. As he started chewing, two things happened. Alice brought in her duck platter and placed it in front of him, and simultaneously, an unbearable pain shot up his chest.

"How do you like the appetizers?" his girlfriend's mother

asked eagerly.

The sentence was barely out of her mouth before Camden lunged to his feet. He braced one of his hands on the table. The other clamped over his mouth. He felt almost like he was going to throw up...if one could possibly throw up fire. "I think I'm going to be sick," he mumbled from between his fingers.

Kristie's eyes widened in horror, while her mother merely looked insulted.

"Bathroom?" Camden managed to gasp out. In his haste, he couldn't remember where the bathroom was, though Kristie had shown it to him earlier.

Instead of answering, Oakley just snickered, being less than helpful.

Kristie was on her feet in an instant. She grabbed ahold of his arm and began tugging him down the hallway just off the dining room.

The bathroom was the second door to the left, but to Camden it felt like an eternity before Kristie shoved him inside. The instant the door closed behind him, he collapsed to the floor with a pitiful moan.

Kristie dropped to her knees in front of him and peered into his face. "Cammy, what's wrong?"

As a spasm of pain gripped him, Camden could only clutch his chest and grimace.

"Are you actually sick, or are you dying again?" she asked, fingering the hem of her shirt in anxiety.

"Dying," Camden grunted, slumping to the side. The only thing holding him upright was the edge of the bathtub.

"Oh shit," Kristie cried. Scooting closer, she shook his arm. "Well stop!"

Camden managed to raise an incredulous eyebrow at her demand even though his vision was swimming.

Kristie patted his face, trying to keep him conscious. "Just sprout horns or something," she demanded. "Turn into a demon! Just don't die on me again." She must not have liked what she saw, because she sprang to her feet and raced to the cupboard. She fumbled around for a moment before producing a cloth.

Camden watched through bleary eyes as she ran water onto the blue rag. He doubted a damp towel was going to be of much help when his chest felt ready to explode, but he didn't have the energy to inform her of this.

Scurrying back to his side, Kristie pressed the cool rag to his forehead.

To Camden's disbelief, some of the pain receded. The cold water soaked into his skin, ebbing back the fire that burned just under the surface. The red around the edges of his vision retreated, and it was easier to breathe. "Cold," he mumbled. "Need cold."

Kristie practically lunged over him in her attempt to get to the bathtub. She turned the cold water on full force, then reached over and grabbed his hand. She shoved his arm under the flow of icy water.

At his small noise of approval, she scrambled to her feet. Her knee almost caught Camden in the face as she leaned over him to the spigot. She gathered water between her hands and brought it down to him, splashing it across his chest. "Does that help?" she asked hopefully.

On his frantic nod, she cupped her hands under the water again and repeated her actions. She continued covering him in the cold water, patting it against his skin as quickly as she could get it.

By the time the burning inferno in his chest began to retreat, they were both nearly drenched. Kristie's top was soaked through, and all of the hair below her shoulders was a darker shade due to the water.

Camden's entire outfit was a mess. It didn't look as if there was a dry spot on him, but he was no longer in pain. Grabbing her wrists, he stopped her from getting more water. "I'm okay," he wheezed. "I'm good. Thank you." He leaned his head back against the rim of the tub and took a shaky breath. "That was bad," he confessed.

Kristie let out a sigh of relief and collapsed next to him. She was half kneeling, half sitting with water from the floor soaking into the knees of her pants. "That was scary." She slung an arm on top of the rim of the tub and rested her head on her hand, staring at him.

Camden turned his head to look at her, blinking away the last effects of whatever his attack had been.

She was shivering. Whether it was from the cold or fear, he wasn't sure. Shifting on the floor, he wrapped an arm around her shoulders and pulled her close. "You saved my life. Once again."

She let out a little laugh and leaned her head against the crook of his neck. "I still think I owe you."

"Nonsense." He squeezed her closer as he gave an amused chuckle. "Think we can easily explain all the water to your parents?"

"Without explaining about your death? No." She let out a little sigh. "We'll just have to change and hope no one notices." Most of the water was on their clothing, but there was a little on the floor in front of the tub. Reaching in a cabinet, she pulled out a towel to mop it up before tossing the towel in a laundry basket.

When she was finished, Camden struggled to his feet with a groan. "Think we'll get away with it?"

As she let him help her to her feet, Kristie grimaced. "Not likely. My mother is obsessed with fashion and clothing. She was eyeing up our outfits the instant we walked through the door, looking to see what designer label we were wearing."

"Designer label?" Camden squeaked. "I don't own a single thing designer."

"Sure you do," Kristie consoled. She took his hand and crept out the door, leading up the stairs to her bedroom. "The shirt you're wearing now is Armani."

Camden screeched to a halt, and his jaw dropped open. "Did you just say this shirt is an Armani?"

"Remember when you asked for my help in finding an outfit to impress my parents?"

"Yeah," he said in disbelief.

"Well, I bought you this," she explained, tugging his hand to get him to enter her room. "I knew you'd never accept it if you knew I paid a hundred and fifty dollars for it, so I never said anything."

"A hundred and fifty dollars?" he squeaked in horror. "You spent a hundred and fifty dollars on me?"

"Close to eight hundred actually," she admitted with a guilty cringe. "The pants you have on were four hundred. I also slipped an extra shirt into your luggage for Thanksgiving dinner."

"Kristie..." he started, but she pressed a finger to his lips.

"Don't worry about it. Please. My parents have a ton of money. Daddy sends it to me in ridiculous sums. I skipped a couple aromatherapy oil massages at the spa. No big deal. You're more important to me than some silly massage."

Camden was stunned. He couldn't believe she'd spent so much money on him. "Th...thank you."

"Like I said, no big deal. I want them to like you, and if that means stooping to their snobbery, then so be it." She lifted her hand and ran it across his chest. "Besides, you look very sexy in Armani." Standing on her tiptoes, she nibbled at the underside of his jaw.

"I *feel* sexy now that I know I'm wearing Armani. I don't want to take it off."

Kristie tilted her head to the side and gave him a thoughtful look. "Perhaps we could dry it and get you back into it." Her hand went to his waist, and she began untucking his shirt from his pants. She slid both hands up his shirt and across his bare chest. "First I want to indulge myself. My parents have you staying in the family room. I won't get to sleep in the same bed as you for the next couple days." Her nails grazed his skin. "I might freeze without you. You're always so warm at night."

"That's the problem, isn't it?" Camden asked. "I'm beyond warm recently. I'm burning up."

Kristie made a small noise of desire. "I don't mind."

The noise she made distracted him from his bodily malfunctions. "I was thinking..." he said softly, running his fingers along her hips. "I want to make those lost oil massages up to you. When we get back home, I'm going to oil you up until your body is nice and slippery."

She shifted so her hip was nestled against his. "That sounds really good."

"I wouldn't doubt if such a thing ended up resulting in oral sex and some really raunchy lovemaking."

"I can hardly wait," she purred. Her mouth was just about to make its way to his when a voice in the doorway interrupted their private moment.

"You skipped out on dinner, insulted my mother, and now you're taking liberties with my sister. Unbelievable."

Both Kristie and Camden's eyes rose in horror to look at the person in the doorway.

Oakley stood with his hand on the doorknob, glowering at Camden.

"Oakley!" Kristie cried, her voice shrill with embarrassment. "This isn't what it looks like."

Oakley crossed his arms over his chest and glared daggers at Camden. "It looks like you guys are fooling around. What else could it be?"

The blonde bombshell shot her brother a pleading look. "Listen, Oak, I can't really explain, but Camden got his shirt wet. I was trying to get him to take it off so I could use the hair dryer on it. That's all."

"You couldn't blow it dry while he's still wearing it?" Oakley asked skeptically.

"Once again, I can't really explain, because it's something personal, but the heat from the blow-dryer would be bad for him. Very bad."

The color left Camden's face at the thought of having a hair dryer aimed at him. It was so much hot air it made him lightheaded at just the thought. He had to swallow before he could talk. "Let's not talk about the hair dryer," he practically whimpered.

Kristie shot him a sympathetic look before turning back to her brother. "Put simply, Camden had a near death experience, and he's still dealing with a few complications."

"Overdose?" Oakley asked in intrigue. "I could tell you were a stoner the moment I first saw you. You just looked like one."

"Oakley!" Kristie scolded. "He did not overdose!" She set her brother with an impatient look. "It has to do with the night he saved my life. By saving me, he..." She trailed off, biting her lip. "Well, it wasn't good."

"So you'd really be dead if it wasn't for bozo here?" Oakley asked.

Kristie motioned for Camden to unbutton his shirt and hand it to her. Once her instructions to him were clear, she turned back to her brother. "First off, don't call him bozo, and second, yes. The...cult members were about to kill me. They wanted to sacrifice me for whatever reason. Camden was the one who stopped them. He ended up getting injured pretty badly."

She was putting it lightly, but Camden supposed that was the best she could do. He doubted anyone in her family would believe her if she revealed he'd been shot, had his neck snapped, and was then resurrected.

Oakley turned to Camden with grudging respect. "Then I suppose I owe you a thank you. We would have been devastated if anything happened to her."

"Thanks, little bro," Kristie chirped as Camden handed over his shirt.

As Kristie entered her adjoining bathroom and plugged in her hair dryer, Oakley spun toward Camden with an almost cruel expression. "You're a lot scrawnier than her usual boyfriends. Must be a new phase." He eyed Camden's lanky upper body and shook his head with a laugh of amusement.

Camden really wished he had a shirt on. Nothing was more awkward than being half naked in front of a stranger, especially one who didn't seem to like him very much.

The hair dryer turned on, cutting Kristie off from the sounds in the room.

At this, Oakley's expression turned downright cold. "I catch you feeling up my sister again, and I will drive your face into the ground. We understood?"

Though Oakley was a year younger than him, Camden felt his stomach drop, and he took a frightened step backwards. If it came down to a fistfight between himself and Oakley, he knew whom he'd place his bet on. It wouldn't be himself. "Understood." Camden gulped.

"Good." As Oakley strode past, he patted him on the back harder than was necessary, probably leaving welts. "I'm glad we had this talk." He squeezed Camden's shoulder roughly before strolling toward the bathroom. "Kris," he called, "let me help you."

Camden winced and stared after Oakley. He was definitely going to have to watch himself around the eldest Taylor boy.

Chapter 5

After the dinner debacle, the Taylors decided to go out for dessert. No matter how emphatically Camden protested that Alice's cooking had nothing to do with him getting sick, the family had insisted they go out. They claimed they wanted to show him around the area.

Kristie told him she thought it was a wonderful idea. Her family was practically addicted to a small ice cream place that was less than five minutes away. She said the ice cream would do him good. It was cold.

This is what finally got him to cave. Keeping cool seemed to help keep his "condition" under control. He couldn't think of anything that sounded better than ice cream.

They were now standing in line waiting to order. Camden's first thought had been his usual favorite, a hot fudge sundae. Upon further analysis, that hot fudge part had him quivering in his Converse sneakers. Rethinking his choice, he decided to go with a plain dish of ice cream. Cold, simple, uncomplicated.

As Camden settled on his order, the last person in front of them received their ice cream, making it their turn in line.

Oakley ordered first. He leaned against the counter, flirting shamelessly with the girl working at the window.

Unable to help himself, Camden laughed and shook his head at Oakley's less than subtle approach. The boy had confidence. He'd give him that. Camden was about to comment on Oakley's behavior to Kristie when someone grabbed his arm. He turned to find a petite woman who looked a few years older than him, probably mid-twenties.

The woman had eyes the color of deep, rich chocolate. Her elbow length hair was a few shades darker than her eyes, falling in loose curls down her back. She was craning her neck to stare up at Camden due to her lack of height. She was lucky if she was 5'4". Her skin was darkly tanned. She looked as if she was of a Polynesian background. She was beautiful in a completely exotic way...at least she would have been if it wasn't for the scowl. "What are you doing here?" she demanded.

Camden blinked in surprise at the strange woman in front of him. "What do you mean what am I doing here?" he asked in confusion. "I'm getting ice cream." His eyes darted to Kristie, sending his girlfriend a questioning look. He was wondering if this kind of thing happened often at this place.

"It's dangerous for you to be here," the woman said with a slight accent.

"Dangerous?" Camden asked in surprise. He took a small step away from her in unease. "I think you have me mistaken for someone else."

She shook her head. "No. You're him, aren't you?" She tilted her head to the side to scrutinize him. "My name is Priya Demenaro. I support what you are doing, but don't you think coming here of all places is a bit too bold? Are you trying to taunt him into attacking first? He'll kill you just for daring to set foot in this building. Taunting him won't result in a fair fight. Stefan would rather slit your throat while you lie in bed for such an insult."

At the fearful tone of her voice, Kristie's parents turned to see what was going on.

"Listen," Camden said, holding his hands up and speaking in a calm, slow voice. "I think perhaps you're confused."

"I'm not confused!" Priya snapped. "I know who you are." She poked a manicured nail against his chest. "I understand that a battle is unavoidable, but not here. There are innocent people among us. I don't want bloodshed to happen tonight."

Camden took a step back, his eyes widening in horror. "Bloodshed? Battle?"

"Camden?" Alice asked, her tone holding more interest than concern. "What's going on? Do you know this woman?"

"No," he was quick to respond. "She thinks I'm someone I'm not."

Priya stamped a foot in agitation. "Do not play games with me!" A stony look suddenly sprang onto her face, and she crossed her arms under her chest. "Get out of my shop."

By this time, the ordering had stopped and nearly everyone was staring at them.

"What?" Camden stuttered, his face flushing in embarrassment.

"Get out," she repeated. "Get out, get out, get out!" By the end, she was screaming. She pointed a finger violently at the door. "I said get out!"

Camden stumbled backwards, holding up a hand in placation. "Okay. Okay." He took another step back. "I'll leave. Just stop yelling."

Priya's expression became suddenly tranquil. "Thank you." Closing the small distance between them, she grabbed onto his forearms. "When the time comes, I will kill for you. All you need to do is ask." Leaning forward, she kissed both of his cheeks. "You are an inspiration." With that, she turned to march away.

"I'm not leaving because *he* got himself kicked out," Oakley stated, his voice full of arrogance. "Whatever this is, it's *his* problem, not ours," he said, jabbing a thumb in Camden's direction. "I'm not leaving until I get my ice cream."

Priya had only gotten a few steps. She whipped around, setting Oakley with a glare. "You'll leave as well." Her eyes flicked to Camden. "Take your cannon fodder with you." Her eyes slid to Oakley in disgust. "Perhaps teach it some better manners." With that, she walked away, hips swaying as she entered the employee area, the rotating door swinging shut behind her.

"Cannon fodder?" Oakley cried in protest...once Priya was out of hearing range of course. "What did she mean by cannon fodder?"

Kristie jumped in, saving Camden from trying to come up with an explanation that he didn't have. "Who knows? She's obviously unbalanced. We should just get out of here and forget this whole incident."

"So no ice cream?" Ward asked, shooting Camden a look of annoyance.

Oakley was busy glaring at his sister. "Or maybe your boyfriend is a freaking terrorist who is going to get us all killed. You heard what she called me! Cannon fodder!" He pointed an accusing finger at Camden. "He can't be trusted! Guys like him do this all the time. They go to Europe for the lax drug policies and wind up in a terrorist training facility."

"Oakley," Alice chastised. "That is enough!"

"Let's just go," Kristie pleaded, sending the door Priya had disappeared through a nervous glance. "Please?"

Dale nodded his head in agreement with his daughter. "Perhaps that's for the best."

Taking Camden's hand, Kristie led the way out of the building. Under her breath, she asked, "What was that all about?"

"I have absolutely no clue," Camden whispered in return. "I've never seen that woman before in my life. Scout's honor."

Kristie sent him a devilish grin. "You're no boy scout. A boy scout wouldn't be half as dirty between the sheets." Her face grew suddenly serious. "Okay. Then she was just some crazy lady. This has nothing to do with the fact that you're a medical anomaly."

"Nothing at all," Camden agreed, but as he glanced at his girlfriend's guarded expression, he knew neither of them really believed that.

Chapter 6

Camden was lying on his bed, the pullout couch in the Taylor family room, staring at the ceiling. He couldn't sleep because he kept running the day's events through his head. He'd effectively made Kristie's family hate him. He didn't think he'd ever made a worse first impression in his life.

He groaned as he recalled the stony silence in the car after the ice cream shop debacle. "I'm a complete screw up."

"Talking to yourself?"

Camden gave a holler of surprise and jerked upright.

"Shh!" Kristie whispered from the doorway. She tiptoed across the room to the couch and slipped under the covers to lie next to him. "I was forbidden to come down here once my father was in bed for the night. I missed you, though. I figured you were worth the risk. Just be quiet. If we wake anyone up..." She shrugged. "Well, no one would be happy to discover us in bed together."

As she settled in next to him, Camden said, "Your family hates me."

She shot him a narrow-eyed look. "Oh, they do not. They understand." She slung an arm and leg across him, hugging his waist. "Besides, who cares if they do? I still like you."

"I care," Camden hissed into the near darkness, broken up only by the faint illumination from a lamp in the hallway. "They—"

A hand clapped over his mouth, silencing him. "Shh! You're going to wake someone up. Also, I didn't sneak down here to talk to you. I can talk to you all day."

"Then what did you—holy hell!" Camden gasped loudly when her hand shot down his pants and her fingers squeezed around his penis.

"This is what I planned on doing," she purred in his ear. "I came down here to fool around with you a little bit. I want you to put your big, warm hands on me." She moved to straddle him, her hands still stroking him beneath his pajama bottoms. "You use those magical fingers of yours well enough, and I'll..." She leaned in and whispered something that involved her mouth and his reproductive organ.

In one swift motion, he flipped her over and knelt between her legs.

She giggled in delight, and Camden placed a hand over her mouth. "You'll wake your parents. Shush," he warned.

Kristie pressed her lips tightly together and bobbed her head.

"Good. Silence is the key. You need to stay perfectly quiet." As he said this, he stroked a nipple through her nightie.

She squirmed and bit her lip. "That suddenly seems like it might be challenging."

Camden's expression turned mischievous. "It's nice to know I'm that good." His hand slid under her nightgown, his fingertips grazing up the inside of her left leg. As he progressed, a surprised expression leapt across his face, and he asked, "No panties?"

"Didn't figure I'd need them."

Camden groaned. His fingers slid teasingly along her, stroking with an intimate familiarity. He knew her body, and he knew what she liked.

Kristie gave a soft whimper and raised her hips when he slid a finger inside of her.

At that moment, there was a creak of the floorboards shifting as someone came down the stairs.

"Shit," Kristie hissed. Nudging Camden off of her, she rolled off the side of the bed. She scrambled underneath and lay flat on her stomach on the rug.

She was just barely out of sight when Oakley appeared in the doorway. He sent Camden a less than friendly look. "You sure made quite the first impression."

Camden laughed nervously, more worried about Oakley spotting Kristie than any insult hurled his way. "I've been told I have a tendency to do that."

Oakley's eyes narrowed. "That wasn't a compliment."

"No. I figured not."

Oakley crossed his arms over his chest and leaned against the doorframe. "Seeing as tomorrow is Thanksgiving, do you think you can keep yourself under control, at least for a couple of hours?"

Camden bobbed his head emphatically. "Yes. Of course." He would have agreed to almost anything if it got Oakley to leave the room.

"Good," Kristie's brother said. "I don't want you ruining the holiday for my mother." His hands balled into threatening fists. "You mess this up and..."

Camden could guess from past experience where this was going. "You'll drive my face into the ground?" he supplied.

Oakley grinned. "Exactly." He uncrossed his arms and edged out of the room. "I'm glad we had this talk." His eyes bore into Camden's, his expression less than friendly. "I'll see you in the morning." With that, he turned and retreated up the stairs.

He was halfway to the top when Kristie came scrambling out from under the bed. "How dare he threaten you?" Her eyes flashed with rage and she stormed toward the doorway, tiny hands balled into angry fists. "If he thinks for a second..." She went to march up the stairs after her younger brother, but Camden lunged to his feet and grabbed her around the waist just before she exposed herself to Oakley.

"Kristie," he scolded under his breath, pulling her back into the shadows of the family room. He nearly toppled to the floor when she lifted her feet off the ground in a stubborn struggle to get free. "Settle down," he pleaded.

"I'm not letting—" She gave an indignant squawk when Camden's hand clamped over her mouth, quieting her raised voice.

He held her tightly, her back pressed against his chest. He stayed silent, except for a few grunts as he struggled to keep her from hurting him in her rage to get loose. When he heard Oakley's bedroom door close and was sure no one else was within hearing range, he finally released his hand from her mouth.

Kristie craned her neck to glare at him over her shoulder, unable to do more with his arms still pinning her own down to her sides. "What the hell do you think you are doing?"

Camden arched an eyebrow in incredulity. "*Me*? What do you think *you're* doing? What exactly were you planning to do? How are you going to explain to Oakley how you heard what he said? Are you going to admit you were hiding under the couch? That will only make his issues with me worse."

His explanation took the fire out of her eyes. She settled at his logic, her shoulders visibly relaxing as her muscles eased out of their attack position. "You're right. I was only going to make things worse."

Camden's restraining grip transformed into a loose hug. "He'll come around. He's your brother. It's his job to be overprotective."

"I suppose," Kristie sighed. She spun in his arms so she could look up into his eyes. "I just don't like that he's giving you such a hard time."

"I think I can handle it," Camden said with a smirk. "Unless he tries to kick my ass, that is. Then I'm in trouble." At that comment, his expression grew suddenly serious. "Are you sure it doesn't bother you that I'm not more like a jock?"

Kristie rolled her eyes in response to such a statement. "You know," she cried, feigning enlightenment, "you're right! I do want a steroid junkie. It doesn't matter that sex with you is the best I've ever had. It also doesn't matter that you're a total sweetheart or that you sacrificed your life for mine. None of that matters. All I care about are muscles! Big, rippling muscles." She gave a derisive snort. "Come off it, Camden. You're stuck with me. You're going to have to come to terms with that."

He chuckled low in his throat. "It will be tough, but somehow I'll manage." Leaning in, he kissed the tip of her nose. "Sometimes it's just so hard to believe that you would want to be with me."

"Well believe it," she scolded. "You should be more confident in yourself. You're great." Her fingers snaked under his shirt, and she playfully grazed her nails along his chest. "I'd like to show you just how great I think you are...but we've pressed our luck enough." Standing on her tiptoes, she pressed her body to his and kissed him. "I'll see you in the morning."

Camden grazed his hand along her shoulder as she stepped out of his reach. "See you tomorrow," he agreed.

With one last sultry look over her shoulder, Kristie disappeared up the stairs.

Camden watched her leave with longing. He would love to just wrap her up in his arms and burrow under the covers, holding her until the sun came up, but that wouldn't win him points with her family. Regret hounded him, but he let her go. He had to. Just like tomorrow, he had to prove to her family that he was right for Kristie Taylor.

Chapter 7

Camden had managed to skate through the morning of Thanksgiving without incident. They'd had deli meat and potato salad for lunch. That had probably helped. All cold foods. Now they were hanging out in the living room while Kristie's parents put the finishing touches on dinner.

Oakley and Ward had brought out Rock Band, and the four of them had spent the last couple hours attempting to break high scores on the guitar. Not that Camden ever came close. He seemed to hit more sour notes than anything else.

Right now, Kristie was taking her turn. Seeing as how she was perfect in nearly every way, of course she'd caught on to the game as if she'd been playing for years. She was strumming away to Warrant's "Cherry Pie," hitting almost every note with complete ease. She was dancing with the guitar as she played, hitting the notes even though she swayed about.

Camden felt a stab of jealousy. He couldn't hit the correct notes while standing still and concentrating with all his might. It seemed unfair that a girl so good-looking should excel at video games.

As the music blared, Kristie continued to dance, her hips swaying in time to the beat. "Eat it, Ward," she taunted, wiggling her backside at her youngest brother as she hit a multiplier that skyrocketed her score.

Camden suddenly forgot about his jealousy as his hormones forced him to take notice of his girlfriend's derriere. The sexual innuendos behind the song coupled with Kristie singing along as she sashayed her tiny hips was a complete turn on. He stared transfixed, watching as she giggled and twirled in a circle.

She lifted the guitar over her head, mocking the moves of a heavy metal guitarist, and her shirt slid up to expose her stomach.

His nether region took particular interest in her uncovered flesh. Last night on the couch had been a tease that left him wanting. They hadn't gone this long without sex since they'd started dating, and he was beginning to feel antsy.

"That's not your cherry pie," a voice growled in his ear.

Camden jumped in surprise at how close Oakley was to him. He hadn't even heard him approach. At the anger in Oakley's voice, Camden gulped. "No," he agreed. "Of course not."

Oakley's eyes darkened. As he opened his mouth to say something else, Camden was saved by Alice poking her head into the room.

"Dinner will be ready in ten minutes. Go get cleaned up," she trilled.

Camden took that as an excuse to inch away from Oakley. "Well, I better get going."

To his relief, Kristie lifted the guitar strap over her head and handed it to Ward. "Let's go, Cam. Mom's serious when it comes to punctuality for dinner."

Glad for the escape, Camden followed her up the stairs, practically running Kristie over to get away from her brother.

Luckily, she didn't seem to notice. She calmly led him into her bedroom and over to the large stack of their luggage. It was more like her large stack of luggage and his duffel bag, but he'd never voice that out loud.

She'd begun riffling through one of her bags with an expression of concentration. A moment later, she produced the designer shirt she'd bought him and a pair of black slacks he would guess cost a small fortune. She tossed them to him then pulled out an outfit for herself. Without any warning, she pulled her shirt over her head and tossed it to the bed.

Camden gave a yelp at the sight of her topless form. "What are you doing?" he hissed in a panicked whisper.

One of her eyebrows arched as she shimmied out of her jeans. "Changing?"

"In front of me?" he asked in horror, clutching the clothing she'd tossed to him to his chest like a protective shield.

A puzzled expression flitted across her face. "Um...yeah." Her eyes searched his for an explanation for his odd behavior. "You've seen me naked a hundred times. Why do you all of a sudden sound like a frightened virgin?"

Had he not been so panicked, he might have taken offense to that. As it was, he was too worked up to even fully process her statement. "Your brothers will know we're changing. Together."

"So?" she asked, obviously not seeing the big deal.

"So?" Camden cried. "They already hate me. If they knew we were changing in front of each other and that I wanted to touch your magnificent breasts, they'd kill me."

Kristie chuckled in amusement at his concerns. She sidled over and slid her arms around his neck. "We can tell them you changed in the bathroom," she said with a nod to the adjoining room.

"Oh," he said with relief. "Well..."

Reaching down, she unbuttoned his slacks. With one hard yank, she dropped them to his ankles. A wicked smile on her face, she caressed him through the front of his boxers with her palm. "They'll never have any idea I did this." She slid her hand along him with familiarity for a moment before pulling her hand back. "Now get dressed."

Feeling much better and slightly amused by her bossy attitude, Camden stepped into the pants she'd given him. He was exceptionally careful, knowing she'd paid more for this outfit than he had on his entire wardrobe.

Kristie dressed herself in an expensive-looking dress. Once she had it mostly on, she turned her back to him. "Zip me up?" she requested.

Taking the zipper tab between two fingers, Camden slowly did up the dress. Once it was zipped, he leaned in and kissed the back of her neck. "You look beautiful."

She tossed him an impish grin over her shoulder. "Of course."

With a laugh at her confidence, he slipped into the shirt she'd bought him and quickly did up the buttons.

When he was finished, Kristie took his hand. "Thank you for doing this," she said in a whisper.

He smiled, lacing his fingers through hers. "I don't mind as long as it makes you happy. I just wish I wasn't coming off as such a jackass."

At his comment, Kristie's eyes widened in shock. "No one thinks you're a jackass!"

"Your brother caught me oogling you downstairs."

Kristie burst into giggles. "He probably thinks you're a jackass," she admitted. On her boyfriend's sour look, her laughter intensified. "Come on! It's funny!"

Camden couldn't help but grin in response. "Okay. Maybe a little." As they exited her room, they met Ward in the hallway. All humor drained from Camden. "I was in the bathroom," he said hastily.

Ward's face screwed up in revulsion. "Disgusting," he grumbled under his breath. Aloud to Camden, he said, "Okay."

Realizing Ward thought he was discussing a trip to the toilet, Camden waved his hands frantically in the air. "Oh! Not that! I wasn't...I mean...that's not..." He couldn't find the right thing to say, but it didn't matter. Ward rolled his eyes and trotted down the steps.

Kristie's arm was suddenly on his shoulder, causing Camden to jump. "Relax," she instructed.

He bobbed his head. "Relaxing." Trying to appear braver than he felt, he tightened his grip on her hand and marched down the stairs. They entered the dining room as a united couple, almost as if daring someone to object.

Alice's eyes lifted to them and she made a cooing noise. "Don't the two of you look adorable in your fancy clothes? You guys didn't have to get all done up for this."

"Yes we did," Kristie whispered out of the side of her mouth as her mother sashayed over.

Alice pulled her daughter into a hug. "You look beautiful, darling," she gushed. Her gaze shifted to Camden, and he saw her fingers twitch. He recognized this action immediately because his own mother would do the same thing when she was dying to straighten his messy hair. Giving up on his scraggly locks, she grudgingly asked, "Armani?"

He nodded, aiming for nonchalance, pretending as if this was something he wore often.

"Lovely," Alice said, though her tone was strained. With that, she spun on her heels. "Everyone to the table!" she chirruped. "I'll go get the turkey."

Kristie led Camden to the lavishly decorated table and they both took a seat.

Moments later, Alice appeared with the main dish.

Dale followed behind her with a bowl of mashed potatoes and a boat of gravy. He walked to the side of the table and leaned between Camden and Kristie to put the items down.

As soon as the gravy passed by his ear, Camden stiffened. Steam was rising from the dish in wisps. He watched the heat rise from each platter of food and felt suddenly dizzy. When her parents retreated to grab more dishes, Camden grabbed his girlfriend's hand under the table. "Kristie," he managed to get out between clenched teeth.

Her head whipped in his direction and her eyes widened. "Camden, no," she begged.

Closing his eyes, he tried to get a hold of himself. He breathed in slowly, assuring himself that it was only food. He hadn't had a problem with food until the past couple days. He could deal with this. Mind over matter.

Then suddenly, the heat slammed into him. He nearly slid out of his chair.

"Camden," Kristie warned under her breath.

His eyes shot open and he found her entire family staring at him.

"Something wrong?" Oakley asked almost snidely.

Camden could barely see him because his vision was swimming. It wavered like the pavement on a scorching day, shimmering like a mirage. "I..." He swallowed hard. "I..."

Kristie's hand was suddenly on his arm. "He hasn't been feeling well lately," she offered. "We actually made a trip to the hospital two days ago." She rubbed his arm sympathetically. "Food seems to make things worse."

Alice actually looked concerned. "You were in the hospital?"

Kristie bobbed her head in answer. "He was. Camden has been having some...issues. This reaction is in no way a slight to your cooking skills. I promise."

Alice's lips tightened, but she didn't comment.

Camden was beyond worrying about hurting anyone's feelings. His body felt like it was going to implode. Stories of spontaneous combustion didn't sound as funny or outlandish as they might have a week ago.

As heat raced through him, he bolted to his feet. "I have to go," he managed to strangle out. With that said, he raced toward the bathroom. Explanation be damned. He was going to fill the bathtub with ice water and plunge in, Armani pants and all.

He reached the bathroom and wrenched the door open. Before he could reach the bathtub, heat roared through him, driving him to his knees. He prayed he lost consciousness, that sweet oblivion would take him.

Instead, searing pain raced up his sternum. Camden opened his mouth to scream, but what came out wasn't sound; it was fire. Flames forced their way up his throat and scorched past his lips.

He expected to feel excruciating pain, but the fire escaping his throat seemed to alleviate it. As terrified as he was, the fire was soothing his spasms of agony and he welcomed it. It made the pain bearable. As it flowed from his mouth, it seemed to pour out his discomfort in a steady flow. When the fire slowly died out, it took the pain with it.

His relief was short-lived when he heard the back of his pants rip open. Something heavy rolled out, hitting the floor with a thud. His hand that was clutching the doorknob suddenly lost its firm grip.

His head shot up to the doorknob above him to find a claw with three curved talons gripping at the doorknob instead of a hand. It was then that he also noticed he'd set the curtains on fire.

At that moment, Kristie stepped into the doorway. "Cam..." Her voice trailed off and she stared at Camden in absolute horror. She spun quickly on her heels to block the sight of someone approaching behind her. "Maybe we should give him a little space. He looks really sick." As she said this, she swung the door shut behind her back, effectively hiding him from view.

Her voice faded to mumbling and Camden returned to his problems. The bathroom was on fire and he had claws, not hands. That made extinguishing the blaze difficult.

An idea popped into his head and he spun toward the shower. As he spun, there was a loud crash behind him. The contents of the bathroom counter hit the floor and scattered across the tile. His tail twitched in irritation at the inconvenient placement of toiletries.

That action took a moment to make its way into his mind. His *tail*? Camden froze, afraid to even glance over his shoulder. He didn't need to, though. He could feel it swishing through the air at his back, flicking almost as a cat's would.

He pushed that thought down, deep down. Right now, he had to worry about not burning the house down. He could freak out over his massive tail later.

Lunging forward, he latched onto the detachable shower-head and pulled it toward him. He fumbled with it, trying to clasp it between clawed hands. When he finally got a good grip, he aimed it toward the burning curtains.

Pushing the button that would release a jet of water, he gave a moan of disappointment when he realized he would first need to turn on the faucet. It had taken him this long to grab the stupid showerhead. He couldn't afford the time it would take him to twist the knob that would get the water flowing.

He closed his eyes with a groan at the solution that entered his mind. "I can't believe I'm doing this," he grumbled. Taking a deep breath, he swung his tail around. He curved the end of it around the faucet handle and twisted.

The sound of the water spraying through the showerhead invaded his ears, and his eyes flew open. It had worked, but at what cost to his fragile sanity? He'd used his tail to turn on the shower. It was just one more thing to suppress. There seemed to be more and more of that every day.

Swallowing thickly, he trained his attention on the fire. He blasted the flames with the chilly water, frantically shaking the hose to give himself more slack.

Above the sink was a smoke detector. Even though he was doing a good job of putting out the inferno, the smoke still reached the detector. It started to screech, the sound nearly deafening him.

As the fire stuttered out completely, Camden could hear raised voices coming from the hallway. It was probably asking too much for the Taylors to ignore the alarm.

With a sigh, he reached a hand over and shut off the water. He jumped in surprise when he noticed that he did indeed have hands again. That was one good thing. Though the situation right now looked bleak.

The fire alarm had stopped ringing, but there was no hiding the singed curtains. There was also water all over the floor. He caught a glimpse of himself in the mirror and groaned. His tail had ripped out the backside of his pants and boxers. Why was his ass always hanging out recently?

He was debating climbing out the bathroom window as a means of escape when the door flew open.

The entire Taylor family stood in the hallway, and not one of them looked pleased. Kristie was biting her bottom lip in concern, but the second she saw the curtains, her hands rose to cover her mouth.

"Oh dear," Alice whispered, her eyes widening in horror. "What..." She trailed off at a loss for words.

It was Dale who finally spoke. "You were in here smoking pot, weren't you?"

Camden's eyes widened and he shook his head vehemently. "No! I...I wasn't."

"Then how the hell did you catch the curtains on fire if you weren't smoking?" Kristie's father bellowed.

Oh, Camden had been smoking all right. Just not in the sense they were thinking. There was nothing he could do to explain himself either. They'd never believe him. So he just stood there, unable to say anything in his own defense.

Dale's angry gaze flashed to Kristie. "You brought a damn pothead into our home!"

"No! Daddy, it isn't like that!"

"I think that's exactly what it's like." Dale's eyes slid back to Camden. "And to think I was defending you to the boys." He turned his back to his daughter. "Just get him out of my sight. I've got to spend the rest of the evening figuring out how much damage he's done to our home."

That was all the encouragement Camden needed. Without a word, he marched past the Taylors. He kept his eyes on the ground, avoiding eye contact. He was nearly to the front door when he felt a hand on his arm.

"Let's go to the tree house," Kristie said quietly.

Nodding, Camden followed her across the lawn, his heart sinking further into his gut with every step. Each second that stretched on drew him further and further into depression. He stayed silent as they climbed into the tree house, and Kristie pulled the rope ladder up so no one could follow them. When she turned to face him, he spoke first, getting the jump on her. "So this is it then?" he asked despondently.

Kristie's arms, which had been crossed tensely under her chest, fell to her sides. "What do you mean?"

"I mean, this is where it ends for us. You dump me in your tree house for ruining your life, and I slink back to campus with my tail between my legs." He gave a cruel snort at that, because it very well might be a literal thing.

Her expression seemed genuinely puzzled. "Break up with you? Why would I do that?"

Camden spun to face the window, his hands clutching the sill as he stared out into the darkness. He didn't want her to see the anguish on his face. "Because you're afraid of me," he offered.

"Afraid of you?" she asked in surprise. "Camden, I'm not—"

He spun to face her, cutting her off mid-sentence. "I saw the fear on your face when you saw what I'd become."

Kristie shook her head, making a small noise of disbelief. "I was afraid because the bathroom was on fire, and I was terrified because I thought you might get hurt!" She moved forward, gripping his forearms. "I was afraid *for* you, not *of* you."

His expression softened upon hearing the honesty in her voice. "Really?" He was afraid to even hope that she wasn't appalled by what he'd become. "You're not breaking up with me because I'm a hideous monster?"

"Hideous monster?" She gasped in disbelief. "Cammy, did you not see yourself? It was amazing! You... I think you're a dragon." Her eyes sparkled with excitement. "You're a dragon, right? I don't know much about them because I never thought they were real, but that's what you looked like."

"I...I think you might be right," Camden said, amazed by her enthusiasm.

"You were absolutely gorgeous," she gushed. "The tail alone was magnificent. Add in the scales..." She shook her head with a laugh. "They were the prettiest green I've ever seen in my life. It was amazing."

In that moment, while she gushed over his dragon form, Camden realized he didn't want to be with anyone else the rest of his life. He grabbed her face between both hands and he kissed her. He kissed her filled with the knowledge that he'd never be able to survive without her.

She made a happy sound in the back of her throat and wrapped herself around him, her body molding affectionately into his.

Camden ended the kiss. He pulled back just enough so he could look down into her face. "I love you," he said softly, his voice thick with emotion.

Tears welled in Kristie's eyes and she drew in a sharp breath. "That's the first time you've ever told me."

"I never realized how...alone I would be without you."

"Well, you will never have to be alone," she assured. "I'll stick with you, no matter what you turn into."

Camden leaned down and kissed her again. "How did I ever get so lucky to hook up with you?"

"You?" Kristie asked in surprise. She jumped up onto him, wrapping her legs around his waist. "I'm the lucky one! My boyfriend is a totally badass fire-breathing dragon. How many girls can say that?"

Camden slid his arms underneath of her, supporting her weight on his forearms. "Your father would probably kill me for such an act on his property, but I want you. Right here. Right now."

Her arms slid around his neck and she gave him a devilish grin. "He'll be preoccupied with the bathroom. He won't even have to know."

Heat raced under his skin at her words. This time, it didn't even worry him. It felt natural, more under control. Maybe now that he'd finally shifted, things would be better.

Letting the heat dance almost teasingly under his skin, he walked her to the inflatable mattress. At her comment of her father being preoccupied, he felt the need to say, "He's probably never going to forgive me for that."

"He doesn't have a choice," Kristie stated in a matter of fact tone. As Camden lowered her to the mattress, she reached a hand up to run it through his scraggly hair. "We're a package deal. If he has a problem with you, he has a problem with me."

His chest welling with gratitude, he lifted her hand to his mouth and kissed it. "Did I mention that I love you?"

She smiled, a blush creeping up her cheeks. "You may have."

Leaning over her, he braced himself on one arm. He lowered his mouth to hers, his free hand stroking her stomach.

One of her arms slipped about his waist and she began tugging his shirt from his pants. The other was running through his hair, holding his mouth to hers. When he broke away to kiss a path along her jawline, she giggled. "I sure hope this old mattress holds up."

Camden watched her with hunger racing through his veins. "We'll have to put it to the test." Even to his own ears, his voice sounded different than usual, more arrogant. He didn't lack passion in the bedroom, but at times he found himself short of confidence. Tonight, he oozed it.

"Sounds like fun," she informed him with an eager grin.

He slid a hand up the inside of her thigh, his fingers disappearing under her dress. "Sounds like a ton of fun," he growled as his hand slipped higher on her thigh.

She shivered and arched off the mattress when he skimmed his fingertips along the front of her panties.

"I want these off," he demanded.

She bobbed her head in compliance, a small smirk on her lips at his domineering tone. She slipped out of her underwear while he self-assuredly removed his belt.

He was on her a moment later, kissing her with a passion he'd never experienced before. His kisses were hot and hard, his mouth demanding.

She yielded to him. Camden could feel her heart pounding frantically in her chest as his hands pushed the bottom of her skirt up. He slid the fabric until it was bunched at her waist. He wanted to get her fully naked, wanted to hold her glorious breasts between his hands, but he couldn't wait. He had to have her. Now.

He fumbled with the button of his pants, then scrambled free of the tattered garment. He didn't even bother with his shirt. As soon as he was free of his bottoms, he forced his way inside of her with a groan.

Kristie gave a breathy hiss and slid her legs around his hips to draw him deep. "Oh yes, Cammy."

A pleased chuckle escaped his lips as he began to move inside of her. He captured her mouth with his, quieting her soft whimpers as his hips thrust forcefully against hers.

When he gripped her hips and increased his rhythm, driving harder and deeper into her, Kristie's head fell back against the mattress and she moaned his name.

In no time at all, he felt her body spasm, felt her orgasm around him. He let himself go, climaxing almost violently. His manhood twitched inside of her with its release, drawing another cry from her throat.

"Cam, that was the best. Ever." She lay panting, her arms limp above her head.

Camden slumped to lie next to her. Her position left her breasts exposed, so he leaned over to press gentle kisses along the fabric of her shirt, nuzzling her affectionately. He indulged himself for a few moments before pulling back to regard her seriously. "I don't know what came over me. It was like..." He trailed off, unsure of what he could even say to describe the changes to his body.

"It's the dragon in you," she reasoned. "From what little I've read in lore, they're very possessive." She snuggled up against his side. "Grr," she growled into his ear, nipping it between her teeth. "I like it."

He chuckled and slipped an arm around her shoulders. "Me too."

As she stared up at him with trust in her eyes, Camden did something he should have done a long time ago. With a soft, tender kiss, he rolled her underneath him and made gentle love to her, showing her with his actions just what she meant to him.

Chapter 8

Camden awoke with a start. In his dream, a woman had been screaming at him while waving an ice cream cone in his face. At least he'd thought it a mere dream until the yelling continued.

"Hello?" An unfamiliar woman called out loudly despite the early morning hour. There was a huff and then she continued. "Do not insult me by hiding. I know you're up there. Damn it! Acknowledge me!"

Kristie lifted up onto one elbow and stared down at him, looking perplexed. "I think she's talking to us."

"I can hear you up there," the woman cried.

Kristie held the sheets across her chest and inched to the small window of the tree house. She peered over the lip of the sill, then glanced over her shoulder at Camden. "It's the woman from the ice cream shop."

"That would explain the ice cream cone," he grumbled. "My subconscious was screaming for me to run."

"I just saw your human," Priya informed him shortly. "I'm not going away until you speak to me."

"Wonderful," he griped. Crawling toward the window, he peered down at their intruder. "Give me a minute, will you? Let me get some clothes on. We don't all wake up raring to go."

"It's eight o'clock," Priya argued up while he hopped around trying to get into his pants. "I've been up for hours."

"Congratulations," Camden said in a tone much shorter than he'd intended. "Some of us had a busy night."

Kristie followed his lead. She pulled her dress over her head, not even bothering to search for her bra. As a last second decision, she scooped up her panties and slid into them. "Make her stop yelling," she demanded. "She's going to wake everyone up."

Camden tossed the tree house ladder over the railing. "She's freaking insane. Do you think she'll listen to me even if I beg?"

Priya stood on the ground in front of the ladder tapping her foot impatiently. Her large brown eyes were full of fire as her nails incessantly tapped against her hips. "It's about time."

Camden slung a leg over the ladder and started down toward her, wanting to get this over with. He had no idea what the woman could want from him, but after their last meeting, he doubted it was anything good.

As he descended, Priya gave a choking laugh. "You shifted form in Armani? What were you thinking, destroying perfectly good clothing?"

Camden was beyond being embarrassed. If there was anyone left in his life that hadn't seen his ass this week, he'd be surprised. He hit the ground next to her and crossed his arms over his chest. "Shifted form?" he asked. "So you know what I am?"

Priya's eyes flashed in annoyance. "Don't talk down to me. Of course I know what you are. Every supernatural being in this area knows what you are." Her expression darkened. "For someone about to overthrow the local dragon spearhead, you sure act very casual about it. Your attitude makes me wonder if you'll be any better at governing our people than him."

"Wait," Camden said in confusion as Kristie climbed down to stand next to him. "What? Who? What are you talking about?"

At his confusion, Priya's expression lost its certainty. "You're not here to take over the local dragons?"

His eyes widened. "No! Of course not! Why would I..."

Priya suddenly looked ready to panic. "Then what are you doing here?" She put a hand to her forehead. "Why would you enter Stefan's territory unless you were planning to take over? He's going to kill you! I thought you to be an arrogant, power-hungry maniac, but it's far worse. You're just an idiot." She reached forward and gripped his forearms. "You entered the territory of a heartless, murdering rapist with no intention of overthrowing him. It's suicide."

"I...I didn't know," he stammered in response. "I didn't know what I was until last night, let alone anything about territories."

"How could you not know what you are? We're born this way. We're raised knowing the rules."

"I wasn't born this way," Camden argued. "It's a recent thing, two months tops." On her disbelieving look, he took a deep breath and filled her in on his story. He didn't see the harm in it at this point. She already knew what he was. "I was murdered then resurrected by a witch. I didn't come back human. I came back like this." He shrugged one shoulder. "I don't know anything about dragons or territories. Last night was the first time I ever shifted form. I fought it before. I thought I was dying." He gave a laugh that lacked humor. "Whoever you think I am, I'm not him. I'm just a guy with shitty luck who happens to breathe fire."

Priya looked as if she might faint. "The others can't know." Her eyes locked onto his. "They thought you were a savior come to rescue us. They've had the first bit of hope in years. They were ready to revolt, to follow you into anarchy." A look of resolve spread across her face. "We can fake it. We can pretend you're some fierce warrior, and when the time comes, I'll fight Stefan myself. We can't lose this hope. They've been abused for too long."

"You said he'd come after me." Camden's voice was wary as he reminded her of her earlier words. Priya's people wouldn't be the only ones to think he was starting an uprising. Their enemies would as well. "I'm still in his territory. If he comes after me before you fight him, he'll kill me." He had no false hope that he could take down a powerful tyrant. Beau maybe, but him? He wasn't made for this sort of thing. He couldn't even defeat dragons in video games. He had no hope with the real thing.

"People are dying." Priya's voice was an emotional plea. "Children." Her dark eyes widened beseechingly. "Please. Just give me a little bit of time. That's all I'm asking of you. Time."

Camden glanced at Kristie, though he already knew what his answer would be. He was into self-preservation, and he knew his odds of winning a fight if attacked, but he wouldn't be a coward and let innocent people die.

Kristie gave a silent nod of approval. Reaching out, she took his hand in a show of support.

It seemed the decision was made. Turning to Priya, he nodded. "Of course I'll help. Whatever you need."

Priya gave an exhale of relief. Her whole demeanor became more relaxed, almost friendly. "I'm so pleased to know you are just a clueless guy who is willing to help and not some egotistical maniac."

Before he could decide whether or not he should be insulted, she continued, "I know this is a lot to throw on you, but I need you to be a leader. I know you don't know much about our ways, but I'll help you fake it. They need to believe you."

"What happens if we win?" he asked curiously. "I can't be expected to keep up the act and lead people I know nothing about."

"We'll worry about that when the time comes. Odds are we'll both be dead by the end of the week, so it really won't matter."

"Story of my life," he grumbled.

Priya gave a sharp bark of laughter that caught him off guard. "After being brought back from the dead, dying is kind of old hat to you, huh?" She sounded more awed than amused.

"Last time I died, I came back as a dragon. I don't care to repeat the process. Who knows what I'll come back as next."

"Yeah," Priya said in amazement. "I can imagine your concern." She eyed him for a moment before saying, "Perhaps we should go inside and talk. I'm sure you must have a million questions about what you are. It's best if I can give you as much information as possible about us and how we live our lives."

"That would be—"

Camden was interrupted by Oakley, who came storming across the lawn. "Who the hell do you think you are? You've got a lot of nerve showing your face around here after wrecking our holiday!" Oakley's face was bright red with anger and his hands balled into fists.

Camden knew without a doubt that Oakley was going to hit him. He braced for it, but he didn't even think to fight back.

When Oakley reached Camden, he hit him with a right

hook that could have taken down a professional boxer.

To Camden's disbelief, the fist flying into his face didn't faze him. It barely even registered on his annoyance meter. He rubbed his jaw in surprise. "That didn't even hurt," he said in amazement.

"Well of course not," Priya scoffed. She looked at Oakley in disappointment. "Why would you do that? Did you want to break your fragile little fingers?"

"On him?" Oakley asked, his voice sounding thoroughly offended. "Fragile?"

Before anyone could answer, Dale came rushing out of the house. "Krissi!" he cried in relief. When he reached his daughter, he pulled her into a tight hug. "Where were you? I was so worried!"

Kristie glanced at Camden, her distracted expression giving away that she couldn't fully concentrate on her father after everything they'd just learned. They'd had a lot of information dumped on them, and she no doubt wanted to discuss it. Turning back to Dale, she blinked in confusion. "You told us to get out."

A horrified noise escaped her father. "*That's* why you never came home last night?" He released her from the hug only so he could look her in the eyes. "Honey, I didn't mean all night. I just meant while I looked at the bathroom. I would never kick you out. You are welcome here as long as you want to stay."

"And Camden?" she asked pointedly. "Him to? Because if not, I will march in there, get my bags, and leave."

Dale's eyes shot to Camden. Without answering, he said, "Let's all go inside where we can talk."

No one had a chance to respond to Dale's suggestion, because Ward suddenly lunged around his father at Camden.

Moving with a quickness he didn't know he possessed, Camden dodged Ward's assault. As the boy went sailing past, Camden put a hand to his back and gave a little push.

Ward went flying passed him, stumbled, and fell flat on his face on the ground. He rolled to his back and glared daggers at Camden. "You're a dick," he snarled.

Camden's eyes widened at the barked insult. Ward hadn't been exactly friendly with him, but he'd never been openly hostile like Oakley until now. Apparently, setting the bathroom on fire was the youngest Taylor's last straw.

"Your humans are out of control," Priya complained with another stamp of her foot. "Their behavior is unacceptable."

Camden cringed. "Stop calling them that."

Her dark eyes slid to his. "Would you rather I call them cannon fodder? I was trying to be polite."

Oakley seemed to finally notice Priya's presence. "Why is the hot chick from the ice cream place here?" he asked in confusion.

Priya's gaze snapped in his direction, fire evident in her eyes. "And now it insults me."

"It?" Oakley asked in offense. "*It?*" He crossed his arms over his broad chest. "And *it* just complimented you."

"It speaks to me as if we are equals." Priya's eyes swept to Camden. "Do you always permit them to speak to you in such a way?"

Kristie's lips pursed in irritation at the insult to her family, and Camden flushed with embarrassment. Things had suddenly grown very awkward. He wasn't sure if all dragons treated humans this way or if Priya was just prissy, but there was no way he could explain her to the Taylors. Not without sounding insane.

It was Mr. Taylor who finally spoke. "Are we not going inside then?" He looked imploringly at Kristie. "I'm trying to make an effort here, baby. It can only go so far unless both parties participate."

"Now's really not a good time, Daddy."

Oakley's face turned red with fury. "Why are you even making an effort, Dad? This stoner ruined our holiday and set the house on fire! He doesn't deserve for anyone to be nice to him."

Kristie poked a finger into her brother's chest. "You've had a problem with Camden since the moment we showed up! You haven't made a single thing easy for him."

"He isn't good enough for you," Oakley argued. "I could tell right away what a nightmare he was."

"We are wasting valuable time," Priya stated in aggravation. "If they will not follow your orders, then you should simply snap their necks and be done with it."

"Now wait just a minute, young lady," Dale said angrily to Priya.

"*Young lady?*" Her voice came out an insulted squawk.

While everyone around him argued, Camden's head began to swim with all the confusion. He was suddenly light-headed. He took a shaky step backwards. Not realizing the teen was still on the ground behind him, he stumbled into Ward and fell to the ground, his arms pinwheeling in the air. He hit the earth with a dull thud and a startled grunt escaped his lips.

This effectively halted all arguments. "Camden!" Kristie and Priya cried at the same time. They both rushed to his side and dropped to their knees to check on him.

Kristie shot the other woman an annoyed look and placed a possessive hand to Camden's chest. "Are you all right?"

Ward gave the women a look of disbelief. "Why did no one care when I fell?"

"Shut up," Kristie and Priya said in unison before turning back to Camden.

"All this arguing isn't good for him." Kristie gave her family a glare. "Don't you get the fact that all his health problems are because of me?" Her gaze lifted to her mother who had been standing fretfully to the side of the group. "It isn't a slight at your cooking." She then looked to her father. "And he wasn't getting high in the bathroom. It's all related to his health problems. Seeing as they're a result of me being alive, I would think you'd be a little more understanding."

"Kristie," Dale began, but she cut him off.

"Not now, Dad." She held a hand up to ward off any more on the subject. "I can't deal with this right now." Tossing one of Camden's arms over her shoulder, she began helping him to his feet.

Priya stood by with a nervous expression but made no move to help. It was Oakley who finally came forward and offered Camden a shoulder to lean on.

Camden hesitated to take the offered support, nervous at having Oakley so close. He debated telling the teen he didn't need any help, but he might fall over without the extra assistance.

"I'm not doing this for you," Oakley said under his breath. "I'm doing this for my sister."

"Noted." Camden spoke quietly, not wanting his girlfriend to hear the exchange. He didn't want to be the reason of any more strain between her and her family. He'd never meant for any of this to happen.

"Give us an hour to speak with Priya," Kristie said to her

father. "Then we'll come in and have a family talk."

Dale glanced at Priya uncertainly before nodding in agreement. Silently, he put a hand on his wife's shoulder and began ushering her toward the house.

Ward gave Camden one last glare before following.

As soon as the Taylors disappeared into the house, Priya's attention jumped to Oakley. "Mortal boy, please assist us in returning Mr. Harrison to his lair."

Oakley's eyebrows rose. "His lair?"

Priya nodded in the direction of the tree house. "I suppose the word lair is being charitable. I've never seen such an unsecure warren before. Not exactly a fortress, is it?" She shook her head. "And in a tree to boot."

Oakley looked at his sister for guidance.

With a roll of her eyes, Kristie said, "Just help him into the tree."

With a shrug, Oakley began carefully helping Camden up the rope ladder.

They were only up a few rungs before Priya spoke with disdain. "I do hope he has more pants nearby. This look is not becoming in a leader."

"He looks fine to me," Kristie replied sharply. With that, she helped push Camden up the last few steps into the tree house. Once inside, she and Oakley looped Camden's arms over their shoulders and led him across the room to deposit him on the mattress.

Oakley crossed to the window and leaned against the sill. He crossed his arms over his chest with a smirk of amusement as Priya followed them into the small room with a look of awe.

"*This* is your lair?" she asked in disbelief. "It's so...pink." She looked around her in shock. "It's unguarded. Where do you keep your treasure?"

"Treasure?" Oakley asked. "What is he? A pirate?"

Kristie waved his question off.

Camden directed his answer to Priya. "This isn't my lair. I only slept here last night because her father kicked us out of the house."

Priya gave a gasp of horror, her hand flying to her heart. Her eyes were so wide it was nearly comical. "Such insolence."

Camden continued as if she hadn't spoken. "And I don't have any treasure. My most valuable asset was a pair of Armani pants that now have a hole in the ass."

"Every dragon has treasure," Priya argued.

"I've only been a dragon two months, and I haven't known about it a day!" Suddenly, his statement sunk in, as did who their company included. Both Camden and Kristie slowly slid their eyes toward Oakley.

The boy's eyebrows had shot into his hairline. "Dragon?" he asked with a laugh. "Really?" He laughed again, louder this time. "She *is* crazy."

Priya turned to Camden in shock. "They don't know?"

"Of course they don't know!" Camden cried. "What was I going to do? Introduce myself by saying, 'Hi, I'm Camden, Kristie's oddball boyfriend. By the way, I'm a dragon who sometimes spouts flames and catches curtains on fire'? That didn't really seem like an option."

"I wouldn't have used the word oddball, but other than that, it's fitting," Priya said with a shrug. Then her expression became one of concern. "They are in danger just by associating with you. You need to make sure they are at least well protected." Her gaze shot to Oakley in curiosity before sliding back to Camden. "Either tell them what's going on or distance yourself from them. You obviously care for these creatures or you would have killed them for their disobedience already."

Oakley's eyes narrowed. "Listen, lady, I don't know who you think you are, but you have a lot of nerve coming to my home and talking to me like this."

"Who do I think I am?" Priya repeated his words with barely restrained anger. "I am a purebred dragon. I am of a superior race than you. How dare you question me?"

"It's hard not to question the crazy lady who believes herself to be a dragon."

"Believes?" Priya squawked in outrage. "*Believes*?" Her nostrils flared, and Camden was sure he saw a wisp of smoke trickle out.

Priya snorted again, the steam rising unmistakably into the air this time. She stalked toward Oakley with violence in her eyes. She'd barely made it halfway to him before her hands transformed into talons. The nails at the end became dangerously sharp. Her skin rippled, becoming blue iridescent scales before their eyes.

When she reached Oakley, she grabbed him by the front of his shirt and yanked him toward her. With his face inches from her own, she growled. "I could eat you for a midnight snack, boy." Her tongue flicked out, long and pointed like a snake's.

Oakley's eyes widened and his pupils grew large. He stared at Priya as if seeing her for the first time. It took him a moment before he was able to speak, but when he finally did, it wasn't with the fear Camden expected. "Is it wrong that I am absolutely turned on right now?"

Priya inhaled sharply in surprise and released her grip on him. She took a stumbling step backwards. Her body returned to its human form, the claws disappearing.

"Can we please just discuss things like adults?" Camden asked wearily. "We've got a lot to cover in a small amount of time." He swung his gaze pointedly to Oakley. "Yes, I'm a dragon. Yes, supernatural creatures exist. Life as you know it is completely different. Blah, blah, blah, blah, blah. While you're dealing with that knowledge, can we move the conversation forward?"

Priya seemed to recover herself. She shook her entire body as if shaking off the encounter with Oakley. "Yes," she was quick to agree. "Yes, let's get started." She put more distance between herself and Oakley, crossing her arms.

"First," Camden said. "In regard to Kristie's family, I think it would be best to keep them in the dark." He held up a silencing hand when Priya started to protest. "They will be just as cautious if we tell them the cult who caused a scene at the college last year has tracked me down. The cult excuse worked last time. It will work now."

Oakley was finally able to drag his eyes away from Priya. "It worked last time?" he asked in shock. "It *wasn't* cult members last time?"

"No," Camden said calmly. "It was vampires." He held Oakley's gaze, letting him see the unusual seriousness in his eyes. "When we dealt with the vampire attack, I was murdered. I was shot in the chest and then had my neck snapped."

Oakley flinched, the skin around his eyes tightening at that blunt description.

"My best friend is a witch," Camden continued. "She managed to bring me back to life. It wasn't easy, and even though she was able to do it, I didn't come back human."

Kristie sank to the mattress next to Camden and took

one of his hands into hers. "He died for me, Oakley," she said softly. As if to make sure her brother truly understood the situation, she added, "I love him."

Oakley looked at his feet. Whether in shame of his own actions or embarrassment of his sister's open emotion, Camden wasn't sure. After a moment of silence, Oakley looked up at him with questioning eyes.

"All of the problems I've been having are due to being brought back as something less than human. I wasn't smoking pot in the bathroom. I was breathing fire. That was my first time, so it didn't go very smoothly. And I wasn't insulting your mother's cooking that first night. Heat sets me off. Steaming hot food was a bad idea."

"As was a blow dryer," Kristie added with a pointed look to her brother.

"My God," Priya breathed. She ran her hands through her thick black hair before looking at Camden in horror. "You are behaving like one of our teenagers. It's as if because you are newly one of us, your body is being forced through dragon puberty."

Oakley snorted with laughter, but did his best to cover it up with a cough.

"No, no, no," Camden argued desperately as if he could change his body's mind. "Human puberty was bad enough. I'm not going through that again!"

Priya shot him an annoyed look at his denial and continued with her own train of thought. "The bigger concern is how we are going to hide this from the other dragons."

"Hide it?" Oakley asked inquisitively. "Why does he need to hide it? I mean, I get keeping the rest of my family in the dark, but why others like you?"

Priya set him with a serious look. "Because there is a very bad man out there who is looking to kill your future brother-in-law."

"Brother-in-law?" Camden squeaked. "Let's not get crazy."

Kristie shot him a dirty look, but turned her attention to her brother. "The man who runs this territory thinks Camden came in to take it over."

"He thinks Mr. Harrison is a powerful enemy not just some newborn goof," Priya offered in explanation.

"Hey! Mean!" Camden protested, but no one seemed to be paying him any attention.

"Everyone has to believe Camden is here to help them overthrow this man, or they will never have the courage to fight."

Oakley's expression became accusing. "So you're going to lie to them? You're setting them up to fight someone more powerful than themselves with only bonehead here to back them up?" he asked with a wave in Camden's direction. "You're lying about a life and death situation. It's like sending them to the slaughter."

Priya spun on Oakley with a vicious snarl. "I would not allow my people to be slaughtered! I will be the one to fight Stefan. I just need my people to occupy his guards so I can get to him. I want them in as little danger as possible. All I ask is a chance to rip that man's throat out with my bare hands."

Though Priya's words were grave, Oakley's lips curved into an affectionate grin. "I have a hard time arguing with anything this woman has to say." He leaned back casually against the window frame, once again the picture of ease. "So what's our plan?"

Priya snorted and rolled her eyes. "The plans do not involve you, human child. You are useless to me, nothing more than cannon fodder."

No longer fazed by being referred to as the "human child," Oakley merely gave her a lecherous look. "I can think of quite a few ways I can be of use to you."

"Oakley!" Kristie chastised the sexual innuendo in her brother's tone, sounding appalled.

He shrugged. "I've heard orgasms really help women unwind. I'm just trying to be helpful. You know, do my part."

"No wonder I'm so stress free," Kristie whispered to Camden.

Camden gave a bark of laughter that he covered with a cough. "Seriously, Oakley, we've got important things to discuss."

Priya shot Oakley a dirty look. "Precisely." She turned to Camden, ignoring anything further Oakley might have to say. "The first thing we need to do is keep you from acting like a rampant teenager."

Camden's expression soured. "Did I mention how much I hate this?"

Priya waved him off. "Regardless..." She took a deep

breath, and Camden just knew she was about to get all bossy. "In our meeting with the local dragons, we need to keep you from doing anything stupid. First rule—no setting anything on fire. Adults rarely ever do such a thing. Random fires are started by the weak and immature."

"Please," Camden said sarcastically. "Keep insulting me. It makes me feel that much more eager to help."

Priya ignored his comment and continued. "Also, try to control your instincts to fornicate."

Camden choked on his next breath, gagging on air while Kristie patted his back. "Excuse me?" he finally managed to wheeze. "Did you just tell me to control my fornicating?"

Priya pointed to a burn mark on the side of Kristie's collar bone. "I see that you've mated. That's wonderful, but it does have certain side effects."

Camden looked at the tiny mark on Kristie's neck in surprise. He'd felt the fire in his throat on more than one occasion during their night of lovemaking, had felt it hot in his mouth while he kissed her, but this was unexpected. Surely she would have protested if he hurt her. "Mated?" he asked Priya in confusion. "What are you talking about? I didn't even know…"

Priya rolled her eyes and let out a loud sigh. "Children know this. You're a loose cannon, running around mating with people unbeknownst to yourself."

Kristie was gingerly fingering the red welt on her throat. "Can you just tell us what you're talking about?"

Priya let out another sigh. "I am talking about the basics. Dragons choose a mate for themselves, someone to spend the rest of eternity with." On the blank stares that greeted her, she added, "Much like werewolves." On their continued confusion, Priya huffed. "You don't know of werewolf customs either? Have you been living under a rock your entire life?"

"Yes," Camden confirmed. "I have. It's called humanity."

Priya waved a hand in the air. "You need to shake off your mortal way of thinking." She snapped her fingers, red nails glinting in the sunlight. "Pay attention. I'm going to have to cram years worth of information into a few minutes. You are simply going to have to survive with the fundamentals. Lord help us if someone asks you a question that requires an intelligent response."

Oakley chuckled. "She's so rude. I love it."

"Now..." Priya pressed on, ignoring his praise. "Many supernatural beings mate. Those that do tend to mate for life. It is a bond beyond any other. Unlike filthy humans," she said with a sneer in Oakley's direction, "we are loyal to our mates. They are for life."

Camden shifted his position on the bed, gently patting Kristie's knee. "So it's like the equivalent of a promise ring?" he asked nervously.

Priya pinched the bridge of her nose and closed her eyes. When she dropped her hand away and locked him with her piercing gaze, there was annoyance in her eyes. "No. It's nothing like a promise ring." She threw her hands up in apparent disbelief. "It's a lifelong commitment more binding than marriage. I cannot believe you are mated and have no clue of what it entails." Taking a deep breath, she elaborated. "Werewolves are most widely known for mating. Their cultures are more barbaric than ours. Their inner wolf choses their mate. The person doesn't have a choice but to comply. Their inner wolf will have them bite their mate, leaving a scar to mark them as taken. For us, it's more of a choice than a reflex. We have a choice of who we would like to spend the rest of our lives with. A werewolf will do most things subconsciously. We make the effort to mate."

She studied them for a moment, making sure they were still following her explanation. Seemingly pleased, she pressed on. "If we are with someone who we feel we would like to spend our lives with, we attempt to brand them. If you are meant to be with that person, if your dragon approves, you will leave your mark on their flesh. During mating, if that person is not your other half, it will not work. It will be as if the person is flame retardant."

Oakley raised his hand. "How exactly does someone of your kind choose a mate? How does your inner dragon know the difference between trying to scorch someone and choosing a mate?"

"Mating is always done during sex. Our dragon is just an extension of ourselves. We know the difference between passion and anger."

Oakley thought on that a moment before his shoulders tensed. His eyes shifted to Camden, their blue depths full of hostility. "You branded my sister? You branded my sister during *sex*?"

Camden tried to make himself invisible, but it didn't seem to be working. "I...I..." He didn't know what he was more afraid of, being suddenly mated or his mate's brother murdering him.

Priya didn't seem to notice the tension. "He did," she agreed. "And while that is wonderful, it can be potentially hazardous. If he is hitting dragon puberty, he is going to be craving sexual intercourse to begin with. When we mate, it has the same effect. Mating couples..." She trailed off and bit the tip of one of her nails. "I had a friend who I didn't see for three years after she mated. It was just non-stop sex."

Kristie perked up at this. "Three years?"

Oakley shot her a look of disgust. "He *branded* you."

"And now it's like we're married," she gushed. "We get to have sex for three years straight."

"Kris," Camden said weakly. "I didn't even know what I was doing. I don't think—"

Oakley talked over him. "You want to have continuous sex with *that*?" He made a gagging noise. "He's not even your type!" He began counting off examples on his fingers. "He's a total mess. He has zero fashion sense. He doesn't have an ounce of muscle on him. He's a spaz."

Kristie came back with a list of her own. "He is an exceptional lover. He cares about me. He doesn't treat me like a bimbo. He died for me—"

Oakley made a roaring sound of annoyance. "Enough with the whole dying for you excuse. Yes, we are eternally grateful he didn't let you get killed, but are you really prepared to spend the rest of your life with him because of it?"

She waved to the burn mark on her neck. "Apparently I am!"

When Oakley made a sound of disgust, Camden went to jump to his own defense, but Priya spoke first. "You are not helping. You either need to get over your issues, or you need to leave." Her expression was stern, giving no room for argument. "Right now. Make your choice. You either stay and attempt to help, or you stop wasting our time and leave. We have things to attend to that are more important than your dislike of Mr. Harrison and his poor fashion sense."

Oakley sulked a moment before grumbling, "All right. I'll behave."

"Good," Priya said with an authoritative air. "Now, another important issue is tail maintenance. It—" She broke off with sharp surprise when Oakley once again raised his hand. "What?" She all but snapped the word at him.

"I have one more question." He crossed muscled arms over his chest as he gave Priya a winning smile. "Are you mated?"

Priya blinked at him in surprise. "Excuse me?" Her eyes flicked to Camden and Kristie with embarrassment before returning to Oakley.

"Are you mated?" He repeated the question, his eyes locked intently on her blushing face.

A noise that sounded close to mortification escaped the normally overconfident dragon's throat. "No," she admitted.

Oakley's grin grew. "Where do I apply for the job?"

Camden watched Priya go from embarrassed to angry and back a few times. A wisp of smoke escaped her right nostril, causing him to smirk. This was either going to be the most amusing or the most frightening holiday break of his life. He just wasn't quite sure yet which it would be.

Chapter 9

Camden stood in the center of Kristie's tree house feeling more than a little foolish. The tree was jam-packed with men and women he'd never met before, most of them gawking at him in wonder. He wasn't sure what made him more uneasy, the awe or the faces full of skepticism, like that of the woman standing in front of him now.

"Camden," Priya said with a wide yet somehow tense smile as she took his arm and tugged him forward. "This is Sage. She is the sister of our late leader's widow."

Camden gave the woman a look he hoped conveyed his pleasure at meeting her as well as his sympathy for her sister's loss. "Hello," he said, offering a hand for her to shake.

Instead of greeting him, Sage's eyes slid to Priya. "Why does his face look like that? Is there something wrong with him?"

Priya's eyebrows rose and she tilted her head to take in Camden's odd countenance.

He quickly wiped his face clean of any expression, and in an attempt to fix the situation, he said, "I'm very sorry to hear about your loss."

"Why?" Sage asked without the slightest hint of mourning for her dead family member in her voice. "You'd merely be overthrowing him instead of Stefan, now wouldn't you?"

Camden's hands turned clammy as he stared at her, uncertain of how to respond to her blunt statement. Priya had not prepared him for this sort of thing, and he was feeling the pressure.

Kristie jumped in to handle the question for him. "Camden wasn't looking to overthrow anyone. We just happened to be in town for the holidays. We only decided to take a stand because of how poorly this group is being treated. You must understand we never would have come here looking for trouble. We're not violent people."

Sage gave a grunt of disbelief. "Sure." Her tone was dry and lacking any conviction.

Camden's jaw dropped and he glanced at Priya for assistance...or perhaps an explanation as to why this woman was so coldly removed from something that greatly affected her.

Priya shrugged, but didn't comment as Sage turned to examine their surroundings. "Such an odd location choice for a lair," she commented critically. "I thought green dragons preferred a place near water or in thick forests."

"Well, I tried to set up shop at the public pool," he teased, "but I got kicked out for violating their 'No Shapeshifting' rule."

Priya gave a bark of laughter, but pressed her fingers to her lips to cover it up and quickly forced her expression back to neutral.

Sage merely stared at him, obviously not understanding.

"That was a joke," Oakley offered, speaking up for the first time since all of the dragons had filed into the tree house.

Sage looked at him, and jumped as if shocked to discover him standing there. Her gaze swung back to Camden. "Do you permit all of your humans to speak so freely?"

Camden arched an eyebrow and shot a quick glance to Kristie's brother. "He is in no way *my* human."

Sage's expression turned to alarm. "We have an unclaimed human just wandering about?" Her eyes had gone wide and she was looking at Oakley as if she thought he might contain a deadly plague.

"I belong to Priya," Oakley explained with a wicked grin.

"I didn't realize you were keeping any humans," Sage said with surprise to her fellow dragon.

As Priya tensed, Oakley's grin widened. "I was a gift from Camden, kind of like a peace offering." He winked at Sage. "I'm a sex toy sort of gift."

Sage's eyebrows rose nearly to her hairline and one of her delicate, ridiculously thin hands went to her chest. Her gaze swept back and forth between Priya and Camden.

Priya's eyes had widened in disbelief. She choked, coughed, and when Oakley patted her back, she pressed a palm to his chest. After a comment such as he'd just made, her dismissive gesture came off instead as intimate.

Sage blinked slowly, then her lips crept into a deliciously wicked grin. "Well, if that's the type of offering you bring, welcome to the community." Her eyes roved appreciatively over Oakley before shifting to Camden. "Mr. Harrison, you have my full vote of confidence." She ran her hand along Oakley's chest as she walked away to mingle, nails dragging across his shirt.

Oakley gave an alarmed yelp and inched toward Priya. "Please don't loan me out to her."

Priya's eyes darkened as she gave one last cough. "You are my sex slave, aren't you?" She shoved him away. "Sage was already hard to deal with. I didn't have her full respect *before* she thought I had a human sex toy. If loaning you out will improve my status with her..."

On Oakley's horrified expression, Camden shook his head with a laugh. "She's just kidding." He frowned when Priya arched a brow. "You're kidding, right?"

"For your sake," Priya said, patting Oakley on the chest, "you'd better hope so." With that, she clapped loudly to get the attention of the tree house's occupants. "Shall we get this meeting underway?"

There were a few grumbles of agreement, and every eye swung curiously to Camden.

"Please. Have a seat." Priya frowned at the only chairs available in the tree house—bean bag chairs. When Camden attempted to sit, she grabbed his shirt and yanked him to stand next to her. She then shoved Oakley out of view and into a bean bag chair to her left. "Ladies and gentleman, I would like to introduce to you Camden Harrison. He's the man I've been telling you about." After a moment of silence in which everyone stared, she elbowed Camden in the ribs.

He winced at the sharp jab to the side with her bony appendage before forcing a grin. "Hi. I'm Camden...obviously." He didn't get to say anything else because three hands shot into the air. "Um...yes?" he asked cautiously.

"What is your plan for killing Stefan Marcello? He is a very powerful, unforgiving being who will not sit by quietly while you take over. You do have a plan, don't you?" asked a man with red hair.

Camden took a deep breath and started in on the script Priya had gone over with him. "I do have a plan, and it doesn't involve any of you getting physically involved with Stefan. I simply need you to help me get to him. I need his guards out of the way. It doesn't even have to be by violent means. If you can trick them into leaving Stefan unguarded, all the better. Priya and I will be the ones going in to deal with Stefan ourselves."

"Priya?" the man asked. "You're taking her in with you?"

Camden nodded, trying to appear more confident than he felt. "Yes. As I told Sage a moment ago, I'm not looking to lord over this area. I only want to help you obtain your freedom. When I leave, I intend to let you handle your own affairs. Priya has offered to step up and become a leader for you during the transition. She's willing to risk her life, to go in and fight for everyone's freedom. She's a good woman. You should give her a chance."

"You're leaving?" a petite woman asked in surprise.

"Yes," Camden said, stressing the word. "My..." He paused. Priya had mentioned that dragons were nearly immortal. Most of the people in the tree house were at least half a century old. She felt it best he omit the fact that he was barely legal to drink. It would dampen their faith in him. "My girlfriend is human," he explained, sliding his arm around Kristie's waist. "She's in college, so we will need to get back to the university when break is over."

"Will Priya's gift be staying?" Sage asked. As aristocratic and snobby as she might appear, her eyes roved over Oakley with obvious interest.

"Well," Camden said slowly, "Oakley is in college as well. I believe his school is in another state. I assume he will be leaving within the week as well."

"So he wasn't a permanent gift? He's a loaner?" This seemed to interest Sage even more. Camden worried it was because she was hoping to get Oakley loaned out to *her* at some point in the future.

"I *could* be a permanent toy," Oakley said quickly. "I'd be willing to relocate schools if Priya decided she wanted to keep me. Exclusively," he was quick to add.

Priya's eyes lowered to him in startled surprise. "You'd

stay? For me?"

Oakley grinned, his expression wicked and suggestive. "I think it would definitely be possible to convince me."

Sage gave him a wistful look. "Priya, you are a lucky woman. Humans don't usually enjoy our brand of pleasure. Last toy I kept ran back to his mommy because I 'frightened him'. He thought it was unnatural and off-putting for a woman to snort smoke when she's angry."

"I find it sexy when Priya snorts smoke," Oakley said. "It means I've at least got her attention."

Priya fiddled with her hair for a moment in embarrassment. "Could we please stop discussing my human? We have more important issues to deal with this afternoon."

A hulking, dark-haired man at the back of the room stood up. His appearance hinted at a Polynesian background, and his tan, weathered skin attested to many hours spent outdoors.

Priya nodded in his direction. "Yes, Pius?"

"Forgive me, Priya, for being so blunt," he said apologetically, "but are you attempting to take down Stefan because you are looking out for the best interest of the community or because his second in command raped and tortured you?"

The tree house grew deathly silent. Kristie reached out to grip Camden's forearm, her expression one of horror.

Priya stood frozen in shock. Her face had visibly paled, and her hands were trembling.

For the first time since he'd met her, Camden didn't see the tough as nails dragon. He saw a fragile, terrified woman who'd been the victim of abuse. The sudden crumbling of her rough exterior worried him.

Priya's mouth opened, but she didn't speak. Instead of words, a soft injured sound escaped her.

It was Oakley who finally spoke. "How dare you question her intentions and bring up something so personal? She's been doing nothing but look out for this group since the moment I met her."

Pius shifted his gaze to the teen. "I did not wish to bring up such unfortunate events, but I need to assure she has her priorities straight. I need to know that if she has a shot at Stefan, she'll take it and not be distracted by personal vengeance. Stefan must be the top priority. Not Carl."

Priya had been staring at Oakley in shock, but her expression suddenly hardened, and her gaze swept to Pius. "I have one target, and that is Stefan Marcello. I won't be engaging with Carl unless I have no other option. I want to keep what happened to me from happening to other women. Stefan is the biggest offender. The others only follow his example. He's the one abusing instead of protecting his own people. Stefan is the one who needs to be taken out. Kill him and the others scatter and become powerless. I know what I need to do."

"Then you have my full support," Pius said with conviction. "You should have everyone's support." He looked at each person in the small room in turn, his eyes lingering on theirs. "If any of you wish to have any sort of a normal life, you must snatch this opportunity." He pointed a finger in Camden's direction. "This man is willing to risk his own life to help us. Priya was telling me he runs his own territory surrounding the college. He knows something about leadership. We should take his advice and this opportunity."

Camden flinched. Saying he ran his own territory was a technicality. Priya had told him that there were no dragons living in the area surrounding the university, at least none she'd heard of. If there had been any, they would have tracked him down and demanded his pledge of fealty. This lack of dragon population made Camden ruler of the territory by default, not by any effort on his part. There was just no one else to challenge for the title.

"He has my vote," Sage spoke up suddenly.

Silence followed her statement for half a minute. Then low murmurs of excitement began to spread throughout the tree house.

"Sage is known for never supporting anyone. Not even her own brother-in-law," Priya whispered in Camden's ear. "Earlier, when she said you had her vote of confidence, I thought she was being sarcastic. She's cruel that way."

"She's that bad?" Kristie whispered from Camden's other side.

"She's as cold as ice," Priya whispered back, ignoring the commotion in the room. "She was constantly undermining her brother-in-law's authority. We all thought one day she was going to challenge him for control."

"It never came to that because he was murdered, though," Camden guessed.

Priya shrugged one shoulder. "At first, people thought she might have been the one responsible. Then, when Stefan came out of the woodwork, people suspected they'd worked together."

She glanced at Sage before her dark eyes slid back to Camden. "I didn't believe it. They might both be taciturn and would make a beautiful couple, but neither is keen on sharing power." She shrugged. "There are still a few people who don't fully buy into her innocence. They think she was double-crossed by Stefan, that things got out of her control. Her backing you is huge. If she's willing to follow someone else, the others will believe in your capability."

"It's quite possibly a political move," Oakley murmured from his seat next to Priya. "A pretty smart one at that. What better way to get back into everyone's good graces than to support a man you know won't stay long to contend for power? If you win and Camden leaves, it will be the two of you battling it out for control. She has better chances there than challenging a merciless dictator." His gaze lifted to Priya's and their eyes held. Never raising his voice, he asked, "Do you trust her?"

"Not at all," Priya whispered through clenched teeth, though she had a patient smile plastered on her face. "I don't think she's a murderer, though." It seemed as if she'd had enough of the reaction over Sage's announcement, because she clapped her hands to get everyone's attention. "People! Please! Settle down." She waited a moment before continuing. "It is wonderful that we have Sage's support, but we would like it from everyone. Will you join us?"

The room grew quiet. Camden felt uncertainty creep in the longer the silence stretched. He knew they were asking a lot of these people, perhaps too much. He wouldn't blame them if they turned their backs and continued on with their lives.

In the stillness, a man's voice said, "I'm with you."

Following this, a woman's voice chimed in as well. "Me too. I want to see Stefan get what he deserves."

Slowly, other voices spoke up. Members of the dragon community threw their support to him one voice at a time. Camden's breath escaped him in a relieved whoosh. They were now one step closer to overthrowing a tyrant.

"Cut Stefan's head off and burn the body," Sage threw in

vehemently.

Camden choked, then punched his chest to fight back the coughing that followed. "Yes. Good advice. Thank you."

"You should piss on the ashes," Sage added. "If I had a dick, I would do that." She frowned. "I don't, though."

"Once again," Camden said awkwardly. "Thank you...I think."

Sage smiled, her expression smug. "You're welcome."

Kristie's eyebrows rose. "And I thought *you* were crazy," she whispered in Priya's direction.

"Welcome to the supernatural community," Priya whispered back.

Camden rolled his eyes. He still thought Priya was a bit nutty, but she was harmless...mostly.

The dragon in question offered him one last smirk before addressing the assembled group. "We will kill Stefan Marcello," she said firmly. "We are not backing down from this, no matter the cost. With that in mind, if there is anyone who wishes to challenge this decision, speak now. This is the only chance you will have to address the community on an alternative plan." Silence answered her statement. "So that's it then?" she asked, sounding relieved. "No one objects to the plan?"

"I do." A low voice answered her from the ladder. A moment later, a head popped into view. The man's body followed, and he stood in the entrance to the little house. He stood with his feet braced apart and his knees dipped as if he was ready for battle.

The man had long dark hair that hung into his eyes, unsuccessfully attempting to cover a patchwork of scars that traveled up the right side of his face. From cheekbone up to forehead, he was a network of scars and pockmarks.

He wore an open, floor-length faux leather jacket over a tight gray t-shirt. The jacket's hood was pulled up over his head, putting his eyes in ominous shadows. His pants were black leather, matching the glove on his right hand. There were finger holes in the glove, showing off the burnt flesh of his hand. A large sword was strapped across his back, the handle visible over his shoulder.

"Therius Thorn," Priya said evenly. Her voice came out strong, but Camden felt her stiffen next to him.

"Priya," Therius greeted in amusement. "Slumming it as

usual." Moving in a blur of supernatural speed, he swiveled to the glass case behind him that held Kristie's dolls and kicked it in with a booted foot.

Glass shattered, the shards sprinkling to the floor amidst gasps of fear from the assembled group. "Oops," Therius said cruelly. "I hope that wasn't important."

Pius moved threateningly in his direction.

Therius whipped two revolvers from the waistband of his pants. One lifted to point at Pius; the other pointed at Priya. "I wouldn't move if I were you."

Priya inhaled sharply, but didn't give any ground.

"I'm taking it this isn't one of our guys," Camden whispered, his arm going protectively around Kristie.

Priya shook her head a fraction of an inch. "Decidedly not. This is Therius Thorn, Stefan's mercenary." She swallowed and her petite hands quivered. "He…" She shook her head, unable to continue.

Seeing the pure terror on Priya's face made Camden realize they were in way over their heads. If she was this frightened by someone that merely took orders from Stefan, they were all in trouble.

"Now that I have your attention…" Therius shook his head slightly to toss hair out of his eyes, exposing more of his scarred face, yet the guns never wavered. "I have a message from Stefan." His lips curled into a wicked grin. "He wanted me to tell your pathetic little group that you will all be dead before the week is up." His eyes flicked to Camden, though his body never moved. "Anyone who follows you will die. You will be personally responsible for the horrific punishments that are doled out to these people. Can you live with that?"

Camden stayed silent, but his stomach flipped with anxiety. He didn't want to be the reason people got killed, let alone hurt. "These people just want their freedom."

"Not my problem," Therius said carelessly.

"People being treated like victims and prisoners in their own town isn't your problem? It should be if you have a soul, however little it might be," Kristie snapped in annoyance.

Therius' head whipped in her direction. "Shut your human up, or I will."

Camden stepped protectively in front of his girlfriend. He knew this man could probably kill him without breaking a sweat, but he was too blinded by rage to care. He took a step toward Therius, his fists clenched with anger. "Listen you comic book reject," he snarled. "Don't you ever threaten my girlfriend, or I will personally tear you limb from limb." He continued toward Therius, his shoes crunching on the broken glass littering the floor. "You're going to leave here right now, because no matter how badass you think you are, you aren't going to be able to take out all of us. You are going to have twenty-some pissed off dragons all gunning for you if you fire even a single shot. I don't think even someone as skilled as you likes those odds." He jerked his head toward the ladder. "Get the hell out of *my* territory, and give your boss this message. *We're* coming for *him*."

Therius' demeanor never wavered, but Camden saw the displeasure in his eyes. He thought he'd been sent to bully some passive, frightened pushovers. He didn't like being sent into a possible riot. It was written plainly in the blue orbs of his eyes.

"I'll deliver the message," Therius said coolly. "I'm sure Stefan will be glad to know the names of everyone present. He'll want to know who's committing treason." His eyes swept the room, lingering on each person in turn. "If any of you want to be on the winning side, Stefan will welcome you back into his fold. The rest of you...you've just signed your own death certificates."

With that, he jumped from the tree, not even bothering with the ladder. He landed in a graceful, effortless crouch. Then he stood, straightened his jacket, and strode across the Taylors' property to disappear through the gate in the front yard a few moments later.

It was a full minute before anyone spoke. Sage, who'd been pressed along the back wall during Therius' visit, let out a shaky laugh. "Well, we sure showed him."

"We?" Camden asked incredulously.

"Well, you," Sage reluctantly admitted. "But we were all backing you up."

Camden looked around at the faces in the room. Everyone was staring at him with eagerness. Expressions were full of gratitude, awe, and trust. "Fudge," he grumbled. He'd gone and done something brave. Now all these people...dragons believed he was some type of fearless leader.

"We can do this," Pius said energetically. "We can defeat

Stefan. We can be free."

Out of the corner of his eye, Camden saw Priya's satisfied smile. "We can defeat Stefan," she chimed in. "And we will."

He was distracted from the murmurs of agreement when Kristie slipped her arms around his waist. "You're my hero," she gushed.

"Not you, too," he groaned.

"You've always been my hero, but this is..." She grabbed his face in her hands, stood on her tiptoes, and kissed him.

Camden stumbled back a step and was forced to wrap his arms around her waist. The kiss was intense and had a flair of drama to it that left him breathless. It reminded him of when Lois Lane kissed Clark Kent for the first time on Smallville. The way she'd hopped up on that stack of newspapers in her sexy heels... His inner geek had all but swooned.

And why was he thinking about Lois Lane when he had the hottest girl he'd ever met kissing him as if she couldn't get enough? With a chuckle, he pushed all thoughts other than his girlfriend to the back of his mind and returned her kiss.

When Kristie finally pulled back, she gazed up at him with adoring blue eyes. "That was some Karate Kid shit right there, fighting for my honor." She kissed him again, sliding her hands down his chest. "God, I want to have your babies."

Camden backed up a step with a nervous laugh at the sudden and extreme jump in topic. "Yeah, but not right now. Right? Like twenty years from now...if we're still together." There was a look in her eyes that unnerved him, causing him to take another step back.

"I would do it now if you wanted," Kristie purred as she closed the small space he'd created between them and fiddled with the top button of his dress shirt. "I just want you. All of you."

Priya shot Kristie a forced look of amusement. "They recently mated," she said in way of explanation to the group. "On those overshared words, we can adjourn the meeting so they can get back to their alone time."

As he walked toward the ladder, Pius clapped Camden on the shoulder. "Congrats, man. I know it takes forever to find 'the one'. It took me seven hundred and fifty years to find my mate."

Camden smiled weakly and snatched Kristie's hand in his

own when her fingers drifted to his belt buckle.

Pius' eyes followed Camden's hands and he smirked. "Like I said, very lucky." He turned to Priya with a wicked grin. "Remember, dragon mates tend to run in families." He sent a pointed look to Oakley, which earned him a glare from Priya. Laughing, Pius leapt from the tree house.

Camden kept a forced smile on his lips as everyone slowly followed after Pius. His hand gripped Kristie's tightly to keep them from wandering in places less than appropriate in public. When everyone besides Priya and Oakley had gone, he turned to his girlfriend in surprise. "What was that all about?"

The second he released her hands, she slid them up his shirt and along his stomach. "I don't know," she practically moaned. "I just want you. I can't think around it." She stepped in against him, pressing the front of her body to his.

"I told you," Priya said in a bored tone. "You've mated. The urge to have sex and procreate doesn't mess with you alone. It hits her, too. She can't resist, nor can she restrain herself."

Camden flinched before shooting Kristie an apologetic look. "I'm sorry. I never meant to drag you into all of this."

"As long as you make love to me tonight, I don't care." Her words were a breathy whisper in his ear as she stroked his collar.

Oakley jumped out of his seat and grabbed his sister by the shoulders. Gently, he eased her away from Camden. "Someone needs a cold shower before dinner." He glanced in Priya's direction. "You're staying, right?"

She blinked in surprise. "You want me to stay for dinner? With your human parents?"

"That's how things usually work. You've been hanging out in our tree house all day. You can come in for some food."

"Human lifespans are very short. I am honored they would spend some of their precious time with me."

Oakley rolled his eyes with a laugh. "Why does something as simple as dinner have to be weird with you? It's just dinner. Not a gift of our precious human lifespan."

With an uneasy stomach, Camden watched the assembled group as they lightheartedly chatted. They all looked happy and positive. He couldn't bring himself to think that way. This situation was bad. Even if they managed to defeat

Stefan, people were probably going to die, people he cared about.

"Well," Priya said to Camden as she turned to look at him. "Your teenage hormones served you well here. Everyone thought you were terribly brave for standing up to Therius. They didn't seem to even suspect you were merely a slave to your primal instincts. Being newly mated on top of that didn't hurt either. It gave you more reason to be rash."

As Camden looked at her, he asked the one question that had been weighing on his mind since the topic had been spoken for all to hear. "Why didn't you tell me you'd been raped?"

The tree house fell suddenly silent and the cheerful mood evaporated. It was like someone had sucked it instantly out through the tiny window.

"I didn't think it was any of your business," she said coldly. The carefree attitude she'd slowly eased into disappeared instantly, and she was once against the distant and detached woman he'd originally met. "Like I told Pius, it won't affect my duties. Beyond that, it isn't your concern."

Realizing she thought he was questioning her ability to do what needed to be done, Camden shook his head. "I'm not worried about your duties," he said gently, trying to ignore the glare Oakley was sending him. "Priya, I'm worried about how it has been affecting *you*. That...it's horrible."

"Tell me about it." Though her tone was harsh and confrontational, she crossed her arms self-consciously over her chest.

"Have you talked to anyone about it?" he asked. "Are you getting any help?"

"No. For your information, I am not. I don't need help. I am handling everything just fine on my own. What I need is for you to butt out of my personal life." She flopped down onto the mattress with an aggravated huff. "I am so tired of everyone treating me like a fragile piece of glass that might break at any moment. I can handle myself just fine! I thought perhaps I'd found people who saw me for something other than a victim, but here that ugly fact is being dragged out for everyone to see once again."

Letting go of his sister's arm, Oakley sank to the mattress next to Priya. "If it makes you feel any better, I still think you're smoking hot. I wouldn't think twice about jumping into bed with you. If that's not treating you the same, I don't know what is."

Camden wasn't sure how wise it was to talk to a rape victim about sex, but he wasn't dealing with regular people.

Instead of shying away as a normal woman might, Priya beamed at Oakley. "Really?" she asked with a hopeful expression. "You still want to have sex with me?"

A wolfish grin spread across Oakley's lips, and he eyed her for a moment in appreciation. "Sure do. A woman who breathes fire and can kick my ass... Call me a sadist, but that is damn hot."

As thrilled as Camden was to see Priya perking up after his painful question, watching Oakley's shameless flirting was nauseating. "Do you think we can go in for some dinner now? Your parents hate me enough without us being late." He spoke the words pointedly to Kristie's brother, trying to get him moving in the direction of the house.

Oakley's flirtatious grin fell and he shot Camden a look of annoyance at the obviously unwanted interruption. "Why should I care if they hate you?"

Camden's eyes flicked to Priya and a nasty smirk crept up his lips. "You'll care because I don't believe your father cares too much for your love interest either. If I remember correctly, she told me if your family wouldn't take orders from me, I should snap all your necks and be done with it. I'm betting your father isn't going to easily forget that comment."

"I said that before I knew your human, though!" Priya cried out in her own defense, her eyes narrowing at Camden in annoyance. "I would probably frown upon killing them *now*."

"*Probably*?" Oakley asked in disbelief. Shaking his head, he turned to Camden. "Fine. You've got a point. Let's all go do dinner. We can smile and lie to the ignorant humans."

"That's the spirit," Priya chirped, patting Oakley on the knee.

"That was sarcasm!"

Priya shrugged and climbed to her feet. "Well, it's the truth." She straightened her suit jacket and smoothed a wrinkle out of her black skirt. "Let's lie our asses off and make these humans think we're normal."

"I am normal," Oakley grumbled.

"Your life is no more normal than mine anymore," Priya

argued. She grabbed him by the front of his shirt and pulled him toward the ladder. "Get over it."

Camden watched them disappear down the ladder, chatting and flirting as they went. Shaking his head in disbelief at the odd turn of events where those two were concerned, he lowered his gaze to Kristie to find her staring up at him. "What?" he asked nervously.

"I wanted to apologize," she said softly.

"Apologize?" he asked in confusion. "For what?"

"For going insane?" She offered the suggestion with an embarrassed laugh. "For clinging all over you in front of everyone like that. Mostly for freaking you out with my ridiculous comments."

She rolled her eyes in annoyance and kicked at a broken shard of glass. "I'm sorry. I don't know what came over me. I just had this burning desire. It hit me so hard," she explained a little breathlessly, "that I couldn't even think about fighting it."

Her eyes held his and there was a seriousness in them that wasn't normally there. "I always want you, Camden. I want to be with you. I want to touch you. But this..." She shivered. "I had no control over it. It wasn't me. It was...something else. Having you stand up for me opened some door in my mind that I didn't even know existed." She lowered her eyes and fiddled with her fingers a moment before lifting her chin and holding his gaze once again. "I've never wanted you that badly before. In that instant, I would have gladly given my life for yours. I wanted you in every way imaginable. I wanted your children for crying out loud." She ran her hands over her face before dropping down to the mattress.

His heart plummeted and Camden fought to stay calm as he sat next to her. "You don't like having your free will taken away," he said softly. Since the very beginning, she'd been so understanding about this whole dragon thing, but he worried they'd just crossed an unspoken line that was finally too much for her. He couldn't lose her. Not now. He didn't think he'd be able to survive this week without her support.

Cautiously, he reached out and placed his hand on her knee. "It was an invasion of privacy. If there was any way I could take it back..."

Kristie uncovered her eyes and stared up at him, fear in

her expression. "I'm not concerned with that. I love you, Camden, dragon side effects or no. They're only intensifying what I already felt." She placed a hand over his, lacing their fingers. "I'm terrified, not of this power, but of what it might do to you. If what I felt was the tame version of what you are going through..." Her hand tightened over his, her nails curling under to dig into his palm. "Do you love me?"

"You know I do." His words came out in a breathy, nervous whisper. He was worried as to where this was going.

"That's what frightens me." Taking a deep breath, she explained. "When your power rolled over me, I would have gladly died for you, no question about it. You have to fight that. These people could use it against you, use *me* against you. If they threaten me, you might do something stupid, like die for me...again. You can't let that happen. Priya's people depend on you. You're a dragon. You're immortal. I'm just a human, and I'm fragile. Don't let yourself get hurt over something so irrational."

"Kristie—"

"Promise me you won't let that happen. I need you to promise your main target is Stefan, no matter what."

"You are more important—"

"Promise," she said firmly. "I won't let innocent children suffer because your main concern is me. I won't let *you* die." She took a shaky breath and her eyes turned cold. "Promise me or I will leave you. It will be the hardest thing I ever have to do, but I will walk out of your life and never come back. If you love me, you'll do this for me."

"I do love you," Camden said slowly, dread filling his stomach. He was trapped by her words. There wasn't anything he wouldn't do for her, but she was asking something nearly impossible.

"I know you do," she said softly to his confession of love. "This new power can make that backfire on you. For just this week, I can't be the top priority in your life."

Camden sighed wearily and dropped his head into his hands. She was right, but he hated it. An insane idea popped into his head. Before he could curb it, he said, "I'll do this for you if you do something for me." On her puzzled nod, he dropped to a knee in front of where she sat. "Marry me."

Kristie's eyes widened and she sucked in a surprised breath. "What?"

"Marry me the instant this is over. I want to fly to some exotic resort and elope. The semester's nearly finished. Let's take our finals early and leave. If you are going to put me through this hell, then I want you to be my wife when it's all said and done."

"Camden," she said slowly, her voice so soft it was barely audible.

"Wait," he begged. "Let me finish. I know we're young and it's crazy to rush into things, but I've already done the dragon mating thing with you. We're meant to be together. I know it. Pius said some people are meant to be a dragon's mate. It's in their blood. Maybe that's why I came back as this. I came back this way for *you*."

"Camden—"

He cut her off again. "I know what you're thinking. Our parents are going to be pissed. Well, they'll get over it. They'll have a few years to cool down while we finish our degrees. Then we'll have a real wedding, a big wedding. We'll invite everyone we know and do the fancy white dress thing. We—"

"Camden!" Kristie yelled, cutting him off. When she finally had his attention, she grabbed his face in her hands and kissed him. She practically dragged him onto the mattress with her.

Camden's knee hit the mattress between hers and he was forced to brace his hands against it on either side of her legs to keep from toppling over.

Her arms slid around his neck and she opened her mouth to him with a soft coo of desire.

Camden pulled back long enough to ask, "Was that a yes?" On her confirmation, his mouth closed over hers. His fingers reached out to graze along the top of her breasts, caressing the exposed flesh of her cleavage before dipping down to graze one of her nipples through her top.

When he brushed his thumb along her breast again, Kristie moaned. She tugged him fully onto the mattress and rolled, forcing him underneath her. She straddled his waist, leaning over him with a purr.

At that moment, a noise of disgust came from the entrance of the tree house. "Ew, gross!"

Camden and Kristie guiltily broke their kiss. They turned their heads to the doorway to find Ward staring at them in revulsion.

"Mom wanted me to see what was taking you two so long." His eyes shifted to the hand Camden had against Kristie's breast. "Guess I have an answer for her."

Kristie quickly jumped off of Camden's lap and ran her fingers through her hair with a nervous laugh. "Ward, wait! We were just...um...well... We're coming," she said finally in defeat. "Wait for us." Shooting Camden an apologetic look, she ushered her brother down the ladder and followed quickly behind him.

Camden lay for a moment looking up at the ceiling with his feeling of dread back. There was no use wallowing in it, though. It was time to go face the Taylors...possibly something more terrifying than the most vicious of dragons.

Chapter 10

Wishing to forget about the incident in the tree house, Camden entered the Taylor dining room a few steps behind Kristie and Ward. Everyone else was already at the table giving them impatient looks.

"Oh good," Alice said brightly. "You found them."

"Yeah, I found them making out in the tree house," Ward said with disgust. He shot Camden a glare before plopping down into his seat.

Mrs. Taylor's lips pursed in disapproval, and her husband's eyes narrowed at Camden in annoyance.

Camden sighed. *So much for the semi-positive family meeting*, he thought dryly. "I...well...it wasn't..."

"So!" Kristie said perkily. "What do we have for dinner?"

Mrs. Taylor's frown lifted at the mention of food. It was the perfect distraction. "Oh! Well, I've prepared Norwegian smoked salmon with potato arugula salad on the side." Her smile widened. "For dessert, I have chocolate ganache with raspberry dipping sauce."

Though Camden wasn't a fan of fish, this was the first time in days the thought of food didn't fill his chest with an agonizing blaze. He sent Alice a beaming smile. "That sounds amazing."

She glanced in his direction, her face full of shock. "Really?"

"Really," he assured as he slid into the vacant seat next to Kristie. "In fact, I'll have the first piece."

Kristie smiled and placed a hand on his knee under the

table. "See?" She addressed her family as she spoke. "I told you a trip to the doctor to figure out Camden's meds would help things."

Camden nodded, trying not to smirk. By going to the doctor, she meant talking through dragon customs and side effects with Priya. And by meds, she meant breathing fire to alleviate his symptoms, but her description was about as good as it was going to get without giving away his secret.

"Well, I'm glad you're feeling better, dear," Alice said as she played host by serving Camden some of the salmon.

"Yeah. Great," Ward grumbled sarcastically. "Now he can make out with my sister without fear of blowing chunks. Whoopee!"

"I do admire your positivity," Priya said brightly to the youngest member of the Taylor family, trying to be optimistic, though it did nothing to help the situation. Her statement hung uncomfortably in the air. Everyone sat in awkward silence as if not wanting to be the first to speak.

Camden was considering bolting from the room and going to hide in the tree house when the doorbell rang. He lunged to his feet, nearly knocking his chair to the ground. "I'll get it," he said, his tone nearly frantic. Anything to get away from the discomfort that lingered in the air...

He didn't wait for an argument. He rushed down the front hall before that could happen. He was at the door before he even considered that the person on the other end might be someone who wished to do him harm. Honestly, until they returned to school, he should always be the one answering the door. He didn't want Therius to show up and hurt any of the Taylors because he'd taunted the other dragon.

Anxiously, he leaned forward and peered through the peephole. When he saw Bradley on the stoop, he let out his breath in a whoosh of relief. Unlocking the door, he swung it open.

His relief was short-lived when he saw Beau standing next to her, looking anxiously at the sun and patting the sleeves of his smoking jacket.

"Bradley." Camden greeted his best friend, purposefully ignoring her boyfriend. "What are you doing here? I thought you were going to Adrian's for the holiday."

Bradley rolled her eyes with a smile. "You know Adrian and Beau can't be in the same room together for more than ten minutes without hackles rising. Imagine them living under the same roof for nearly a week." She sighed, but her lip was still curled in a smile. "Adrian interrogates Beau, so Beau messes with him. You've seen it before."

Camden noted the slight smirk on Beau's lips. He would have thought a vampire might have better things to do than mess with his girlfriend's brother, but apparently he was wrong.

"Anyway," Bradley continued, "I decided to give Adrian, more importantly myself, a break for the evening. I was worried about you. This was less than an hour drive from Adrian's, so I figured we'd stop by. I wanted to check in and see how things were going."

Camden watched the way Beau's eyes slid over him, appraising. He swallowed nervously as the conversation he'd overheard between the two of them came rushing back. Would Beau kill him if the vampire found out he was a dragon? That wasn't something he was willing to risk finding out. "I'm fine," he said with forced cheer. "I'm feeling pretty great actually. Thanks for stopping by to check on me, though." With that, he slammed the door in Bradley's face.

"Camden!" Mrs. Taylor's voice cried out from behind him. "What kind of host do you think I am?" She marched to the door. "If your friends traveled all this way to see you and check on your health, I'm not just going to turn them out on the street." She swung open the door and gave Bradley a bright smile. "Hello, dear. You must be a friend of Camden and Kristie. I'm Mrs. Taylor."

The confused expression Bradley wore over having the door slammed in her face melted into a smile. "I'm Bradley." She offered a hand for the other woman to shake. "I'm best friends with Camden." She motioned behind her. "This is my boyfriend, Beau."

Mrs. Taylor's eyes landed on Beau and she froze. Her jaw dropped slightly, and Camden could practically see the stars in her eyes. This tended to happen to people around Beau. Everyone seemed to love him: mothers, women in general really, babies, puppies, even Camden had to admit the other man was pretty damn badass. Everyone but Bradley's older brother seemed to be in the vampire's thrall. Camden hated to admit it, but the man had charisma, and not just because he was a vampire with supernatural powers.

Beau was the epitome of tall, dark, and handsome. His shoulder-length black hair was currently slicked back off his forehead. A black designer dress shirt, which was unbuttoned at the neck to draw the attention of the female population, was covered by a black, knee-length jacket. The jacket was obviously expensive, possibly custom tailored to fit the man's broad shoulders. Black slacks and polished Armani dress shoes rounded out the outfit.

Camden hated him and admired him all at the same time.

"Hello, Mrs. Taylor." Beau stepped forward to shake her hand as he greeted her. "I'm Beauregard Channing."

"Beauregard." Alice repeated him, sounding love struck already.

"I'm so sorry to intrude, Mrs. Taylor..."

Alice cut Beau off. "Oh, please. Call me Alice."

Beau grinned, showing off his perfect white teeth.

Camden wondered if "Alice" would be so impressed if Beau's fangs were out and noticeable.

"Thank you, Alice," Beau said charmingly. "Once again, I wish to apologize for our intrusion. We just wanted to check on our buddy Camden here. He had a hospital scare before break, and we wanted to make sure he was doing okay."

"That was very thoughtful of you." Mrs. Taylor opened the door wider in invitation. "Well, why don't you come inside? You can join us for dinner and visit afterward. I'm sure Camden and Kristie would be delighted for the company."

Camden made a noncommittal grunt filled mostly with displeasure. In truth, he wanted to be far away from Beau.

"We wouldn't wish to intrude..."

Camden rolled his eyes at Beau's fake concern. The vampire had no problem with intruding on other people's lives.

"Nonsense!" Mrs. Taylor took Beau's arm and pulled him inside the house. "We would love to have you for dinner. It's no trouble at all to add two extra plates. There's plenty of food to go around."

"Oh, he'd love to have *you* for dinner, too," Camden grumbled as he watched them walk off to the dining room.

"Thank you so much for inviting me inside," Beau said with a mocking grin at Camden over his shoulder.

Camden rolled his eyes again. The whole *vampires have to be invited in* thing was a myth. Beau had barged into his apartment on numerous occasions without an invitation. The vampire was just goading him.

"Camden," Bradley said, drawing his attention away from her boyfriend, "I'm so glad you're okay." She moved forward and gave him a hug, kissing his cheek. "I worry about you."

He hugged her tightly in return. Despite being wary of Beau, he was grateful to Bradley for coming to see how he was. She was truly the best friend a guy could have. "You don't have to worry about me."

"Says the guy who got shot and had his neck snapped all in one evening," she said, lips curving into a teasing smile. "I remember having to bring you back from the dead. It's not something I'm going to forget any time soon."

It wasn't something he was going to forget any time soon either. In fact, his newfound fire-breathing abilities were a constant reminder of what happened to people who cheated death. "Are you ever going to let me live that down?" Camden asked playfully in an attempt to lighten his brooding thoughts.

"Never." Bradley looped her arm through his as she guided him into the dining room, following behind Mrs. Taylor and Beau.

When they reached the others, Alice was still holding tightly to Beau's arm. She beamed up at him as she began making introductions. "Everyone, this is Beauregard." Camden could actually hear the purr in her voice as she spoke Beau's name. Oh yeah, she was in love. Alice motioned behind her. "And this is Bradley. They are friends of Camden's that will be joining us for dinner."

"Great." Ward's words were a grumble, but he spoke them loud enough for everyone to hear. "The freak has friends."

Alice ignored this and continued with introductions. "This is my husband, Dale."

Dale nodded politely, though his expression conveyed that he was impatient to move on to dinner.

"This is my son, Ward," Alice continued. "He's my baby."
Ward cringed.

"This is my middle child, Oakley. And—" She broke off in confusion and stared at Priya as if just noticing her for the first time. "Who are you, dear? We never got to introductions." Her eyebrows drew together in uncertainty. "You are the girl from the ice cream store, yes?" She looked at her family as if silently asking why the woman who ran the local ice cream shop was at their dinner table.

"This is Priya," Oakley said. "She's my date for the evening. She's my woman." He wrapped an arm around Priya's shoulder and gave a teasing squeeze.

Priya shot him a dirty look and elbowed him in the ribs, though she didn't shake off his arm. "I'm not your woman. You're my pet to do with as I please."

Dale choked on the water he'd been about to swallow.

Kristie patted her father roughly on the back with a satisfied smirk. "Camden's not looking so bad right now, is he?"

During the awkward silence that followed this comment, Camden noticed Beau staring curiously at Priya. Not wanting the vampire looking too closely at his crazy personal life, Camden clapped his hands together loudly. "Okay! How about we get down to dinner now that the introductions are out of the way?"

Alice released Beau only to rush to the kitchen for more plates and silverware.

Oakley shot Camden a curious look as he climbed to his feet. "I'll go get some extra chairs. Why don't you help me?"

Camden nodded and followed him into the living room.

"Okay," Oakley whispered as soon as they were out of hearing range. "What is going on? You're practically sweating bullets." He paused before adding, "More than usual, I mean."

"Am I that obvious?" Camden asked with a cringe. If Oakley could tell he was nervous, there was no doubt Beau could as well.

"Worse."

"Damn."

"Who are those people?" Oakley asked. "Why do you look so terrified? You look worse now than when Therius showed up."

"Therius caught me by surprise," Camden admitted. "I didn't have time to think about it. I've had plenty of time to think about the things Beau might do to me."

"So they're bad guys?" Oakley whispered angrily. "And you left them alone with my family?"

"They're not bad guys." Camden was quick to assure Oakley of this lest the teen rush out and do something rash. "They're my friends."

Oakley's eyebrows rose in astonishment. "Then why are

you worried about the things Beau is going to do to you?" His face suddenly twisted in disgust. "This isn't a gay thing, is it?"

Camden gave a bark of laughter at the mere thought of Beau being gay. "No! It's not a gay thing. Of course it isn't! I'm worried he might kill me."

"Some friend."

"It's...complicated." Camden shrugged. "He's a vampire."

"Wait!" Oakley hissed the word in an angry tenor and his eyes widened in revulsion. "You invited a vampire into our house?"

"First off," Camden said in his own defense, "I didn't invite him in. Your mother did that." He held up a hand to cut off Oakley's protests. "Secondly, Beau is one of the good guys."

"One of the good guys wants to kill you?" Oakley's voice was skeptical as he led Camden up the stairs to his father's study for more chairs.

"He doesn't *want* to kill me...at least I don't think so." Camden huffed out a sigh as he grabbed a chair from the table in the corner of the room. "Okay, here's the deal. Remember the best friend who raised me from the dead?"

Oakley nodded.

"It was Bradley."

Oakley's eyebrows shot to his hairline. "The little hottie downstairs is a witch?"

"Hey!" Camden flinched. "Don't talk about Bradley like that. She's like a sister to me."

"I don't think you have any grounds to be complaining about sister stuff. I just spent the morning listening about how you branded *my* sister during sex."

"Point taken," Camden said reluctantly. "Let's move on." He dragged the chair toward the doorway. "Bradley raised me from the dead, and Beau knew the chances were good I wouldn't come back human." He grunted in annoyance. "This is a little tidbit of information the two of them didn't feel the need to share with me. I'm sure you can imagine my surprise when I thought I was having a heart attack at the tender age of twenty."

"Couldn't have been fun," Oakley chimed in as he grabbed and dragged a second chair toward the door. "You must have thought you were overdosing."

Camden shot him a sour look. "How many times do I

have to tell you I'm not a druggie? Sure, I'll admit I smoked a little pot in the past, but Bradley slapped me upside the head when she found out. She literally slapped me. Stuck up, goody-two shoes white witch." When he caught Oakley's grin, he stopped his rant.

"I'm just teasing, dude," Oakley said with a chuckle. "I'm thinking not even the Jaws of Life could pry my sister from your side at this point. I'm going to have to get used to seeing your ugly mug."

Camden felt a rush of warm emotion toward his future brother-in-law and the acceptance he finally felt from a member of Kristie's family. He paused, letting his chair go for a minute. "I love her." He wanted Oakley to know he wasn't just dragging Kristie along on this ride without being sure of his feelings for her. That wouldn't be fair. Hell, sometimes he was sure it still wasn't fair.

"I know." Oakley's voice was a grumbled admission of annoyance. "I know she loves you, too. For months, you're all she's talked about. I think I was just thrown by your appearance. I was expecting...not you."

Camden rolled his eyes. "I'd be insulted by that except I was just as surprised as you that Kristie gave me the time of day." He smiled with affection at the thought. "She sees past the trivial, the physical. Your sister sees..." He shook his head. She'd seen right into his soul.

Oakley offered a grunt. "Can we move on from my sister? This is starting to weird me out a little bit. Let's get back to why Beau might kill you."

"Right," Camden said eagerly, picking his chair back up. "Beau knows I'm not human anymore. He's just waiting for me to sprout horns or start eating babies. He said he would *do whatever he had to* when my symptoms started emerging."

"Can't you explain to him that you're not evil?"

"I could try, but what if he has something against dragons? What if he kills me before I get a chance to explain? Look at him, would you want to take him on? Keep in mind he's a vampire who's used to violence."

"Point taken." Oakley started down the steps, moving slowly due to the bulky chair. "Would you like me to pick a fight with him? My parents might kick him out if things get hostile."

Camden grinned, feeling a sense of camaraderie with Oakley. Oddly, the only other guy he'd ever felt this with was Beau. He'd had other male friends, but he would guiltily admit they were stoner buddies. His only true friend had been Bradley. "No. You don't need to start anything with Beau," he said, his voice full of gratitude. "Thanks for the offer, though."

Oakley bobbed his head as they reentered the living room. "Sure thing. I'm not letting some vampire break into my house and kill our guests during dinner....even if that guest is you."

Camden chuckled and shook his head. "Thanks...I think."

Oakley shrugged with a crooked grin. "Don't start getting too comfortable. I still might kick your ass down the road."

"You can try," Camden replied with a confident smirk.

"If you didn't have those supernatural powers, I'd wipe the floor with you," Oakley said with a roll of his eyes.

"Agreed," Camden said with a laugh as they pushed into the kitchen. "Not much incentive to fight fair, is it?"

Kristie's eyebrows rose in surprise as they entered the dining room laughing. It must have been odd to see the two of them getting along so well after their disastrous start.

"Well isn't this nice," Alice said in a chipper voice as she clapped her hands together. She beamed at her eldest son as if he were partaking in something much more amazing than the simple act of excelling at conversation.

"Yeah. Nice." Oakley's words were a grumble as he pushed the chair in his hands roughly toward Beau. "Here you go, dude. Don't fall on it. Wood can be dangerous."

Beau stared at the teen in puzzlement. "Um...okay. Thanks."

Camden snickered and set his chair down in front of Bradley. "Here you go, Brad." He held the chair for her as she sat and scooted it in behind her.

"Thank you, sweetie," she said with a smile. She shot Kristie a grin. "He's such a gentleman."

Kristie nodded. "Yes. He's very polite. He always makes sure I'm happy." As he took a seat next to her, she caressed Camden's shoulder. "He always makes sure I'm pleased with the movies we go to see, the places we have dinner, my preferred positions in the bedroom..."

Mrs. Taylor spat her water out across the table.

Kristie's eyes widened as she seemed to remember everyone who was present at the table. "I meant Yoga positions.

Dang, Mom." Her voice rang nervous and false through the room. "Dirty mind much?" Leaning over to Bradley, she whispered loud enough for the entire table to hear. "I actually meant sexual positions."

Camden groaned and covered his face with his hands. Did she really bring up their preferred sexual positions in front of her family? He didn't have to open his eyes to feel Oakley's glare. He suddenly wished he could sink into the floor.

Bradley, trying to save the situation, smiled at everyone. "I love Yoga." She laughed apprehensively. "Who doesn't love Yoga?"

Silence greeted her.

"Okay," Bradley said with a chirp. "How about we get to dinner?"

"Agreed," Oakley, Alice, Dale, and Camden all said in unison.

Bradley's eyebrows rose. "Sounds like family time has been going well," she said sarcastically.

"You have no idea," Ward grumbled.

Mrs. Taylor shot her youngest child a quick warning look before taking a deep breath. She let it out slowly, then plastered a wide, fake smile on her face. "I agree with Bradley. Let's eat." She reached into the basket of rolls and pulled one out. She shoved nearly the entire thing into her mouth and bit down. Trying to talk around her overflowing mouthful of food, Alice plopped down roughly in her seat. "Dig in."

"Thanks, Mommy." With an appreciative smile toward her mother, Kristie began loading her plate up with food.

Everyone followed her lead and before long, the atmosphere became more relaxed as people concentrated on their food.

Once the color had returned to her face and she regained her poise, Alice turned to Bradley with an expression of curiosity. "So tell me, dear, how long have you known Camden?"

Bradley shot her best friend an affectionate look. "Since we were in diapers. Our parents are friends. We pretty much grew up together."

"That explains a lot." Alice's voice was a mumble that she tried to hide by bringing her wine glass to her lips.

Camden frowned, but Bradley shot him an encouraging smile before pressing on. "Camden is like a brother to me. He's the best friend a girl could ask for."

"Hmmm." Dale's reply was a disbelieving grunt. This sound was followed by an awkward silence.

Obviously having heard enough, Alice moved the conversation away from Camden and trained her eyes on Beau. "Bradley, do tell us how you met Beauregard. I'm sure that's an interesting story."

Bradley shrugged as she speared a small chunk of salmon with her fork. "Not really."

Camden's brows arched at the lie. The circumstances surrounding the way Bradley and Beau met were completely exciting to the point of becoming unbelievable. Taking a bite of food, he silently awaited her reasoning of how her meeting with Beau had been less than electrifying.

"We met at the university," Bradley said. "Beau is an archaeologist. He was looking into a piece of jewelry I owned. He asked me out. The rest is history."

Camden realized she was talking down her relationship to make his seem more thrilling. He appreciated it, but nothing short of Beau biting someone was going to wipe the infatuated look off of Mrs. Taylor's face.

"It was much more romantic than that." Beau cut into the following silence, a devilish grin on his lips. "She leaves out all of the fun parts." He took Mrs. Taylor's hand and dramatically continued. "I was madly in love with her, but she feared I was trying to con her into selling her antique jewelry at a less than desirable price. I asked her out on multiple occasions, but the answer was always no. I started sending a rose to her dorm room every morning. I had chocolates delivered to her at work. I left cute little stuffed animals outside her room. I went as far as to send her a diamond bracelet wrapped in a hand written poem detailing her beauty. The words came from deep within my heart, expressing my undying love." He touched a hand melodramatically to his chest.

Mrs. Taylor's eyes widened, and she breathily said, "How romantic."

Camden rolled his eyes. He'd been there during the brief courtship. There hadn't been any gifts, and Beau had been the farthest thing from a lovesick puppy. He'd been confident going on arrogant, sure that he'd get the girl in the end. There was no way Beau would ever write poetry either. His entire story so far was bullshit.

"The day came for me to leave the university. With my

last attempt, I found her in the campus courtyard. I dropped to a knee in front of her and begged for her love. Still she rejected me."

Mrs. Taylor's eyes shot to Bradley in surprise. "How could you say no to a face like that?"

Bradley was blinking in confusion at Beau. With a half-hearted smile, she turned to Mrs. Taylor. "I suppose I was playing hard to get. I wanted to find out if he loved me or was trying to sweet talk me out of my antique."

"After this brutal rejection," Beau continued, "I gave up. I decided to give up on love as no other woman would ever compare. Brokenhearted, I packed up my belongings and headed to the airport for a job in Tucson. I was just about to board my flight when I heard someone yelling my name."

"It was you, wasn't it?" Mrs. Taylor asked Bradley with delight. "You showed up to stop him from boarding the plane."

"It was me." Bradley's admission sounded more like a question, and she raised her eyebrows at Beau in question. "Right?"

Beau bobbed his head with an encouraging grin that looked out of place on the vampire. "It sure was." He sat back with a sigh of satisfaction. "She called me back just as I was about to board. She raced over to me, threw herself into my arms, and kissed me." He sighed again. "That kiss was the best moment of my life."

"And most fictional," Camden grumbled under his breath. He rolled his eyes at Beau's antics. Where had the dark and brooding version of the man gone? He was more comfortable with that guy.

"That," Alice said, pressing a palm to her chest, "is the most romantic thing I've ever heard."

Kristie's eyes narrowed. She'd obviously had enough of Beau stealing the limelight as well. "If it was *so* romantic, he'd be the one engaged to be married right now instead of us. *We're* the romantic ones."

Camden sucked in a breath of horror at Kristie's disclosure. He'd hoped to survive the weekend before dropping that bombshell on her family. Shit was about to hit the fan.

"*What?*" The word was hollered by three people nearly simultaneously. Bradley was the first to react, her voice a shrill yelp. Oakley's hollered response came next. Alice all but shrieked the word in outrage.

"Engaged." Kristie affirmed the decision with a nod. "We are going to end our semesters early so we can get married as soon as possible."

"*As soon as possible*?" Alice's words were still being shrieked and her eyes were incredibly wide. "I don't think so, young lady."

"Of all the irresponsible decisions—"

Kristie cut her father's angry words off. "We want to do this," she said defensively. "We have a little money saved up. We're going to go somewhere tropical and say our vows on the beach."

"You think everyone's just going to pack up and follow you at the last minute?" Alice asked testily.

"No. I don't." Kristie's voice was reasonable as she conveyed their plans. "We're eloping. No one is going to be there except the two of us."

Alice gasped in horror. "You aren't going to have your own mother at your wedding?"

"When we finish college and get decent jobs, we're going to do the big, fancy wedding." Kristie's words were gentle as she tried to assure her mother of her inclusion in the affair. "We'll invite everyone then."

"You're doing this to get back at us, aren't you?" Alice asked dramatically. "This is our punishment for kicking you out last night."

"We're doing this for us, not using it as punishment for anyone else." Kristie huffed and threw her hands into the air. "Punishment? God, Mom! It's *punishment* for me to get married?

It was Bradley who answered. "You're on board with this?" She directed her question at Camden, her tone borderline reprimanding. "I know you've had this...obsession with her for forever, but I think if you take a step back—"

"Are you implying my daughter isn't good enough for him?" Alice's head reared back and she set Bradley with a haughty look.

Camden could hear the superior tone in her voice. It was quite obvious that Mrs. Taylor saw things the other way around. *He* wasn't good enough for Kristie.

"No!" Bradley's voice was a shocked cry. Her eyes widened as she was not at all used to being admonished. "It's just that...Camden is... Well, he's... He's very focused on his education. As his best friend, I know that he won't be happy with someone who...." She scrunched her nose, trying to convey her thoughts without sounding insulting. "Someone...someone who doesn't value their education as strongly."

"You think my daughter isn't *smart* enough to date him?" Dale asked, speaking up for the first time. "I'll have you know," he said in an affronted tone, "my daughter is currently at the top of her graduating class. She has a good shot at making valedictorian."

Bradley's eyes widened in disbelief and her head whipped in Kristie's direction. "Wait. You're smart?"

Camden had to smirk at this. He'd known everyone perceived his girlfriend to be nothing more than eye candy. He'd held on to the secret of her intelligence because it was so funny to watch her amusement when people assumed otherwise. She was silently laughing at them while they laughed at her.

"I'm very intelligent, actually," Kristie said in confirmation to the question posed at her.

"You little faker!" Bradley said with awe.

Kristie shrugged. "I hate those people who act superior just because they're smart. I'd rather be me."

Camden reached over and squeezed her hand. "One of the many reasons why I love you and want to do this." The look she gave him made his heart swell. He hadn't ever thought a woman would look at him with such love and adoration, especially not one as amazing as Kristie.

"I wasn't saying Kristie isn't smart," Bradley said, quick to correct herself. "It's just... I don't think they've thought this through. They are making a rash and hasty decision. They are rushing, and I think it may be a mistake."

"Finally," Alice grumbled. "Something we agree on."

"Lust can be a very powerful thing," Bradley continued, not knowing the best time to stop. "I get it. I really do. Lust can be...overwhelming. Add wild, animal sex to that, and it's nearly impossible to think clearly. All you can think about is the next caress, black silk sheets, and bloodletting. Trust me. I know."

"Yeah you do, little Bella," Beau groaned, pulling her toward him for a quick kiss.

Mrs. Taylor's expression had instantly switched to concern. It wasn't merely the topic of lust and wild animal sex, though that had gotten a look, too. No. It was Bradley and

Beau's delight at bloodletting during sex. She was a human getting a glimpse into a vampire's sex life.

Camden wondered what her reaction would be if she found out he enjoyed burning Kristie during sex. He was betting the reaction wouldn't be favorable.

With a sound that couldn't be mistaken for anything other than arousal, Beau pulled away from Bradley. "Mrs. Taylor, I think we all agree that these two are too young to get married. They have forever to do such things. Why rush it?"

Camden glowered at Beau, but before he could comment, Priya said, "I don't agree."

This was received by a glare from Mrs. Taylor. "You don't?" Though a question, her words sounded like an accusation.

"No," Priya said flippantly. "They've already mated. Why not get married? In fact, you should be encouraging them to marry. With the amount of sex they'll be having now..." She shook her head. "The urge to mate will be hard to fight now that they've gotten a taste of it. Your daughter was already begging him to impregnate her. I say marry them off before they conceive and you've got a bunch of illegitimate, fire-breath—" She broke off. "I mean, darling grandchildren running about." She winked at Camden, her face full of pride at catching her near slip.

Alice sucked in a breath of horror. "You asked him to impregnate you?"

A blush spread across Kristie's cheeks. "Perhaps that wasn't the most prudent..."

Alice made a sound that resembled a growl. "I...I cannot believe... Go to your room, young lady!"

"*What*?" Kristie's voice rang through the dining room, full of outrage. "You can't just order me around like I'm a child!"

"You are in my house and you will follow *my* orders. I said go to your room!"

"Fine!" Kristie screamed the word with a snarl. She threw her napkin angrily to the table and stormed out of the room.

Camden began to rise to follow her when Mrs. Taylor's finger pointed at his chest. "You sit down. Lord knows I can't have the two of you sneaking off and making me a grandmother."

Dale shot an annoyed look in Priya's direction. "And you," he said in accusation. "You are the last person my daughter should be taking advice from. If I remember correctly, you told Mr. Harrison he should 'snap our necks and be done with it'."

"That was before I got to know your family. Despite the fact that he's trying to get into my pants, your son has been very charming. You should be proud of him."

Both parents shot Oakley a surprised look. "He's what?" Alice asked weakly.

"Do you not know this slang?" Priya tiled her head questioningly. "It means he wants me to have sexual intercourse with him. He's wearing me down, too. I think he might succeed."

Oakley's face lit up with delighted surprise. "Really?"

Priya gave him a pleased grin. "Yes. There is something undeniably sexy about your persistence."

"Oakley!" Mrs. Taylor barked her son's name, sounding close to hysterical. "Go to your room!"

His eyes widened in disbelief. "But I didn't even do anything!"

"Go!"

"Mom," he growled. "You're embarrassing me."

"I don't care!" Alice slammed her palm against the dinner table, making everyone's glasses rattle. "Get upstairs now!"

He sighed in defeat and stood.

Priya followed, climbing to her feet. "If Oakley is banished, I see no reason to stay." She smiled brightly, seeming oblivious to the tension. "Thank you for inviting me." She then turned to Oakley. "I am far too old for you, but..." She grabbed the collar of his shirt and tugged his mouth down to hers.

Oakley gave a growl of approval and hauled her up against his chest.

When the kiss seemed to go on for longer than was publicly appropriate, Camden's eyebrows rose. His dragon friend sure was doing an about face on her outlook pertaining to human cannon fodder.

Priya finally stepped back with a throaty laugh. "I'll see you soon." She backed away, a grin on her face.

Oakley's expression matched hers. "See you, fire cracker." He stood rooted to his spot as he watched her back out of the room. When they finally heard the front door close, he spun back to the dinner table, a wide grin on his face. "I'm going to marry that woman." His face fell when he caught sight of his parents' expressions. "What?"

"To your room!" Alice hollered.

Oakley shrugged with indifference and disappeared into the living room. A moment later, his footsteps sounded on the stairs.

In the following silence, Bradley cleared her throat. "Maybe we should go."

Mrs. Taylor's predatory look snapped in her direction. "Absolutely not. Just because my children are acting like animals doesn't mean we are cancelling dinner. *Someone* has to eat the meal I've prepared."

"Your children are acting like animals?" Ward asked, sounding annoyed. "What did *I* do?" Before his mother could answer, he continued. "Everything was perfectly fine until this oddity came along." He pointed an accusing finger at Camden. "He's completely screwed up our lives."

"Ward," Dale said admonishingly, "that is very rude!"

"It's true, though! He's been nothing but trouble, and now all of a sudden he's got his hooks into Oakley, too!"

"Ward!" Alice hollered her youngest child's name in anger.

"I know. I know." Ward rolled his eyes in irritation. "Go to my room." He pushed back from his seat and threw his napkin to the table in disgust. "I prefer solitude to tonight's company anyway."

As he stormed out of the room, Bradley pursed her lips thoughtfully. "Are you sure..."

"You're staying." Despite the fact that the other woman had doubted her daughter's intelligence, Alice pinned Bradley with a firm look that clearly stated no one else was leaving the table. "We are going to have a nice family dinner." She took a large gulp from the wine glass in front of her. "Even if it kills us all."

Camden swallowed thickly, wishing he had some wine as well to calm his nerves, but he doubted the Taylors would appreciate him asking for some. They already suspected him of smoking pot in their home. Why add underage drinking to that list? He would be twenty-one in April, but he was pretty sure the Taylor's wouldn't care about how close he was to the legal drinking age. With a sound of defeat, he settled back in his chair for a long, alcohol free evening.

Chapter 11

Camden made his way to the Taylors' front door, following behind Beau and Bradley as he escorted them out. Dinner was finally over. Dinner, and to his horror at the extended time at the table, dessert. He'd spent the entire affair sweating bullets.

Funny how he'd merely been worried about Beau discovering his secret, yet he was downright terrified of Kristie's parents thinking poorly of him. He'd rather deal with angry Beau than the angry Taylors. What did that say about his priorities?

Luckily for him, dinner hadn't been all that bad. Despite its disastrous start and all of the Taylor children being banished from the table, the evening proceeded smoothly enough. Beau and Bradley had somehow managed to completely charm the Taylors. Camden even had a little hope that they'd softened Dale and Alice's opinions of him. Bradley had dazzled them with amusing stories about their childhood together, making him seem much more awesome than he really was. All things considered, dinner had been a success, especially if he stopped to think about its beginning. He couldn't have hoped for better.

Still, being around his future in-laws for so long made him nervous. His eyebrows rose at that thought. He thought of the Taylors as his future in-laws. He and Kristie were really going to do this. It was still hard to believe.

Sure, they were young and still in college, probably too young by human standards, but Camden knew what he wanted out of life. Besides, from what Priya said, he'd already bound them together for life anyway. Why not make it official to the human world as well?

"You've got lovesick look on your face," Bradley said as she turned in the doorway to face him and tapped her fist playfully against his jaw in a mock punch.

He grinned guiltily. "I'm that obvious, huh?"

She shrugged. "Little bit." His best friend in the world paused and bit her lip. Finally, she asked, "Are you sure about this whole wedding thing, Cam? No offense, but you've never seemed like the straight-laced, family man type. I just don't picture you married with children."

"Things change." He offered this explanation with a soft smile. "I'm crazy about her." He shrugged. "Having another close call made me realize I can't take anything for granted." He supposed they'd all had enough close calls in the past couple years to get that.

She nodded with an expression of understanding. "If this is what you truly want, I'm behind you one hundred percent," she said. Then her eyes turned sad. "You're growing up. Soon you're going to have babies and grow out of me."

With a laugh, Camden pulled her into a hug. "I will never outgrow you." He planted a kiss against her hair. "You're my best friend," he whispered. "My sister."

On her laugh, he continued. "Who else is going to babysit all of my brats so Kristie and I can have a night out? It will be immortal Aunt Bradley. I'm sure Beau will have turned you by then."

Bradley pulled back slightly, her eyes wide. "You would expose them to that? I would be a vampire! Could children be trusted to handle the supernatural element and its secrets?"

Pulling her close again so Beau couldn't hear, Camden whispered, "They're going to be fully aware of the supernatural element even if they don't learn it from you. We'll find a way to make it work." Louder, he said, "They'll love you."

As she pulled back to look at him, Bradley's eyes were full of inquisitiveness.

His statement had given away that something otherworldly was going on with him, but he'd kept it vague. He silently pleaded with his eyes for her not to give him up. At least not yet. Beau would eventually find out about him, but he hoped for it to be after he got his new abilities under control. If he could prove he had no ill intentions and possessed the capability to keep his secret, maybe Beau wouldn't kill him...or so he hoped.

Bradley nodded, her eyes roaming over him as if searching for evidence of what he was becoming. After a moment of finding no indication, she merely shook her head. "I'll give you some time to sort things out."

Conveying his gratitude with his expression, Camden pulled Bradley in for one last tight hug. "Thank you," he whispered.

Her arms tightened around him. Then she took a step back. "We'll talk when you get back to school."

"Promise." He winked. "I'll have a wedding to plan, so I won't have time to waste. Catching you up will be one of the first things on the agenda."

Bradley laughed, her expression one of disbelief. "I still can't believe you proposed, Mr. I'll Never Get Married."

He smiled at the bold words he'd spoken all throughout high school. With a little chuckle, he shrugged. "I'm crazy. You know that."

"Always have." She gave a little wave and took a step backward off the porch to join Beau on the sidewalk. "We'll see you soon."

He nodded. Then his gaze slid to Beau. "See ya, dude."

In return, Beau rolled his eyes. "Can't wait." Though his words were sarcastic, a grin touched his lips.

As Camden watched the two of them leave, he smiled. He and the vampire had a special relationship. It was one of those love/hate things. He only hoped Beau was in the friendly phase when he found out about the whole dragon situation.

He gave a little wave, trying to squelch his annoyance as Beau slung an arm over Bradley's shoulder and drew her in for a disgustingly long kiss. With a grunt, he tried to shake off his "big brother" feelings. "I've told him before about the groping, kissing thing. It's gross. No one wants to see their sister kissed by some dude." He suddenly had new respect for Oakley's annoyance with him.

Vowing to be more tactful where Kristie and Oakley were concerned, he turned and walked back into the house. He moved as silently as he could, wanting to avoid his girlfriend's parents. Seeing as Kristie had been banished to her room, he doubted they would appreciate him visiting her. That being said, he wasn't going to spend the evening hanging out with them either. He would probably just get a shower and hide in the den for the evening.

He trudged into the den and ran his hands wearily over his face. This had been a long weekend from hell. Maybe an evening alone to quietly organize his thoughts was what he needed. Scooping up his duffel bag, he trudged up the stairs to the bathroom.

Once inside, he took a deep, cleansing breath. Then he stripped off his shirt and tossed it to the floor. "Here's hoping I don't set *this* bathroom on fire."

He climbed out of the rest of his clothing and was under the hot spray of water within a few minutes. He shoved his face under the stream and let the tension ease out of his shoulders. He was finally relaxing when he heard the bathroom door open. He gasped, choking on the downpour of water. "Ocupado," he said on a cough.

He heard the door click shut a moment later and sighed in relief. Having one of Kristie's parents see him naked would just about top off the awkwardness of this weekend. He didn't think he would survive such a humiliation.

Suddenly, the shower door was yanked open.

Camden made a noise close to a shriek. "I'm in here! The bathroom is occupied!" As he was struggling to wipe water out of his eyes, hands slid around his waist. He gave another cry of alarm.

"Camden, shut up!" Kristie hissed in his ear. "Do you want us to get caught?"

He calmed at the sound of her voice. "Sorry. You scared the crap out of me." His vision finally cleared, and he found Kristie staring up at him.

"Who did you think was sneaking into the shower with you, Oakley?" She asked this in amusement, her lips curved in a teasing smile.

He rolled his eyes and shrugged with a grin. "I suppose not." His gaze shot nervously to the bathroom door. "You're not worried your parents will catch us?"

"I wanted to be with you," she informed him. "Besides, I'm starting not to care what my parents think. My mother is being snobby and difficult."

"I think she's just being human," Camden defended gently. "We don't live in the same world she does. The supernatural community operates differently. If I were human, I'd think we were crazy, too." He gave her a lopsided grin. "I get your aggravation, though. We're star-crossed lovers, like Romeo and Juliet."

Horror filled Kristie's face at his comment. "Cam, Romeo and Juliet died." She stepped into his arms and leaned her head on his shoulder.

He could feel her small frame quivering with distress and instantly regretted his words. "Okay, not the best analogy."

"It could be accurate." Her voice was a fearful whisper. "Life just feels so dangerous right now. I worry we aren't going to make it through this."

Camden pulled her tighter against him, caressing his hands along her back. "I promise you," he assured with his lips against her ear, "in three weeks we are going to be on a beach somewhere, making love in the sand. And shortly after that, you'll be celebrating Christmas as Mrs. Kristie Harrison."

Pulling back, she grinned. "I like the sound of that."

He nodded. "Me too." He kissed the tip of her nose. "We're going to help Priya gain control of this territory. Then we're getting out of here. I swear it."

She tightened her arms around his waist and stood on her tiptoes to give him a kiss. "Your confidence makes me feel better."

He gave her another brief, chaste kiss. "Good." With a grin, he pulled her farther under the spray of water and turned her around.

"What are you doing?" she asked with a laugh. "Is it kinky?"

Camden chuckled in response and shook his head. "No. It's just me taking care of my woman," he said playfully. Reaching to the shower's shelf, he grabbed a bottle of girly shampoo. He squirted some of its contents into his palm and rubbed his hands together to lather them up.

He then stepped up against her back, temporarily blocking her from the shower's spray. Being careful to not let any shampoo run into her eyes, Camden began to lather it into his girlfriend's hair. He curled his fingers into her locks, massaging tenderly at her scalp.

Kristie gave a soft moan and tilted her head back in enjoyment. "Mmm, that's good."

He chuckled, leaning down to press a kiss to her shoulder. "If I remember correctly, I owe you a few naked massages."

"You do," she mumbled. "But this doesn't count. The ones you owe me came with the stipulation of oral sex followed by raunchy lovemaking."

He smiled, continuing to caress her scalp. "That's true. I do remember making promises to that effect." He stepped backward so he could tilt her head so that her hair was in the stream of water. "I fully intend to pay up. I'm going to get you all wet in our shower back home. Then I'll carry you to the bedroom, your body dripping. I will proceed to lick every last drop from you." He leaned in and brushed his lips across the side of her throat, his words a whisper. "Then I'll concentrate solely between your thighs."

Kristie moaned, pressing back into him. "I like the sound of that."

"Me too." He knew there was no way to hide his erection, so he didn't even try. He pressed himself against her backside, his eyes practically rolling back in his head in pleasure at the feel of her soft, slippery curves.

He fumbled with the cap of the shower gel as he tried to convince his body to keep from getting too excited. When he finally managed to get some into his hands, he ran them along her shoulders, massaging as he soaped her up. "That time isn't now," he said regretfully. He rubbed his thumbs between her shoulder blades, trying to force away her tension. "That should maybe be saved for the honeymoon. We'll be in some big, fancy hotel on a tropical island."

"I totally agree." She rolled her neck, lavishing in the attention. "I have a small amount saved up that we can use. It will be fun."

"No way," he argued. "There is no way I'm letting you pay for our honeymoon. That's my responsibility."

"But—"

He cut her off. "I will borrow from my dad. He was willing to pay for us to go on vacation with them now. I have no doubt he'll help me out."

Her eyes became thoughtful. "We can move into my apartment. Daddy paid for it through next year when I graduate. I wouldn't expect him to cover my rent after I'm married, so I'll tell him not to make any further payments."

He nodded his agreement. "My parents either. I'll call them when they get back and tell them I'm moving out." He felt her shoulders tremble under his hands.

"This is really going to happen," she breathed.

"It is." He wrapped his arms around her waist and began running his soapy hands across her belly. His body had started to calm, but upon such alluring contact, his libido stirred again.

With wicked intent, he slid his hands upward until they were caressing the undersides of her breasts. He felt her body respond like he knew it would. When she pressed her buttocks back against his groin, he slid his hands upward until he cupped her breasts. He caressed his soapy hands across her skin, making her slippery. Upon hearing her breath catch at the teasing strokes, he rubbed his thumbs along her nipples.

Kristie moaned and leaned her head back against his shoulder. "You're so good at that."

"You know what else I'm good at..." He trailed off, letting a hand travel down her belly. He slipped it between her thighs and stroked her very gently, his index finger circling the sensitive nub of flesh at the apex of her legs. He grinned into her hair when she whimpered.

"You're very good at that," she agreed on a sigh.

Unable to help himself, Camden grabbed her right leg and lifted until her foot slid into the soap shelf. Now that he had better access, his erection pressed persistently at her opening. He was in the process of easing into her body when he froze. He then withdrew on a groan. "We can't do this."

"We can't?" she asked in disappointment.

"No." He kissed her shoulder to take some of the bite out of his words as he guided her leg back down to the tub floor. "I can't do this in your parents' home. It doesn't feel right."

Kristie sighed, but nodded. "Yeah. I don't want them angry with you." She reached an arm up and wound it around the back of his neck. Pulling his mouth down to hers, she kissed him over her shoulder. "You're such a gentleman."

He stroked one of her breasts again, though this time it was less sexual and more possessive. "Sometimes it is really hard to remain such a boy scout." He grinned and pinched her nipple before turning off the water. "The only reason I

am able to contain myself is because I want to do this right."
He grabbed a fluffy towel from the nearby cupboard. "I don't
want you to be forced to remain silent because your parents
might hear. I want to make you scream."

He pulled her out of the shower to stand next to him on
the bathroom's cushy throw rug. He wrapped the towel
around his shoulders and pulled her in against his chest, co-
cooning them both in the large towel.

"Mmm," Kristie mumbled, wrapping her arms around his
waist. "I can't wait to get back home."

"Me either." Leaning over her shoulder, Camden drew fire
up from his lungs and let it tickle in his throat. He then let it
out in a small, caressing burst against her skin. "Seeing that
my fire doesn't leave any marks aside from our original mating, I'm curious to explore this as well."

She giggled and squirmed against him. "It's so crazy that
you are putting fire on me and it doesn't burn. It just gets
warm and tickles."

He wrapped the towel tighter around them and was just
about to pull more fire from his chest when there was a cry
of alarm from the hallway.

Kristie's eyes locked onto his and widened. From the hall
came the sounds of a struggle followed by a series of loud
crashes. "What is that?" she asked worriedly.

Moments later, Oakley's voice hollered out. "Let go of
me, you oversized lizard!" His statement was followed by an
inhuman growl.

"Shit." Camden cursed in alarm. "Dragon."

Shattering glass sounded in the hallway beyond, followed
by the thump of footfalls that were clearly larger than human. Someone ran up the stairs, then Mrs. Taylor's screams
rang through house.

"I think it's *dragons*. Plural." She pushed frantically away
from him and began digging through their pile of discarded
clothing. She yanked Camden's shirt over her head, covering
herself to her knees. Then she shoved her arms into her robe
and tied it firmly at the waist.

Camden was right behind her. He clumsily struggled into
his pants as he raced toward the bathroom door. He yanked
it open and stumbled out, Kristie hot on his heels.

He'd barely entered the hallway before he was grabbed
by the throat and tossed a good ten feet. He hit the wall with

a pained grunt and slid to the floor. Carpet dug into his el-bows as he stared up at the ceiling for a moment, unable to breathe.

"There's the girl." A gravelly voice that could only belong to a transformed dragon barked out commands. "Get her."

A moment later, Kristie gave a frightened cry.

Camden struggled to merely prop himself up on his el-bow. "Let them go." His demand was weak and he was hack-ing with the effort to force air through his lungs.

"Sorry." The response came from a dragon who had a tight grip on Oakley's neck. His forked tongue slithered out between blue-tinted lips. "Boss's orders. I'm sure you under-stand."

The second dragon, whose scales were a sickly yellow-green, yanked Kristie viciously against him. "Mr. Marcello wants to drive home a point to you. You don't challenge someone of his power without expecting to lose a few lives. We thought your humans might be a good place to start."

The dragon holding Oakley let out a guttural laugh. "Tell Priya I said hello. I want her to know that after I torture her little boy toy, I'm going to hurt her again. I will make her bleed and cry and beg for death. Just like last time."

Oakley emitted a rage-filled growl. "You're the one who raped Priya." His accusation was filled with fury and he struggled against the dragon, his face turning red with his anger. "I'll kill you for what you did to her!"

"Ooh!" The man Camden assumed to be Carl by the story they'd heard let out an amused laugh. "This one's got some fire in him." He yanked on Oakley's throat, drawing a ragged gasp of pain from the teen. "Maybe I should show him what real fire is like." He chuckled, his eyes trained on Camden. "Would you like to see your friend go up in flames?"

Though his entire body hurt, Camden forced himself to his feet. Once there, he lost his balance and stumbled into the wall. "No. Please," he begged the dragon, his voice fear-ful. He did not want to be responsible for the death of his girlfriend's brother.

Carl's lips curved into a wicked grin. "Once you see what Stefan does to him, you'll wish I'd been merciful and given him a crispy death in his own home." He gave a mocking sa-lute. "You're going to regret ever stepping foot in Stefan's territory. I promise you that." With that, he dove backwards out the large window behind him, shattering the large pane of stained glass.

"Oakley!" Kristie screamed in horror as her brother disappeared with Carl. She struggled against the man holding her, fear for her sibling plain on her face.

There was a thud as Carl hit the ground outside. After some shuffling, the trunk of a car slammed shut. A moment later, the dragon's voice hollered up through the broken window. "Throw the girl down to me!"

The dragon still in the house began yanking Kristie toward the broken window. She screamed and fought against him, kicking her feet out at the frame in an attempt to keep herself from being pushed out.

Rage began building inside Camden as he watched the dragon manhandle his girlfriend. All he'd wanted to do was visit Kristie's family for the holidays, not start a war. These innocent people had been tossed into the middle of things because Stefan Marcello couldn't play nice.

A snort escaped him that was less than human. He pushed off the wall with a newfound strength given to him through his recently acquired dragon genes. "Ward," he said darkly, addressing the boy hiding in his bedroom doorway. "Get me the sword you have hanging on your wall."

Ward's eyes widened, but he darted quickly into his room.

Camden closed his eyes and tried to block out the screams of his girlfriend, the screams of her terrified family. He concentrated on forcing his body to transform into his dragon form. He was no good to them human.

He felt his body shift, felt things move that never should. He waited through the process anxiously, because he'd never shifted on purpose. When he thought the procedure was done, and when he felt he couldn't wait any longer, his eyes flew open to assess the situation.

His eyes opened just in time to see Kristie go out the window. He cursed. The words that escaped him were much deeper and frightening than his normal voice.

Mrs. Taylor gave a squeak of fear as she stared at him, her eyes wide as her hand went to cover her mouth.

The dragon at the window flinched at the growl in Camden's voice.

The momentary hesitation of fear from the other man gave Camden enough time to move forward and strike his tail out. It curved around the yellow dragon and slammed into the window, effectively blocking any escape.

The dragon spun to face Camden, his nostrils flaring with alarm.

From outside, a vehicle started up and sped away, tires squealing as it peeled out onto the road.

"Looks like the getaway vehicle decided not to wait." Camden's voice was a low, menacing growl. "For immortals, you guys sure are impatient."

The dragon's eyes flicked around the hall as if looking for an escape route, unease plain in the man's shoulders.

"You're not going anywhere," Camden threatened. He spotted a large vase on the hall table, and he rolled his eyes at what he had no doubt was an overly expensive item. Swishing his tail around, he whisked the vase up with his tail and brought it swiftly into the dragon's head. Sure, it was hokey, but it was effective.

The dragon's eyes rolled back in his head as the glass contacted with his skull, and he fell unconscious to the floor.

"Don't you get back up," Camden warned, though the man couldn't hear him. "There are plenty more overpriced vases around this house. I'll break 'em all." He saw Alice shift unhappily out of the corner of his eyes. His gaze swept to her. "Oh, sor..." He broke off with a cough and cleared his throat. "Just a sec." Focusing his attention, he pushed back his dragon form to return to his human one. As he did, he glanced backwards at the seat of his trousers. "Another pair of pants ruined. Damn tail." He shook his head to clear it before returning his attention to Mrs. Taylor. "Sorry...again." He cleared his throat. "I won't really break all your vases."

Alice was staring at him somewhat fearfully. "It's no problem. Really." She rushed out the words a little too quickly. Her eyes were a little too wide as she stared at him.

Ward took that moment to come crashing back into the hallway, sword dangling at his side. He took one look at the downed dragon and grinned. "Cool." His eyes slid to Camden, and he held the sword out. "What did you need this for?"

Camden shrugged, though he took the sword by the handle. "I don't know. Aren't you supposed to kill dragons with a sword?"

"Dragons," Ward said in amazement. "Totally awesome."

Camden's expression darkened. "Yes. Totally awesome

that your siblings have been kidnapped by murderous supernatural beings hell bent on killing all of us."

"Well except that part," Ward admitted meekly.

Camden sighed and ran his free hand over his face. "I have to get them back."

"Camden?" Alice spoke in a voice so quiet he barely heard her. "What can we do?" Her gaze flicked back and forth between him and the downed dragon, her expression one of disbelief.

"You can start by getting me some rope—no. Chains. He may burn through rope." He glared down at the dragon. "We need him tied up. I require some answers from him."

Mrs. Taylor nodded slowly. "Yes, of course." She leaned toward the stairs and hollered down to the landing of the first floor. "Dale! Dale, bring us the chains from the shed. The ones for your truck!" She turned back to Camden with wide eyes. "Now what?"

Camden moved to stand above the unconscious dragon, fearing the man might wake up at any moment. "We need to get Priya back here," he said, trying to keep the desperation out of his voice. "She'll know what to do."

"Priya?" Alice asked in surprise. "Priya as in Oakley's little girlfriend? The weird one?"

Camden flinched. "I don't think the future ruler of the local dragons would appreciate being referred to as Oakley's little girlfriend."

"That woman is the future *leader* of...of...of people like you?" Alice's voice was full of astonishment.

Camden nodded, giving her an apologetic look. "I know. Kinda scary, ain't it?"

Chapter 12

Camden stood over the chair of the bound dragon, staring down uncertainly at their hostage. Priya was on her way, should be there any minute actually, and he couldn't wait for her to get there. He wanted her to take this situation off his hands. He didn't know the first thing about interrogations.

Alice stood in the corner of the kitchen, pressed against the wall. She was keeping herself as far away from the dragon as she could even though he was currently in human form. She was frightened, yet her curiosity was strong enough to keep her from fleeing the room.

Dale was in the hallway just outside the kitchen, keeping an eye out for Priya.

Ward was sitting on the kitchen counter, watching the scene with open fascination.

Turning his back on the Taylors so he could fully face the stranger, Camden said, "I know this is probably a stupid question, but would you mind telling me where they took my girlfriend?" As an afterthought, he added, "Telling me where her brother is would be appreciated as well."

The man spat at Camden, his face contorted with rage. "You can go to hell. I'm not telling you anything."

"Yeah..." Camden drawled the word out with disappointment. "I was assuming that would be your answer."

"I do not appreciate that type of language in my house." Alice's voice came sharply from her corner of the room as she reprimanded their unwanted guest.

Camden glanced over his shoulder just in time to see her

face pale as she seemed to realize who she was speaking to. He would have been amused if the situation wasn't so grim.

With a sigh, he addressed their captive. "Hurting someone I care about isn't going to help Stefan keep control of this territory. It's only going to make those in revolt angrier. These humans are innocent. You have nothing to gain by hurting them."

"Humans die by the hands of supernaturals every day. I don't understand why you and Priya care about their survival so much. They are no more than shields for higher beings. They are insignificant. None of our kind should value or mourn the lives of mortals. Most don't, not even your own men. Only the two of you, the ones Stefan is trying to make a point to, are torn up over the death of these inferior creatures."

In that moment, Camden saw Beau for what he really was. Beau was one of the good guys through and through. The man in front of him was the type of person Beau hunted down. The vampire might seem cold and calculating at times, but he wasn't evil. This was the type of monster Beau had feared Camden might be transformed into with the onslaught of his new powers, but Camden didn't have that type of evil in him.

Feeling irate that people this malevolent even existed, Camden took a menacing step forward. "I have a vampire friend who hunts men like you." A grin spread across his lips that could only be described as cruel. "Being a member of the supernatural community, I'm not sure if you're aware of what vampires do to their victims. They tear their throats out and leave them to slowly bleed to death."

Sure. He was lying. He had no clue what Beau did to people he hunted, but this man didn't know that. Once Camden had witnessed Beau torture a man, at least he'd witnessed the start of the torture. That quick glimpse had been more than enough.

"I watched him torture a man once," he continued conversationally, as if the event hadn't disturbed him on every level. "It wasn't something I ever want to witness again, let alone be subjected to." He crossed his arms and stared down at the now nervous-looking man. "Don't make me call in my vampire friend."

"Your vampire friend is unnecessary." The comment came

from Priya as she entered the kitchen. "I'm sure there's nothing torture-wise he does that I'm not willing to do."

"The crazy lady is here," Dale commented dryly as he trailed her into the room.

Priya ignored this and instead marched purposefully toward the restrained dragon. "Pierre Mondeau, you French bastard."

"I've been in the states for nearly three hundred years." The dragon snapped the words out in irritation.

"Only because the restrictions on the supernatural community are stricter in France, not because you like it here so much."

"That does not make me any less an American citizen. The humans accepted me with open arms." A mocking, cocky smirk curved his lips. "God bless America."

"Just another example of how primitive a society they are," Priya grumbled in annoyance.

Pierre's eyebrows rose in surprise. "I thought you were fond of the little vermin now. That is the recent rumor."

Priya gave a huffy sigh. "Just because I find one of them attractive, that doesn't make me a human advocate." Her eyes narrowed. "Besides, my sex life is none of your business."

"It used to be my business." Pierre all but purred the words, his voice thick with suggestion.

"You used to date this clown?" Camden asked in disbelief.

Priya shrugged, her lips pursed in disgust. "I was young and stupid, barely two hundred years old. When I realized what a sadist he was, I got rid of him fast." Her hands went to her hips as she stared Pierre down. "It was only after we broke up that I found out the really nasty stuff he was in to. He wasn't above rape or torture for political gain, nor sabotage or threats. Basically, this man is a real douche bag." Her expression turned downright evil as she took a step closer to the restrained dragon. She straddled his lap and put her face directly in his, her eyes boring into him. "And if Pierre here thinks I'm going to let our past affect how I do my job, he's extremely wrong." Lips quirking into a devilish smirk, she added, "In fact, our past might make me even better at this."

She stared at him in silence for a moment. Her dark eyes flashed, her pupils widening at some sign of fear she seemed to see in him. "You should just give up Stefan now and save yourself the pain."

"You wouldn't torture me," Pierre said with an amused laugh, yet his eyes held fear.

"Mr. Harrison?" Priya glanced over her shoulder at Camden. "Could you bring me that rather large kitchen knife?" Her finger pointed to the knife block on the counter, and her expression was one of impatience.

Alice finally stepped away from her corner. "Should we put the extra pool tarp under him?" she asked with concern. "How much blood is there going to be? I watch a lot of CSI, so I know leaving of bunch of blood in my kitchen could get us into trouble."

Ward's eyes widened at his mother's fretful words. "We're really going to do this, then? We're going to torture a strange man in our kitchen?"

Alice shrugged a noncommittal shoulder.

When Ward looked to him for confirmation, Camden let out a sigh. "It appears we are. He hasn't left us much choice in the matter." His gaze shifted to Dale, who'd been alarmingly quiet during the entire affair. The man's lips were set in a firm line, but there wasn't a trace of indecision on his features. Mr. Taylor was obviously prepared to do whatever was needed without argument. This caused a second, wearier sigh to escape Camden, as he felt he'd brought this upon the family. With a shake of his head, he looked to Priya. "Well?"

"Go get the tarp," Priya answered. "We can burn it when we're done."

Alice and Dale both scurried out of the room.

As they did, Priya climbed up from Pierre's lap and sashayed over to the knife block. In all the confusion, Camden had forgotten she'd asked for one of them. She fingered the handles sticking out of the top as she eyed up the selection. "Pierre, you know I am capable of violence...if the ends justify the means." She picked out a knife at random and slid it from the block. "You're already dead. You know that. You were dead the moment the getaway car sped off without you. Let's not make your death drawn out and overly violent. I would hate to mess up this pretty kitchen. Besides, I always did hate the sound of your screams. They tend to be horribly shrill and panicky."

"Priya, baby..." Pierre wheedled.

Priya turned in the direction of the kitchen doorway when

the Taylors returned with a large pool tarp between them. She gave them a brisk nod of appreciation before turning back to Pierre. "Don't *Priya baby* me," she said to their hostage with annoyance. "My human is in danger. I've no time for games."

She smacked the flat end of the knife against her palm. "The longer you take, the more concerned for Oakley I am going to get. The more concerned I am, the angrier I'm going to get with *you*." To emphasize this, she pointed the tip of the knife at his left eye.

"I've been tortured before," Pierre said callously. "What makes you think now will be any different?"

Priya laughed, though it sounded more cruel than amused. "You've taken a dragon's mate hostage. That's a big no-no in our community, even for you guys. Retribution is to be expected. I can do whatever I want to you without a single repercussion."

Pierre's eyes widened with horror. "What? No one said you'd been mated. It was assumed a cold-hearted bitch like you would stay single for all eternity."

"I wasn't talking about me," Priya said with a growl of exacerbation at the insult. "I was talking about him." She pointed with the knife in Camden's direction.

Pierre's eyes slid to Camden and realization filled his face. "The challenger is mated. The girl is a dragon's mate."

"Mated?" Alice asked curiously. "What does that mean?"

"I don't know," Ward said, feeling the need to offer his input. "It sounds gross, though."

Priya heaved a sigh. "It is the supernatural equivalent to being married."

"They got *married*?" Alice shrieked this in outrage and spun on Camden. "When did this happen?" she demanded angrily.

"Last night." Camden's voice came out a meek squeak as he took a step away from Mrs. Taylor.

"Last night?" Dale roared.

"You two got married last night and we weren't invited?" Alice whined in dismay. "My daughter *did* get married without me. She hates me!"

"She doesn't hate you." Camden was about to try to soothe Mrs. Taylor's injured feelings, but Priya beat him to an explanation.

"Dragons mate during sexual intercourse. It's a sex ritual. A dragon will burn his brand into his chosen life mate's skin. I highly doubt you wanted to be present for that." She stamped a foot in irritation. "Does no one know the rules?"

"You branded Kristie during sex?" Ward asked with an amused laugh. "You are in so much trouble!"

Camden's gaze swept anxiously to Mr. Taylor. The man's expression wasn't friendly, but he sighed in resignation. "You two have a lot of explaining to do when this is all over, but right now I just want to get my children back safely." He nodded to Priya. "Do what you have to do."

Priya grinned in delight. "Thank you. Now give me that tarp." She took the proffered sheet of plastic and quickly spread it out along the floor. Then, with no apparent effort, she hefted up the chair holding Pierre and carried it to the center. She dropped it roughly and unceremoniously down on the center of the tarp. Then taking a step back, she stared at their captive with a thoughtful expression. "Where to start…"

"Priya," Pierre said, squirming anxiously in his chair. "This really isn't necessary."

Her eyebrows rose as she picked up the knife she'd set down so she could spread out the pool tarp. "You don't think?" She glanced about the room, knife dangling casually from her fingertips. "I don't see Oakley about anywhere. Trust me, I would notice. He'd be trying to grope me, or he'd be giving Camden a hard time about banging his sister. Those are kind of his two favorite things." Tilting her head inquisitively to the side, she asked, "Where's Oakley, Pierre?"

"I'm not telling you anything." Pierre spat the words with contempt. "I hope Stefan cuts off all of his fingers."

Before Pierre had time to even take his next breath, Priya shoved the knife deep into his stomach. "Where's Oakley?" she asked through gritted teeth.

Pierre gave a holler of pain that had Camden squirming, but the dragon's response was cruel. "They'll castrate him, you know? Make it so he's impotent. There is no bigger insult than stealing the chance to breed away from a rival. Dragon progeny are so hard to come by. A man who is unable to produce offspring… Well, a lover like that isn't even worth having. They'll ruin him, making him too tainted to be accepted by the dragon community. Even if you win, you'll be an outcast with him by your side."

Priya's jaw clenched and she twisted the knife, drawing a grunt of pain from Pierre. "Where are they?" she asked angrily.

When his groan trailed off, Pierre's gaze slid to Camden. A malicious chuckle escaped him, vibrating through his chest. "You know what they'll do to the girl? They'll carve out her ovaries. No anesthesia. Just raw pain. The louder she screams, the deeper they'll cut her."

Camden felt something inside of him snap. With an animalistic roar, he was across the room with speed a human didn't possess. He heard the loud swish of his tail as it sliced out through the air before he even realized he'd shifted form.

Before, if asked what he thought a dragon might look like, he would have described a Godzilla-like creature, something massive. In this form, he wasn't much bigger than when he was human, so it didn't make maneuvering, or grabbing Pierre by the throat, difficult. "I guarantee you are going to regret ever laying your scaly hands on my mate." He pulled his arm back, noting the way his claws gleamed in the kitchen's florescent lighting.

"Camden, don't kill him!" Priya was backed up against the kitchen table where he'd shoved her during his blind rage. "He wants that! If you kill him, we'll never find out where she is!" She yelled this desperately, her dark eyes large with shock at his outburst.

Camden paused and glanced at her over his shoulder. "I have no intention of killing him yet." With that, he rammed the pointed tips of his claws into Pierre's gut next to Priya's knife wound. "That would be too quick for this piece of shit."

Following Pierre's agonized scream, Priya's alarmed voice asked, "Camden, how much do you know about torture?"

"I know it's supposed to hurt," he said darkly. He flexed his hand, which caused his claws to extend and slice through Pierre's gut with barely any effort.

"Camden!" Priya barked his name firmly to get his attention. "I know you're worried about her, but you have to be careful! We have professional torturers for a reason. You torture someone when your emotions are involved, and people end up dead before you want them to be. I am begging you to torture with your head, not your heart."

"That's not something you hear every day," Ward commented wryly.

Camden stared at Priya for a moment before taking a step back. "You're right," he said regretfully as he retracted his claws from Pierre's abdomen. "You take over."

"Thank you." She gently nudged him out of the way. "I just hope you didn't puncture anything vital," she chastised, peering thoughtfully at Pierre.

"If it helps at all," Camden offered, "I didn't feel anything go *pop*."

"Most organs aren't going to pop," Priya said with annoyance. "They aren't balloons."

"I will never look at balloons in the same way," Ward said with a cringe.

Priya shot him a dirty look. "You aren't as cute as your brother. I'll hurt you without thinking twice about it if you begin to annoy me."

"Honey," Alice said nervously to Ward, holding a hand out to beckon him to her side, "maybe you should let her do her job."

Priya arched her eyebrows at Ward, silently conveying that she agreed with Mrs. Taylor. Then she turned her attention back to Pierre. She bent down in front of him to better assess the damage Camden had done. "I think we're cool. He doesn't seem to be dying." She glanced up into Pierre's face and must have seen something in his expression, because she suddenly yelled, "Don't you dare!"

Pierre snarled in response. A forked tongue protruded from his mouth, and it was only then that Camden realized the man's eyes had turned reptilian.

Priya got right in his face, her hands grasping the arm rests of the chair. "If you shift form to heal yourself, I will jam toothpicks between your scales." Her voice held a threatening tone that had Camden instinctively shrinking back. Pierre grew very still, and Priya's lips quirked at the power she had over him. "Toothpicks are the worst, aren't they? It's agony, worse than bamboo shoots under the fingernails." She glanced over her shoulder. "Do you happen to have any toothpicks, Mrs. Taylor?"

Alice perked up at the opportunity to be helpful. "I've got an entire box!"

With a crooked grin, Priya watched Mrs. Taylor scurry to a kitchen cabinet and riffle around inside. "Isn't she adorable? She's like one of those Stepford wives."

Dale's eyebrows rose. "Did you just compare Alice to a robotic trophy wife?"

Priya nodded. "Yep." Missing Dale's look of disbelief, she grabbed the sword that was lying against the table leg and leaned on it as if it was a cane, her eyes on Pierre. "You stay in human form, and we slice up your organs and appendages with this sword. You shift into dragon form and I use the toothpicks. Not the best options really."

As if on cue, Alice cried out with delight. "Ooh! I found the toothpicks!" She scampered over to Priya, her blonde curls bouncing merrily.

"Yeesh," Priya said with a cringe. "She's terrifying, isn't she? It's Martha Stewart meets the Jigsaw killer."

Alice pulled one slim toothpick from the expensive look-ing holder and held it out toward Priya, her cute pink nail polish seeming out of place for their current activities. "Who's the Jigsaw killer?" she asked sweetly.

"He's this crazy guy who tortures people," Ward ex-plained. "It's from a movie."

Alice paused and thought on that. Finally, she shrugged. "If we have to torture people in our kitchen, I'd not hate it if it resembled Martha Stewart's. She's amazing."

Ward groaned and slapped a hand to his forehead. "Only you would take that as a compliment."

"Her or Kristie," Camden said with amusement despite their circumstances. For the first time, he was seeing where his girlfriend got her quirkiness from.

"So what would you like me to do with this?" Alice asked angelically as she held out a single toothpick and arched an eyebrow.

Pierre's eyes followed the toothpick avidly, his expression becoming more and more alarmed. As Alice took a step clos-er, he gave a cry of panic. "All right! I'll tell you whatever you want to know. Just keep her away from me!"

Camden's brows shot up. It was true *he* found Mrs. Tay-lor to be somewhat frightening, but it surprised him that Pierre did as well.

Priya didn't hesitate to jump on the man's weakness. She leaned toward him, her voice eager. "Just tell us where Stef-an is taking Oakley and Kristie."

Pierre hesitated only a moment. One glance at the toothpick still held out by Alice, and he turned to Priya with wide eyes. "He's having them taken to his main dwelling, the big place on Rodeo Drive."

"The giant mansion that looks like a castle?" Priya asked. "The one that's impossible to break into and is guarded by his biggest, meanest thugs?"

Pierre bobbed his head, seemingly frantic to please her. "He knew you'd attempt some sort of rescue. He wanted to take them to the place where he knew the defenses were impregnable."

"Damn it." Priya gave a soft hiss and pushed away from him in disgust. "I was hoping he'd taken them to one of the smaller properties because there'd be so many to sort through." She turned to Camden and bit her lip with concern. "This is going to be nearly impossible."

He rolled his eyes, trying not to appear as nervous as he felt. "Good thing I specialize in nearly impossible."

"Well, I hope you have some of your dumb luck saved up." Priya's attention shifted back to Pierre. "Thanks for the information. You always were a deplorable traitor." She hefted the sword up, and with a battle cry, she swung it around.

The blade sliced through Pierre's neck, severing bone easily. Before anyone in the room had time to react, the man's head toppled to the floor.

Camden's eyes widened in horror as the spinning head came to a stop at his feet. "Priya!" He gasped her name in shock. "You killed him! You actually killed him!" He backed up a step and wiped his sneaker on the tarp as if to wipe away any germs left by the decapitated head. "I can't believe that just happened." He ran his hands along his face, feeling overwhelmed. "I don't understand. He gave you what you wanted."

"When I left him..." Priya shook her head, anguish filling her eyes. "When I refused to go crawling back to him, he burned my best friend's house to the ground with her inside." Her eyes lifted to Camden's. "She wasn't a dragon. She was a vampire, a vampire that was far from fire resistant." She tossed the sword down to the tarp. "I think I owed him."

"What a horrible, horrible man," Alice said with disapproval. "The world is better off without him in it."

Camden's jaw dropped and he stared at his future mother-in-law with alarm. "Wait. You aren't even a little upset that Priya just beheaded a man in your kitchen?" His voice squeaked embarrassingly at the end of his question, causing him to flinch.

"That man was obviously a bad person," Alice said with a shrug. "It's apparent that the supernatural community works a little differently than what we're used to. I trust that Priya knows what she's doing."

Camden blinked in disbelief. "You trust Priya?" He practically shrieked the words with incredulity. He then waved his arms around, motioning to the chaos that had transpired in their kitchen. "You're okay with all of this, but you've given *me* such a hard time?"

Silence filled the room. Then Alice frowned. "You've gotten flak from us because you've been so secretive about your alternative lifestyle. Had you just been honest..."

"Honest?" Camden cried. "Honest? Things were just a little too complicated for that."

"Well, honesty is very important in our family," Alice said huffily. "If you would have told us from the beginning that you were a fire-breathing dragon and not a pot head, I think things may have went a little differently."

Camden gaped at Alice in disbelief. Was she honestly suggesting that he should have laid his entire secret out on the table from the get-go? That he should have known they would be okay with their daughter's boyfriend turning into a dragon on occasion?

"That," Priya added to the discussion, "and not mating with your daughter the first chance he got. That's kind of extreme."

Camden rolled his eyes at Priya's input. "Thank you for the help." Changing the subject, he said, "Instead of going on about how atrocious I am, could you please tell us how we are going to rescue Kristie and Oakley?"

Priya's focus seemed to snap back to the problem at hand. She whipped her cell phone from her pocket. "I'll have Pius gather everyone together. Stefan wanted a war. Well, he got one when he kidnapped Oakley."

As she began pulling up the number she wanted, Camden stared at her expectantly.

She stared back, her expression blank. "What?"

He simply continued to stare, waiting for her to comprehend what he was waiting for.

It took a moment, but realization finally dawned in her eyes. "Oh! Kristie too. Shame on him for taking your woman."

Camden rolled his eyes once again. "Your sincerity amazes me." As she turned her back to speak to Pius, he fixed his attention on the rest of the room and rubbed his hands together. "All right. We're off to go start a war and get people killed. I'll try to find someone to send over who can take care of this body..."

Alice waved him off. "Don't worry about us, dear. We can handle things here. Maybe Google will have advice on the best way to dispose of a dragon. That Google has everything."

Camden pinched the bridge of his nose. Had she actually just suggested finding body disposal tips on Google? "Okay. Um...thank you...I suppose." He turned to Priya as she shoved her cell phone back into her pocket. "So we're set? Pius and the others are meeting us?"

Priya nodded. "Yes. He's very eager to kill people."

Camden clapped his hands together. "Fantastic." Sarcasm was thick in his voice, but he doubted she noticed. He turned to the Taylors. "I guess we'll be back as soon as possible. Try not to worry."

Ward hopped off the counter and sauntered over with an obstinate expression on his young face. "I'm coming with you."

Camden's eyebrows rose. "Um...I don't think that is such a good idea. This is going to be dangerous."

"This is my brother and sister we're talking about. I don't care how dangerous it is."

"You're human," Camden pointed out gently.

"I don't care," Ward said stubbornly. "I'll be careful. I'll hang back and help evacuate my brother and sister to safety while you guys do the fighting. If those monsters have done anything to them, they might need the assistance."

"I hate to admit it," Priya said, "but that isn't a bad idea. We don't want to be distracted with getting hostages out. No doubt there will be more than just Kristie and Oakley. If he follows us in, Ward will know the way back out. It's kind of perfect actually."

Camden turned his attention to Alice and Dale. "I'm not agreeing to anything unless it's okay with you two."

Both parents paused, obviously feeling reluctant to send their son off into a supernatural war. "Well..." Alice said slowly.

"He's an adult," Dale finished for her, placing any future blame on his head to save his wife the guilt. "I'm not going to make such an important choice for him. Whatever Ward decides, I'll back him."

"Me too." Alice put a supporting hand on her husband's arm, though her face was drawn with worry. Everyone in the room turned to look at Ward.

"I'm going," he said firmly. "There's nothing you can say that will make me change my mind."

"Wasn't gonna try," Priya assured him. "Prepare yourself, kid. It's going to be a bloody ride."

Chapter 13

Camden sat in the passenger seat of a black, unmarked van. He, Ward, and Priya were a half mile from Stefan's home, where Oakley and Kristie were being held. The area was thickly wooded, but he could still see the lights of the house like a beacon in the darkness calling out to them as if in challenge.

It was frustrating to be so close to the structure where Kristie was without rushing in immediately. His mind was going through dozens of horrible scenarios while they waited for the last of the dragons to arrive. Sage was one of those still unaccounted for.

Pius was in a van behind them with more of Camden's "followers" waiting for a signal from Priya on when to move in. It was simply a waiting game until the rest of their group showed up.

"I don't like waiting," Camden complained even though he understood why they were. It still set his nerves on edge and caused his concern for Kristie to mount with each passing minute.

Priya suddenly spun on him with a glare. "You think I *like* waiting? You think I like sitting here knowing how fragile Oakley is and picturing the things they're probably doing to him? I hate it," she said angrily. "In fact, I'm freaking out a little bit right now. I'm worried sick, and I don't like it. I'm not used to this feeling."

Camden stared at her for a moment in stunned silence. Finally, he let out a whistle that he followed with an amused chuckle. "Oh my God, you like him. You actually *like* like him.

I knew you liked him, but I thought it was sort of like how a person likes a puppy that follows them around. I didn't realize you had genuine feelings for him." He paused before nodding in confirmation at this discovery. "Wow. That must be a tough pill to swallow."

"It is," Priya said darkly as she crossed her arms over her chest in annoyance. "I don't like caring about other people. It's weird."

Camden shook his head in amusement. "It must be scary finding out you're more human than you thought."

She glared at him in response. "It is." She opened her mouth to complain some more, but there was a rapping on her window.

Pius stood outside her door, his hands shoved deep into his pockets. He waited patiently while Priya opened her door.

"Yes," she said, sounding breathless and nervous all at once.

"Everyone is here except Sage. I don't advise waiting much longer. If she decides to show, she can catch up."

Priya sucked in a surprised breath. "You think she's betraying us?"

Pius shrugged. "You never know with Sage. Her allegiances have never been her top priority. I just know she isn't here. You make your own assumptions from that."

Priya took a deep breath before nodding. "Okay. We proceed without her."

"Are you okay with that?" Pius asked cautiously. "She's a powerful ally to lose."

Her face grew stern with determination. "Sage is a powerful ally, but she isn't much help in a fight. We can do this without her."

He nodded his agreement. "I'm going ahead to plant explosives on the gate. Give me three, four minutes, then follow after me." He went to turn away then paused. "Watch out for Therius. He won't hesitate to kill any one of us once we're discovered on the property."

This time when he went to turn, Priya reached out and grabbed his arm. "Thank you," she said quickly. On his puzzled expression, she explained. "For giving us a chance. Many of these people value your opinion a great deal. If you hadn't sided with us, I doubt tonight would have happened."

Pius grinned. "A man radical enough to hold such an important meeting in a tree house just might be crazy enough to pull this off. That's the way I look at it."

"Are any of us in the supernatural community ever truly sane?" Priya asked with a small laugh.

"Never." With a wink, he disappeared into the darkness.

As soon as he was out of earshot, Camden gave a groan. "I hate lying to them! These people are going into a fight thinking I'm something I'm not. It isn't right."

Priya slid out of the van with Ward's sword in hand. "They think you're a man with a lot of nerve who isn't afraid to help people in need. Are they wrong?"

"No. But—"

"Then shut up and get yourself ready." When Ward used the sliding door on the side of the van to get out, she went to him. "Try to avoid anyone seeing you as best as you can." She held the handle of the sword out to him. "If you run into anyone, use this. Decapitation is the only way to kill a dragon."

Camden frowned. "Then what was with the freaking out when I clawed Pierre if decapitation is the only way to kill one of you guys...I mean, us guys?"

"You can kill one of us in conventional manners," Priya explained as Ward took the sword from her. "We can be killed by stab wounds, bullets, and even sliced organs. With those methods, we don't stay dead, though. Our bodies heal the damage and bring us back. I was worried you'd kill Pierre before we got the information. If we had to wait for his body to heal that amount of damage, Oakley and Kristie would have been dead."

"So you weren't just kidding with the whole good cop/bad cop thing in an attempt to frighten Pierre?" he asked in surprise as Priya surveyed the extensive display of bladed weapons in the back of the van.

She slid a large knife into a holster on her thigh, then shot him an annoyed look over her shoulder. "No, I wasn't kidding." She shook her head and turned back to the weapons. "You scared me, alright? You went crazy. And I lied to Pierre. He *was* dying. You sliced the hell out of him. Had we not frightened him into talking right away, we would have lost him for who knows how long."

Camden suddenly felt sick to his stomach. Pierre wouldn't be the first person he'd ever killed, but all the others had been during an attack when he'd been forced to fight for his life.

This felt much more wrong. "I...I didn't realize I'd killed him."

"You didn't kill him." She explained this logically as she handed a matching knife over to him. "I sliced his head off with Ward's sword."

"Had he been human or had you not reacted so quickly, I would have screwed us over." Camden said this in quiet horror as he very carefully eased the knife into one of the deep pockets of his corduroy cargo pants. "I almost got Kristie and Oakley killed without even realizing it."

"You're young," she said flippantly. "In time, you'll learn."

"I'll learn?" Camden asked in horror. "I'll learn to better torture someone? What kind of life do you expect me to lead?"

She shrugged carelessly. "If you plan to live for the next century, you can't possibly expect for all of it to be peaceful. One day someone is going to come into your territory and challenge you. You will be glad of the things you learned from me about torture then."

Camden rubbed his temples, feeling tired. "Lucky me."

Priya handed him a giant sword. "Quit wallowing in self-pity. It makes you look pathetic."

Camden rolled his eyes and took the sword. "Thanks for the pep talk, chief."

Priya grabbed a sword for herself and slid it into a sheath she had strapped across her back. "I'm not here to make you feel good about yourself. I'm here to teach you how to kill dragons and keep you alive."

"I appreciate that," Camden said honestly.

Spinning to face him, she grabbed his belt buckle and pulled his pants away from his body. In her right hand, she held up a pistol for him to see before shoving it into the waistband of his slacks. "A temporary kill isn't as good as a decapitation, but it will do." She let go of his belt to allow his pants to snap back into place and returned her attention to the van. Grabbing a gun of her own, she shoved it into the back of her black leather pants.

"I've been shot in the chest before," he said with a grimace. "I remember how well it does the trick."

Priya offered Ward a pistol as well before smiling up at Camden. "You really are impossible to kill. I definitely picked the right guy to help me overthrow this corrupt regime."

Camden grimaced as she slid the van door closed. "I'm not impossible to kill. I've died before, and apparently, I can die again. I'm just impossible to keep dead."

Ward shook his head in amazement. "I can't believe you died. That's crazy."

Camden shrugged. "It's not like I planned on getting myself into that situation. A really bad ass vampire was trying to kill your sister. I saved her. Then this jackass human shot me, and the vampire snapped my neck. Kinda sucked."

"So you *died* to keep Kristie safe?" Ward asked in awe as they began following Priya along the dark road that led to Stefan's home. "*Damn*. That's intense." He loped along beside Camden, his eyes wide with amazement. "What happened to the men who killed you?"

"Well, the guy who shot me...he was human." Camden grimaced. "I kind of accidently shoved a stake through his chest. That's part of the reason why he decided to shoot me. He was pissed about the fact that he was dying."

"You shoved a stake into a human's chest?" Priya whispered as they marched along the roadside. "That's vicious."

"I said it was an accident," Camden hissed. With a deep breath, he continued. "Anyway, the vampire that snapped my neck was killed by Beau, the vampire who joined us for dinner the other night."

"Wait!" Ward's voice was a shocked cry. "That guy was a vampire?"

Camden grinned widely. "Yep. He could have bled you dry at any moment." Even in the darkness, he could tell Ward had gone pale. "I'm just kidding. Beau is one of the good guys...usually."

Before Ward could respond, Priya shushed them both and drove her elbow roughly into Camden's ribs. "Boys, quiet time now. We're getting close."

That statement was enough to sober Camden up. He was so close to Kristie, yet so far away. He could be less than a mile from her, unable to help while she was being tortured. It made him sick to his stomach just picturing it. "I'll do whatever you need if I can get her out of there alive," he whispered.

"I need you to shut up," she whispered back.

Camden nodded, clenching his jaw with anxiety. He and Ward followed her silently the last few yards to the gate of Stefan's home. As they approached, Camden noticed Pius's bulky shape crouched in front of the gate and could hear the others moving quietly behind them.

This was happening now. They were starting a war. He knew with a certainty this uprising would be violent; people were going to die.

Priya must have seen the fear on his face, because she grabbed his forearm and stared intently into his eyes. "Listen to me. These men are evil. You can't hesitate in killing them, because they won't hesitate with *your* life." Her fingers tightened on him. "Please tell me you're not crapping out on me. I can't do this without you."

"I'm not crapping out on you," he assured. "I just don't like killing people." As soon as those words were out of his mouth, a loud explosion sounded. He watched in amazement as the door on the iron gate in front of them was blown right off its hinges.

Any chance they'd had of rethinking and coming up with a different plan was now past. The first shot had been fired and they would need to proceed with unerring determination. "It doesn't look like I have much choice anymore, even if I was second guessing myself." He turned to Ward, his expression grim. "Stay back. I don't want anyone to see you. You find Kristie and Oakley. Then you get out of there. Understood?"

"Understood," Ward said with a nod. "I want the opposing dragons to spot me less than you do."

"Good." Priya inched forward in front of them, her eyes trained on the house beyond. "Let's go start a revolt."

Camden shrugged at Ward before following Priya. Already, he could see men rushing outside to check on the damage to the fence. He didn't think they'd quite realized what was going on yet. Then right in front of his eyes, the closest enemy dragon suddenly went down, a battle axe lodged in his forehead, and there was no question of what Priya and her people's arrival meant for Stefan. The war had begun.

Pius went racing forward onto the property with a war cry. He had a sword raised above his head as he raced toward the downed man. As his sword came down, other forms came rushing onto the lawn from the tree line beyond the gate.

Camden winced as Pius's sword decapitated the unconscious man. The body gave a jerk and blood spurted into the air.

Pius was already moving on before the body stopped twitching. He'd yanked his axe free and was lumbering toward the next man.

Instead of backing off with fear as any sane person would, Stefan's men came forward to meet the attack head on. Roars ripped through the night as bodies transformed into dragons.

As Pius reached his third victim, the man was already in dragon form.

Luckily, this second form wasn't like some of those Camden had seen in movies or read about in fantasy novels. Dragon forms were larger than a person's human body, but they weren't as massive as some of the Hollywood portrayals. Dragons weren't twenty feet long with wings. He'd yet to see a dragon with wings. Of course, he'd only seen a handful of dragons, so that didn't mean there weren't any.

Camden was lucky if he was six feet tall. In dragon form, he'd noticed a jump in height. He guessed himself to be at least six-foot-five, possibly closer to seven feet. He'd also gained bulk. Normally scrawny, in dragon form he had gladly supported a good sixty extra pounds, all of it solid muscle. He could just feel the unrestricted power coursing through his veins, but he chose not to change. It was easier to hold a weapon in his human shape. He wasn't as skilled as the others at hand-to-hand combat.

The man approaching Pius must have felt the same way. He didn't even hesitate at the sight of his adversary's weapon. He simply roared with rage and lumbered forward.

One thing legends did get right were the tails. They were massive and heavy, a good weapon. The dragon in front of Pius used his own body to attack. His tail had a row of spikes running down the length of it. He swung that hulking mass around and caught Pius in the shoulder.

Spikes dug into flesh, tearing through skin and meat as if it were butter. The man yanked, dragging the imbedded spikes down Pius's arm.

His face screwed up into a grimace, but Pius didn't react any more than that. He ignored his bleeding, injured arm and brought his axe forward. He hacked violently at the tail, and after three whacks, it separated from the body.

The owner of the appendage gave a high-pitched squeal of agony.

Camden watched with wide eyes as his holler was cut abruptly short by one of their allies, a woman. She swung a sword around into the throat of the screaming dragon.

Priya was suddenly yanking on Camden's arm, dragging him away from the carnage. "We don't have time to waste! We can't wait to make sure everyone is okay. Once he realizes he's under attack, Stefan may kill Oakley and Kristie just to spite us."

Camden nodded his understanding and pushed past the others toward the large staircase leading into the mansion. This wasn't the first time he'd been in a fight that was life or death. He knew what it was like to have to press forward and hope that the people he cared about would live through the night. Of course, he'd died the last time, but the concept still applied. Damn, he hoped he didn't die again. To say that would suck would be an understatement.

They neared the entry, the vicious battle raging behind them. Camden reached for the handle of the massive door, but stumbled back in shock when it opened from the other side.

A man stepped out, a large shotgun wielded in his arms.

Camden was so surprised to see the other man that he froze. He stared down the barrel of the gun and could only think the words, *Not again.*

Luckily, the man seemed just as surprised to see him. Priya did not. She swung her sword around so fast that her movements were a blur. The blade of her weapon caught the man in the jugular. It didn't falter at all as it sliced through meat and bone. At the sword's completed strike, the head of the man tottered for a moment on his neck before rolling backwards into the foyer of the mansion.

"First death is on me," Priya offered as her dark eyes bore into his. "I'll give you a moment to get warmed up, but don't think you're going to get out of here alive without getting your hands dirty."

His response was a look of annoyance. "I've killed before," he reminded her. "I'm not worried about keeping my hands clean. He just startled me, okay?" That was partially true. Just because he'd killed before did not mean he was completely comfortable with it.

Priya shoved the front door open with her foot, and holding her sword one-handed, she grabbed for the gun at her waistband. "Well, don't let it happen again. I might not always be there to save your gangly ass."

"Gangly ass," he repeated darkly. "Yes. Insult me. That will make me want to keep the bad guys from killing you."

Priya glanced in his direction, and in the instant she was distracted, a woman came sprinting from the shadows.

Camden reacted on fear and instinct. His hands only fumbled a fraction of a second before his fingers closed around the pistol in his waistband. In one fluid motion, he raised it up, clicked the safety off, and fired.

The bullet hit the woman in the sternum, sending her stumbling backwards into the wall. She hit with a thud and a groan, clutching at the bleeding wound in her chest.

Priya gave a startled yelp and spun to face the woman. Slowly, she inched forward, peering down to better see the woman's face as she slid down the wall. "This is Marie Claire," she informed him. "She is Stefan's first cousin and a nasty bitch."

Camden stared down at the now unconscious woman and fought not to cringe at the damage he'd done. "Good to know she's a bitch. Harder to feel guilty that way."

Priya hefted her sword over her head, the muscles bulging in her tiny arms. "It looks like we're even now. And do not feel guilty. Marie Claire is an evil troll. A fast one, too. I don't know how you got the drop on her, but I'm grateful. She would have seriously hindered our progress, and it's quite likely she would have killed one of us had you not stopped her first."

Camden stared down at the angelic-looking blonde whose blood was soaking into the carpet at his feet. She looked so small and fragile, worlds away from his idea of a crazed killer.

With a grunt of effort, Priya swung her sword downward, cutting into Marie Claire's neck. The sword cut through carpet and caught in the floor boards below.

Camden flinched and took a step back to keep blood from staining his shoes. "You really didn't like Marie, did you?"

Priya yanked her sword out of the floor with a groan, then stumbled backwards a few steps as she fought to regain her balance. "Was it obvious?"

He blinked in surprise that she even had to ask while she held a sword dripping with blood and wore a sneer on her face. "Nah," he said sarcastically. "Couldn't tell at all."

"Good," Priya said as she marched purposefully toward the massive staircase. "Because I hated her sister even worse. This is business. I don't want them thinking it's personal."

Camden couldn't help but gawk at her bloody sword as he followed Priya up the wide staircase to the second floor. "It's either personal or you're an extremely hostile woman."

Priya shot him a dirty look.

"Let me correct that. You are an extremely hostile woman, but I still feel it's personal. You've decapitated people you know with a hateful expression on your face. If you ask me, this is pretty damn personal."

"I didn't ask you," she reasoned as they reached the landing.

Camden never got to respond, because two men and a woman rushed at them from the hallway to their left.

Priya widened her stance and held her sword at the ready. "Time to earn the name of challenger," she called over to him.

"Yay?" he asked back. His heart was pounding fiercely in his chest and his palm felt sweaty against the hilt of his sword. He adjusted his grip and braced himself.

Priya took the lead. She stepped in front of him with a blur of speed. She swung her sword forward, but these men had been given more time and warning to arm themselves. Her sword clashed against the blade held by the closest man, sending a spark into the air. She spun, her other hand raising her gun toward the second man. She pulled the trigger and a shot rang through the air.

The man stumbled backwards with the impact, his raised weapon acting as a hindrance as he staggered back.

Priya was already moving again before the echo of the shot dissipated. She brought her foot up and kicked the first man in the gut, forcing some space between the two of them.

Camden didn't get to see any more of their skirmish because the lone woman charged him. By the time he reacted, she was too close for him to comfortably use the large sword in his hands. He was forced to go on the defensive, merely deflecting her strikes.

He idly wondered why it was the woman he was up against. He'd already shot one female this evening. He did not want to get a reputation for harming women. He felt guilty enough about hurting *anyone*. Having it be a member of the opposite, fairer sex made him feel even more uncomfortable.

Thinking of the gun made him realize it was still clutched

in his hand, making an uncomfortable gap between his palm and the sword handle. He couldn't keep the apologetic expression off his face as he raised the weapon. It was nothing personal after all. He didn't know this woman. How could he not feel guilty about shooting her?

Not that he had much to feel guilty about anyway. Before he could even get a shot off, the woman caught him in the wrist with a spinning kick. The gun flew from his hand and hit the wall a few feet away, and the sword clattered from his hands to the ground.

The woman's lips curved into a wicked grin. "You're not so tough," she said with a thick Russian accent. "I think perhaps I could kill you myself, save Stefan the trouble." She brought her fist around in a right hook to Camden's jaw.

His head jarred with the impact and he nearly lost his balance. Before he could recover, the woman drove her foot into the back of his knee, forcing him to the ground. She then kicked him in the ribs, sending him sprawling backwards across the floor. Camden felt and heard something inside of him snap, probably ribs.

When his back connected with the ground, he gave a groan of pain at the pressure on his now sensitive midsection. He sucked in a sharp breath as pain shot through his chest in a secondary wave of agony. He attempted to curl into a defensive ball in an effort to protect himself.

As he gasped in anguish, the woman pressed a booted foot to his shoulder and forced him to his back. She swung a leg over to straddle his waist and her left hand wrapped around the back of his neck, lifting his head. Her right hand balled into a fist. Pulling her arm back, she drove her knuckles into his nose.

The impact knocked the back of Camden's head into the hard wood of the floor. Stars burst behind his eyes, and his vision blurred with gray at the edges. He blinked in an attempt to clear his vision, but the woman hit him again. Blood spurted from his left nostril, trailing down his lip.

When she hit him a third time, Camden began fumbling in his pants pocket for the knife Priya had given him in the van. The woman hit him a fourth and fifth time. On the sixth punch, he managed to get the knife free.

Using both hands, he jammed the thick blade of the dagger up into her stomach. The serrated edges and curve of the blade were made for maximum damage. He shoved the cutting edge as deep as it would go before slipping the digits of his right hand through the finger holes in the rounded handle. The holes made the knife easier to grip, made it easier to do damage. Once he was sure he had a good hold, Camden yanked the knife free. Blood dripped from the open wound down onto his white t-shirt, making it look like a homicidal artist's prized painting.

The woman jerked. She then froze for a moment before her hands slid down to her bleeding stomach.

Though it felt heartless, Camden took this moment to jam the dagger into her chest. As she toppled backwards and off of him, he struggled to a sitting position. The knife never left her body and he followed through until he was crouched over the downed woman. He kept the knife imbedded in her chest, but his eyes roved over her in regret. He hadn't wanted to kill her. He hadn't wanted to kill anyone.

Her eyes fluttered closed, her hands gripping the hilt of the knife. While her blood spilled out onto the floor, her feet scrambled weakly at the ground as she struggled through her pain.

He felt pity for her, but knew had their roles been reversed, this woman would not have hesitated to do the same to him.

Priya's voice hollering his name drew him out of his reverie. When Camden looked up, the Middle Eastern goddess tossed her sword in his direction.

His body acted on instinct. When he caught the bladed weapon, he brought it down forcefully into his adversary's neck. With one strong, sure strike, he severed the head from its body, ending the woman beneath him permanently.

Once the damage was done, he sat down roughly on the ground next to the body and stared at the now headless woman. A hand touched his shoulder, and he flinched. His body tensed until he realized it was Priya.

"You did well," she encouraged. She offered a hand to help him to his feet. "Natasha there was in charge of child abductions. Stefan would keep people in line by taking their children. It was a way to guarantee total cooperation from those considering mutiny. It was Natasha who did the dirty work for him. She was abusive. Don't feel guilty about what you did. She had it coming."

He nodded his head. Knowing that the people he killed were evil made him feel better about the act, but it didn't make doing so any easier. He accepted Priya's hand and let her pull him to his feet. "How could someone take a child?" he asked with a shiver.

"They're heartless sociopaths," she supplied. She patted his chest with the palm of her hand. "Just think, the closer we get to Stefan, the farther up the ladder we get. If you think Natasha, the child abusing Russian, was bad, you're in for a terrifying evening." She reached up and wiped a trickle of blood from under his eye. "She did give you a pretty rough beating, though."

Camden nudged her hand away and dabbed gingerly at the damage. "*I* was afraid of that chick. I can't imagine being a kid trapped in a room with her."

As he continued to assess the harm done to his face, Camden surveyed the two dead men lying face down on the floor. Apparently, Priya hadn't had as much trouble as him dispatching her opponents. "Make me look bad," he complained with a nod at the men. "You took out two men in less time than it took me to overpower a single woman."

Priya picked his sword up from the ground and held it out to him. "That came off as kind of sexist." She grabbed her own sword, which Camden had left beside Natasha's body. "Besides, I've had a lot more practice than you. I've been murdering people for centuries. You've only been doing it a few months."

He couldn't help but shoot her a grin. "You are scary. You know that, right?"

Priya started down the hallway their attackers had come from with determination in her stride. "Thank you," she tossed brightly over her shoulder.

He rolled his eyes and followed after her. Bending, he scooped up his gun and slid it back into his waistband. Then he hefted his sword up onto his shoulder. "How do you know where we're going?"

She glanced at him before she went back to cautiously scanning the hallway for signs of more attackers. "I don't," she admitted.

"You...you don't?"

"Nope." They reached a door on the left and she kicked it open. "I'm just following the trail of villains. They're trying to keep us from getting to Stefan. They're nervous. So...wherever they come from, he's deeper within in that direction. Simple deduction, really." She entered the now exposed room, gun drawn. "Help me clear this room, though I doubt we find them on the lower levels. I'm assuming Stefan has Oakley and Kristie in the tower. It's cliché, but he's old. Just in case, I don't want to pass them up. The quicker we get to them, the less likely it is they die."

In silent agreement, Camden followed her into the room. He kept his back to the wall as he called out. "Kristie! Baby, are you in here?" He kicked back the door to the adjoining room and found it empty as well. "Just a bathroom," he called over to Priya.

"No one here," she agreed.

As he made his way back toward the door that would lead into the hallway, Camden paused at a window that showcased the massive lawn below. The battle still raged on beneath them. Figures combated in the moonlight and weapons glinted.

There were downed bodies on the lawn. He wasn't naïve enough to believe them all to belong to the opposition. He sent up a silent prayer that none of them were Ward. Kristie's youngest brother was just a kid, and he was human.

Priya put a sympathetic hand on his shoulder. "The quicker we get through this, the more lives we will save. Stefan is the dictator of this regime. Once he is dead, the others will bow down and relinquish their weapons. They will surrender or they will flee. Either way, the fighting will cease."

Camden turned his back on the window and walked back into the hallway. "Then let's work really hard at killing Stefan."

Priya pushed past him to take the lead. "I'm enjoying this more positive attitude of yours."

They reached another room and Camden cautiously turned the knob, easing the door open. "Only a sociopath would find that to be a positive comment."

She shrugged. "A sociopath or a member of a much oppressed dragon community." She glanced into the room before ducking back out. "Closet," she informed him.

Camden closed the door and followed after her as she continued down the hallway. "So...what do you think the odds are of finding Kristie and Oakley alive? Do you think they'll have hurt them yet?"

Her response was a grimace. "I'm assuming they'll have hurt them. I'm just hoping they're not dead yet. That's the best we can hope for."

Camden scowled at the thought of someone hurting Kristie to get to him. She was innocent in all of this. She was only involved because of her feelings for him.

"I'm thinking there's little over a fifty percent chance they're both still alive," Priya said darkly as they reached another doorway. "I'm trying not to think about it."

That thought made Camden's stomach roll, made him feel as if he'd swallowed a boulder. With a grim expression, he raised his weapon and prepared himself for whatever was behind the door. "Let's just get this over with," he said softly. To his own ears, his voice sounded gravelly and raw.

Nodding, Priya swung the door open and they edged inside.

As he'd done earlier, Camden headed for the bathroom while she cleared the main room. He reached the door and pushed it open. To his surprise, the room was occupied.

A woman sat cowering on the bathroom floor, wedged between the toilet and the wall.

Camden stared down at her in surprise, unsure of what to do. She looked terrified and helpless, but he knew firsthand that looks could be deceiving. "Priya!" His voice was a nervous holler, his tone full of anxiety.

Upon hearing his voice, the woman cowering on the floor whimpered and tried shoving herself even closer against the wall.

"Priya, I have an issue," he said desperately. "I need you in here. *Now.*"

There was a loud sigh from the other room. Then Priya stomped into the doorway. "What could possibly—" She broke off, eyes widening in horror. "Kill her!" she screamed.

Camden lifted his sword and looked down at the cowering woman. She was more girl than woman if you asked him, her face still rounded and full with youth. She barely looked sixteen. Her hair was jet black and done in curls that were so thick he could barely see her big green eyes around it. Hell, she was just a kid. "Priya, I can't," he said, voice catching. "I can't do it."

"Camden, kill her!" Priya screamed, her voice sounding hysterical.

His heart thudded in dread as he looked back and forth between the two women. "She's unarmed," he breathed in horror. "She—" He broke off at Priya's scream of horror.

"Camden, look out!"

He turned in shock to see the tiny girl lunge from her spot on the floor. She had a dagger clutched tightly in her fist and it was aimed for his heart.

He was frozen is shock, unable to even move. Priya suddenly shoving him out of the way was the only thing that kept the blade from sinking into his chest. Instead, it sliced across her forearm.

Priya hissed in pain but pushed forward. She shoved her sword headlong into the woman's chest. With a holler, she shoved harder, ramming the sword completely through until it came out the woman's back. "You're time is up, bitch," she growled, yanking the sword back.

The dagger fell out of the woman's hand and clattered against the tile floor. "So is yours," she whispered. A delicate hand drifted down to touch her wound. When she pulled her fingers away, they were stained with blood. "Stefan will have your head for this," she promised.

"Sorceresses are easily replaced," Priya taunted. "He'll be more upset over the blood we leave on the floor."

The woman's expression hardened. "You will die here tonight, Priya. I at least saw to that." Her eyelashes began to flutter rapidly, and shallow, harsh breaths wheezed past her lips. She convulsed before her head finally came to rest against the wall. She died surrounded by strangers and a puddle of her own blood.

Once the show was over and she stilled, Camden nudged the woman with the toe of his shoe. "Um...do we have to cut her head off?"

Priya flung open the bathroom's medicine cabinet and gave a noise of triumph when she found a gauze wrap. "No. We don't have to behead her," she said as she wrapped the bandage around her bleeding forearm. "She wasn't a dragon. She was a sorceress. Stefan's sorceress."

"Now we are dealing with sorceresses, too?" Camden asked with an overwhelmed tone to his voice. "Well shit."

"She was left here to forfeit her life in hopes that she could bring a few of us down first. Stefan is known for sacrificing others to save his own ass. She knew that. Must have stung like a bitch."

He cringed and stepped away from the body. "No wonder she was so hostile."

"She was so hostile because she was trained to be," Priya corrected. "That girl specialized in poisons and magical torture. In her element, she could make a person writhe in agony without ever touching them."

"Lovely woman," he said sarcastically as he edged out of the room. A thought occurred to him and he asked, "What did she mean when she said your time was up, too?"

"There was poison on the tip of her dagger. Always is. She was hoping to take you, the biggest threat, out of the fight, but she got me instead."

Camden felt his heart drop to his toes. "She was trying to take me out with a poison-tipped dagger?" He studied Priya in concern. "What does this mean for you?"

"It means I've only got a couple hours to live. Tops." On Camden's horrified expression, she patted his arm in reassurance. "Don't look so worried. I'll come back...as long as no one chops my head off that is." She sent him a pleading look of concern. "Please don't let that happen." When Camden nodded his reassurance, she pressed on. "Unfortunately, I don't know how fit I'm going to be when it comes to killing Stefan. I pray I have enough stamina left in me to finish the job."

"If you aren't able to do it, I will," he promised, voice firm with determination. "We've come this far. They've kidnapped my fiancé. I'm finishing this tonight."

Priya nodded, her eyes boring into his. She placed a hand on his arm. "I'll take you as far as I can. I'll sacrifice my life for yours if need be."

Camden shook his head frantically. "There is going to be no *if need be*. You're making it out of this alive. Oakley didn't like me before. If I let you die, he will kick my ass."

"He's a silly human," she said fondly. "He can't kick your ass."

"He would if I fought fair," he countered. "Either that or he'd die trying."

Priya frowned. "I don't wish for Oakley to *die trying*."

"Then get your ass in gear," he ordered. "You only have so much time before that poison starts to affect you. Let's get as far as we can before that happens."

A look of resolve crossed her face, and Priya stepped

over the dead body of Stefan's sorceress. She paused long enough to wipe away the blood on her sword against the woman's back. "Let's do this."

Camden followed her out into the hallway with new motivation. He'd been leery about killing strangers, but he couldn't afford to hesitate anymore. Priya was dying. She needed him to take charge, to be strong.

She marched ahead of him to the end of the hallway toward another set of steps. "From the blueprints Pius managed to obtain, we have another floor before we reach the steps of the tower where Stefan is most likely hiding Oakley and Kristie."

"Tower?" Camden couldn't help but ask with a snort. "I know you mentioned it before, but...really? What century are we in?"

Priya shrugged in response. "Stefan is ancient. He likes to do things the old fashioned way. He doesn't mind being cliché. Things become cliché for a reason—people do them and they work."

He couldn't deny that reasoning, so he simply followed Priya up the staircase, his weapon at the ready.

They were reaching the top of the staircase when a woman jumped into view from the right. She dove at Priya with a howl of fury, and the two of them went tumbling down the stairs in a tangle of arms and legs.

"Priya!" Camden went to race after them when something at the top of the staircase caught his eye. He turned in what felt like slow motion to face the largest man he'd ever seen in his life.

The man took up the entire stairway. His shoulders were tremendously broad, but even bigger was the weapon in his hands. The giant wielded a hammer that was so massive it looked like it should take a dozen men to lift it. He was dragging the mallet behind him, the sound of it grinding into the hardwood floor filling the air. His face was covered by a leather satchel that was bound around his neck. The only exposed bits of flesh were his hands, which were deeply disfigured. They were so damaged that bone poked through the scar tissue in patches. With a mighty roar, the man lifted the hammer over his head and waved it in a bloodthirsty cry.

Camden felt the blood drain from his face. "Oh fuck."

Chapter 14

Camden felt completely and thoroughly screwed as he stared at the inhumanly large man at the top of the staircase. He whirled to look at Priya, who was just coming to a bone-jarring stop at the bottom of the steps.

The other woman, a redhead with an expression of pure hatred, came through the fall with the advantage. She was crouched over Priya as she lifted her right arm up and back.

Before his eyes, she transformed her hands into talons. Sharp claws decorated the ends of her fingertips. She wiggled them in the air for a moment before slicing them down at the woman underneath her.

"Priya!" Camden yelled in alarm.

Priya just barely managed to get her arms up in time to keep the woman's claws from tearing into her face and neck. Still, they gouged into her forearm, slicing clear to bone. Despite her predicament and the blood that now poured freely from her arm, her fear was directed behind him. "Camden, look out!"

He felt the air shift behind him and barely managed to dive out of the way as the giant's hammer came crashing down. As he hit the wall, the hammer hit the floor, causing a floorboard to crack and the ground to shake.

With a grunt, the man hefted the weapon back up onto his shoulder.

"The Executioner!" Priya screamed hysterically. She thrashed underneath the other woman, emitting shrieks of terror. "Let me go! Let me go!"

Camden had never seen Priya look so terrified. Not that it wasn't obvious just by looking at him, but for Priya to be this panic-stricken, the Executioner had to be bad news.

"Camden," Priya shrieked as she struggled to free herself. "Run!"

He never would have abandoned Priya. Even if he wanted to, there wasn't enough time. The Executioner had his weapon ready and was bringing it around again. This time, he swung it like a baseball bat with his intended target being Camden's head.

Camden barely had time to duck the hammer. It hit the wall behind him with a loud crack. The wall shook and dust flew into the air as the plaster fractured.

He was on his hands and knees. When the hammer came swinging down toward him, he rolled, coming to a stop against the Executioner's feet. Thinking quickly, he grabbed the dagger Priya had given him and jammed it into the man's foot.

The giant growled in pain and backhanded Camden across the face, sending him catapulting down the stairs.

Camden collided with the two women, coming to a stop against the wall of the landing's hallway with a bang. Color flashed before his eyes, and he had to shake his head to clear it. "How do I kill this guy?" he asked breathlessly to Priya. "I can't even reach his neck. Even if I could, I'd need a chainsaw to get through that thing."

Priya was struggling to her knees, blood dripping from the numerous gashes in her arms and along her shoulders. "He's human," she said desperately. "Just kill him!"

Those were the only words of advice she could spare him. As soon as her instructions were out, she turned her attention back to the redhead. "Dawn Rene, I killed Marie Claire," she taunted. "Your sister is dead. You will join her in a moment."

Dawn Rene gave a howl of outrage and charged at Priya.

Priya shoved her sword forward, skewering Dawn Rene on the blade of her weapon. "Just kill him," she hollered over to Camden with desperation in her voice.

Seeing as Priya seemed to have her situation under control, Camden spun back around to face the mammoth human being. The Executioner was making his way slowly down the stairs, his hammer slamming into each step behind him as he trudged forward.

"This guy's human?" Camden asked with disbelief, gawking at the man's sheer size and strength. "And I thought Oakley was scary."

The Executioner grunted as his feet stomped heavily down each step. The sound he emitted hinted at a lack of intelligence. This being was meant for one purpose only—destruction. Camden would bet anything that reasoning with this man was going to be out of the question. He seemed like a rabid dog that'd been released on his owner's competitor. There wasn't an intelligent, original thought happening in his brain.

Still, Camden had to try. He had misgivings about his odds and ability to defeat this man in a fight. In a placating manner, he held his hands up. "There is really no need to do this," he reasoned. "Stefan's reign is over. You have to realize that. Why cause more death? Can't you just peacefully walk away and let things happen as they should?"

The hammer swinging at his head was answer enough. Camden hit the ground and rolled. He smacked into something solid, and it took him a moment to realize it was the back of Dawn Rene's legs.

The redhead stumbled over him, landing roughly on her backside. She scrambled to her feet in a flash, her face contorted with rage. "Can't win your own battles?" She spat the insulting taunt at Priya as Camden struggled to his feet. "You need your loser friend to help you?"

Any further mockery was cut short by the Executioner's hammer as it collided with the woman's skull. He'd been attempting to get at Camden through her, his actions testament to his complete disregard for anything other than killing his target.

Priya gave a startled cry. Her nails dug into Camden's legs as she used his pants to pull herself to her feet. When Dawn Rene's head hit the floor, cracking like a soft melon, Priya began sobbing. "He's going to kill us," she whimpered in a soft, terrified voice.

Camden grabbed Priya by the shoulders and hefted her the rest of the way to her feet. "What is wrong with you? Where is the tough-as-nails woman I know? Snap out of it! We can do this."

"No, we can't," she mumbled pitifully. "People don't walk away from the Executioner." She struggled to break free of

Camden's grip. "He has no pity, no sense of reasoning. There is no soul in that man. He's nothing more than a killing machine."

With a sigh, Camden dropped his hands away from Priya and turned to face their adversary. "Looks like I'm alone on this one."

The large man's only response was a growl as he lumbered forward, his feet shuffling along the floor as if he was some type of hideous Frankenstein monster. He only lifted his massive feet when he reached Dawn Rene's body. He didn't even use the effort to go over her. He stepped on top of her, too focused on his target to fully step above, crushing the chest cavity of the already dead woman.

Priya gave a whimper of terror at the crunching of bones. "She's not dead. Not really." Her hands trembled as she took a frightened step backwards. "She'll come back. She'll wake up when her body begins to heal itself. She'll feel it. All of it."

Camden felt sick to his stomach. He wouldn't wish that on anyone, not even their enemies. He understood Priya's fear, but it really wasn't helping him.

Squaring his feet to appear braver than he actually felt, he grabbed for the gun in his waistband with shaking hands. The cold steel felt heavy and reassuring in his palm. It gave him the courage to raise the weapon and aim it at the Executioner's chest.

He fired off the first round, his arm jerking with the kick of the gun. He then proceeded to empty the entire clip into the man's chest.

The Executioner showed no signs of being affected. The bullets tearing into his flesh didn't even slow him down. He kept coming, his heavy footfalls echoing in the hall.

Camden backpedaled, his eyes wide. "Human?" he screeched at Priya. "This thing is human?" When his gun clicked empty, he tossed it to the side. "Now what?" he asked no one in particular. If an entire clip being emptied into the man's chest didn't work, he didn't know what would.

"He's too strong," Priya whimpered from behind him.

"Why is he too strong?" Camden asked with bewilderment, keeping a wary eye on the hammer. "No one should be this strong."

"Stefan injects him with dragon's blood. It makes him stronger, bigger. It also stopped the aging process. As long as he keeps up with the injections, he'll keep living, growing stronger." She swallowed thickly, her eyes trained on the genetic abomination. "He's immensely powerful, but he's still human." At her own words, some confidence returned to Priya's face. "He's only human," she repeated, as if for her own benefit. "He can be killed. It just takes effort." She moved to stand next to Camden, her shoulders straight and pulled back with determination. She sent him a look that clearly stated she was back in the fight and ready to do whatever necessary to win.

He glanced at her with a crooked grin. "Hey, you're back."

"Yes. Well, I just realized that we can in fact do this." She raised her sword up vertically and stared past it at the Executioner. "Let's kill this mother fucker."

"There's the crazy bitch I admire," Camden teased, his eyes never leaving the Executioner. "Where do you suggest we start?"

"I have a very bad and dangerous plan," Priya said hesitantly.

"Sounds awesome," Camden retorted. "Hit me with it."

"He hates women. Stefan taught him to be exceptionally brutal to his female victims." She grimaced before continuing. "If I taunt him, he'll come after me even if you're the intended target. I'll distract him, keep him going in circles. I'll try to stay out of his grasp while you chop away at him."

He didn't like the idea of using her as bait, but he didn't see much choice. They were not going to take this man down without getting creative. "Do we have any other options?"

"No." Her reply was solemn and foreboding.

"Then I guess we don't have much choice."

"Please don't let me get killed," Priya requested. Then she stepped forward in front of him.

Camden watched with admiration as Priya approached the Executioner as if she didn't harbor the slightest fear.

"Hey there, big boy," she taunted flirtatiously. "I'm on your target list, aren't I?" She stopped a few feet away from him and cocked her hip in his direction as if inviting him to come forward to her. "I'm not at the top of the list, but I bet I'm pretty close, huh?" She smiled coyly at him and batted her eyelashes. "Does Stefan give you pictures of me to look at late at night when you're locked up in your cell?"

The Executioner faltered and gaped at her, his eyes wild

behind the leather satchel.

"Do you pleasure yourself while thinking of ways to hurt me? To make me scream?"

Camden couldn't keep the disgust from his expression when the hulking man's eyes widened with interest, his nostrils flaring. These people were monsters! How could they keep an abomination like this alive? Worse than just allowing him to live, they'd pumped him full of dragon's blood to make him practically immortal. It was depraved!

Priya must have seen Camden's expression, because she hissed, "Stop looking horrified and get ready to kill him." To the Executioner, she said, "Does it bother you to know you'll never have me? I won't let it happen. You're beneath me, a shell of what an immortal should be. I'd never let a foul creature like you ever lay a finger on me." When he roared in outrage, she flinched but continued. "You'll never know what it's like to torture me, to hear me scream and beg for my life."

At this, the Executioner picked up his pace. He lumbered toward Priya, his eyes dilated with a desire for violence.

Priya backpedalled past Camden, keeping her eyes on the behemoth that was dead set on killing her. "Now would be a good time to do something," she trilled.

"Oh! Right!" Camden hefted up his sword and braced his feet. Despite his brave face, he couldn't help but cringe as the Executioner reached him. Luckily, just like Priya had predicted, the man marched past him, heading for her instead.

Camden took the advantage and swung his sword into the giant's gut as the much larger man forced his way past. The unforgiving metal sliced into flesh, tearing into the Executioner's body. The other man didn't even slow down. Blood cascaded down the front of him, staining his already grimy clothing, but he didn't even hesitate to observe the damage.

Priya looped around in a wide circle and jogged back toward Camden, her eyebrows raised hopefully. "Well? Did you get him?"

He nodded in response. "I got him. Didn't seem to faze him too much, though. He's just bleeding all over the place."

"Keep going," she ordered. "Like you pointed out, he's only human. Eventually, you'll slice through something vital, or he'll bleed out." She glanced over her shoulder and gave a yip. "Here he comes! Hit him again." With that, she danced a few feet away from him, giving Camden space to wield his weapon.

"Just don't slip and fall on the blood," Camden called to her in warning. Then, as the Executioner approached, he repeated his earlier attack. On this pass, his sword sliced along the big man's arm, cutting clean down to bone at the wrist.

This time, the Executioner took notice of his injuries. He looked down at his bleeding wrist and blinked at it for a moment as if trying to comprehend what was happening. He then simply dropped his weapon to put less strain on his arm. With that done, he continued on his path for Priya.

Her eyes were on the dropped weapon. "You weakened him," she said excitedly. Her eyes slid to Camden, and she grinned. "Keep going. We're wearing him down."

"It's not like I have much choice anyway," he grumbled as Priya once again danced past him like a boxer.

When the Executioner reached Camden on this trip, the large man froze. His eyes finally left Priya and slowly turned to Camden. He seemed to realize the other man was responsible for his wounds. He gave a growl of aggravation and aggression. His arm whipped out and connected with Camden's chest, sending him flying backwards.

Camden hit the wall hard and crumpled to the ground. He must have lost consciousness for awhile, because the next thing that registered was Priya screaming.

"Camden!" Her voice was a terrified shriek. "Help me! Camden!" Anything further she'd been about to say was cut off with a strangled gurgle.

That sound forced Camden to focus. He struggled to his feet, holding onto the wall for support when the room spun. "I'm coming," he croaked out. His voice sounded off to his own ears and he worried he might have a concussion.

Even so, he forced himself forward. Pushing away from the wall, he moved in Priya's direction. His feet stumbled clumsily along once he no longer had the wall to hold onto. The sight that greeted him when his eyes finally focused made Camden's heart drop to his toes. All he could see of Priya was her feet. The Executioner was leaning over her, his massive shoulders straining with whatever he was doing.

As he stumbled closer, Camden's toe caught on the edge of the dropped hammer. He stared at it thoughtfully. With decisiveness, he then hefted up the weapon. Initially, his arms came crashing back down to the floor from the weight of the hammer. "Damn," he grumbled. "This thing is heavy as shit."

Adjusting his grip, he lifted the weapon with a groan. It was heavy, but that meant it would do a lot of damage. A normal human being would not have been able to lift it, but Camden drew on his newly found dragon strength. He hoisted the hammer up and carefully made his way over to the pair on the floor. Once he was directly above them, he raised the mallet as high as he could. Then he drove it down onto the Executioner's skull.

There was a loud crack, and the big man's knees gave way. Though he went down, his hands didn't release Priya.

Camden grunted and lifted the hammer again. He swung it up and over his shoulder before bringing it back down on the man's skull.

The Executioner's body twitched, and his hands finally fell free from the woman underneath him.

Priya sucked in air with a ragged gasp. Coughs tore from her throat as she struggled to get away from her would-be murderer.

"Get out of the way!" Trusting that she would be able to get free, Camden lifted the hammer again.

The Executioner was trying to get to his feet when his own weapon came down on his head once again.

Camden put as much power as he could behind that swing. As he brought it down, he targeted the already weakened portion of skull. It gave way with a sickening crack.

The monster collapsed face down. Though he was prone, his arms still scrambled at the floor, trying to pull his injured body toward Priya. He dragged his injured form along the ground, bringing himself closer to his intended target.

"Hit him again," Priya screamed as the Executioner's hand wrapped around her calf. She kicked at him, but was unable to break free of his vise-like grasp. "Hit him again!"

Camden cringed. He could see the lumpy, uneven area under the mask where he'd already cracked through bone. His lip curled in disgust when he realized the monster wouldn't stop until his baser instincts were cut completely off. He would have to obliterate the brain. Shivering at the thought, he lifted the hammer up and drove it back down onto the Executioner's head. He was going to brain the man with his own weapon.

He brought the heavy hammer down again and again, trying not to heave at the crunch of bone and then later, the squish of brain. He continued striking until the other man stopped moving, until there was nothing left of the Executioner's head but blood and splintered bone and brain matter ground into the fancy Oriental rug under their feet.

Only then did Camden stop. Sweat was dripping down his forehead and his arms were quivering from the effort before he finally lowered the hammer to the floor. He was breathing in heavy gasps and his vision still danced with stars.

"Holy crap, Camden," Priya said from beside him. "That is disgusting."

"It might be disgusting, but I can pretty much guarantee he isn't going to try to hurt you anymore." He was wiping sweat away from his forehead with the sleeve of his shirt when a pitiful keening noise filled the air.

"She's coming back," Priya whispered in horror. She gripped Camden's shoulder, nails digging into his skin. "Dawn Rene is coming back."

Another agonized wail filled the air and Dawn Rene's body writhed on the ground, reminding Camden of Priya's comment that the woman would feel every injury. Judging from Priya's comment that Pierre would be incoherent a long time after being killed, he guessed the healing process wouldn't be fast. This woman would suffer a considerable amount of pain for a very long time. He knew that was Priya's fear, the woman's pain, not the fact that she was coming back to life. She was no threat to them now.

With grim resolve, Camden moved away from Priya. He picked his sword up from the ground on his way over to Dawn Rene. He limped across the hallway, raised the sword above his head, and then brought it down onto the suffering woman's neck.

Priya stared at him, her lips parted and eyes wide with shock.

"I'm not going to sit here and watch someone suffer," he said gruffly. "Evil or not, she's still a human being."

Priya nodded in solemn agreement. The two held eye contact for a moment before she turned and slowly limped her way back up the steps.

It wasn't until now, when the immediate danger was over, that he noticed how battered Priya looked. Her injured arm hung limp at her side and blood was dripping off the ends of her fingertips. Her shirt had a gash in it that sliced along her midsection, giving him a peek at her damaged flesh beneath. Her normally pristine hair was sticking up in a few different directions. Her lip was split and her skin was sickly pale.

"Are you all right?" he asked as he followed her up the stairs. He knew there was no way he was looking even close to his normal self, but Priya looked trashed. She looked like she might fall over dead at any second.

"I'm fine," she said through gritted teeth.

"You don't look fine," he countered in a gentle voice. "You look far from fine."

Priya's head whipped in his direction and her eyes blazed with fire. "I'm *dying*. You knew that. Of course I don't look fine!" A ragged cough tore up her throat at her raised voice. "My body is shutting down. An hour from now, I'm going to be dead." She ran the back of her hand along her mouth, wiping away blood. "We just need to finish this before then."

Camden nodded slowly, trying to keep the pity from his eyes. He knew it would only piss her off. "I'll make sure you come back," he promised.

"You'd better or I'll haunt you for the next hundred years," Priya came back with a hint of a smile.

As they made it to the landing where they'd first encountered the Executioner and Dawn Rene, Priya took a deep breath. Then she limped toward a small spiral staircase to their left. "Well, this is it," she said quietly. "Stefan will be up here. So will Kristie and Oakley...if they're still alive."

"They're still alive," he growled darkly in response. "If either one of them have even a scratch, Stefan is going to be begging for mercy." With that, he marched up the stairs with every intention of finishing what they'd started.

Chapter 15

The walk up the spiral staircase was the most agonizing couple of minutes in Camden's life. He was desperate to see if Kristie was alright, but he dreaded coming face to face with the man responsible for it all. Camden was not a violent man, but he feared he might lose control if anything had been done to his fiancé.

When they reached the door, he turned the handle cautiously and gave a gentle push. The door squeaked open to reveal a small, circular room. The entire room was made of stone, giving it a very primitive look. It was bare and aboriginal, the stones looking ancient and rare. It looked like something out of an old fairy tale, just the kind of place an evil witch would hide out. Other than its intimidating appearance, the room was vacant. "It's empty," he whispered to Priya.

"We're in the tower," she replied just as quietly. "They're probably on the roof. Dragons like open space to fight, especially in their reptilian form. We like the fresh air." Her expression soured. "No doubt he also wanted to keep an eye on the fighting below, see who fell in the war he created."

"The roof?" Camden asked in horror. "Is now a good time to mention I'm afraid of heights?"

Priya pushed him in front of her and entered the room on his heels. "You'd better get over that fear very quickly, because you're about to have more important things on your mind."

Camden cringed as they inched toward a small staircase that was crudely carved into the stone wall. It led to an arched doorway above. "Not very comforting. Can't you ever say anything comforting?"

"That's what your girlfriend is for," Priya reasoned. "I'm here to be practical and help you become a leader. Now that you're aware of your dragon heritage, it is your responsibility to defend that territory of yours surrounding the college. My job is to push you, not coddle. It will help keep you alive."

Camden glanced in her direction to comment when a crack shot through the air. Pain raced suddenly up his shoulder like fire. He hissed at the throbbing sting and looked down to see a tear in his shirt and a trickle of blood. "I think I just got shot," he said in astonishment. "Where was your whole 'keeping me alive' gimmick for that one?"

Priya swore under her breath and yanked him down to kneel beside her at the foot of the stairs. "You got shot? Why'd you let that happen?"

"*Let* that happen?" Camden squeaked in disbelief as she prodded his injured shoulder. "Like I *let* it happen. I can't jump out of the way of a speeding bullet. Who do you think I am, Superman?"

"Absolutely not," Priya said curtly. "Superman never would have allowed himself to get shot. And if he did, the bullet would have simply bounced off of him, not burrow in and mess up his shoulder. You're more like Clark Kent than Superman. You bumble. You're awkward. You're kind of nerdy. Plus, for some unknown reason, hot chicks dig you. Definitely a Clark Kent."

Camden narrowed his eyes at her description of him. "I'm surprised you even know who Superman is. You don't seem like the type to be up on modern pop culture." His voice sounded a little harsh, so he tried to even out his annoyed expression. He wasn't really angry with her, just at the pain currently tearing through his arm.

"Modern pop culture?" Priya asked in confusion. Her eyebrows furrowed. "You do know that Superman is real, right? He's a vigilante hero bred and raised within the supernatural community."

Despite the imminent danger, Camden couldn't squelch down his excited inner little boy, who was currently dancing with glee. "Really?" he asked with wide-eyed delight.

"No. Not really." Priya punched his uninjured arm. "I can't believe you bought that. You can add gullible to that list." With a sigh, she dropped his arm as if realizing there wasn't much she could do without first aid supplies. Then she cautiously pushed up into a crouched position. "On the bright side, if you are good enough to get excited over Superman, you're good enough to keep going."

Camden groaned and lifted to a crouch next to her, keeping his back against the wall in an effort to keep out of the sight of the men just beyond the doorway. "Any plans?" he asked hopefully.

"None that don't involve one of us getting killed," Priya admitted as she stared thoughtfully toward the doorway.

"Awesome," he said sarcastically. "So what's the best out of those?"

Priya rubbed her hands together with a wide grin. "Wow. Camden Harrison, stepping up his game." She peered toward the door. "Well, there can't be many men left up there. Stefan sent the worst of his crew at us. I haven't seen Therius, but he's a front line type of guy. I don't see him waiting patiently up here while a battle is raging on the front lawn." She glanced out a small window along the wall. "He's down there somewhere. I know it."

She stared for so long that Camden felt the need to bring her back. "So there's going to be minimal security once we breach the doorway?"

His question worked, drawing Priya's eyes back to him. "Yes," she said with a brisk nod. "He's probably got a couple sharpshooters up there with him aimed strictly at the entryway. Maybe a few artillery men. It's his last line of defense."

She took a deep breath and set him with a serious look. "I'm going to run through. They'll shoot at me. I'll draw their fire, and you can rush in low and fast. I'm confident you'll get a clear path to Stefan."

"I got shot just approaching the doorway," Camden argued. "There's no way you'll be able to draw their fire and not get shot. It isn't possible."

"I don't plan on not getting shot," Priya said evenly. She rubbed her palms against her dirty pants.

"Wait! You *plan* on getting shot?" He gave her a look of incredulity. "No. You're injured already."

"No. I'm dying already. Whether they pump me full of bullets or not, I'm dead." When he shook his head in disagreement, she grabbed his forearms tightly. "This makes the most sense. You know it does."

"I don't want to sacrifice you," he said softly.

"I don't want Oakley to die." Her eyes were pleading as she tightened her grip on his arms. "I want to do this. If me dying keeps Oakley alive, keeps your mate alive, then it's worth it. Let me do this."

Camden swallowed past a lump of emotion in his throat and nodded. "Alright." He took a deep breath and nodded again. "You're a brave woman, a good leader." He smiled crookedly. "I'd follow you. I intend to once everything settles down."

"A good leader?" she asked with a derisive snort. "I'm not even going to be able to battle Stefan. I'm dying before it even gets to that. I've failed as a leader."

Camden shook his head in disagreement. "You didn't fail. Dying...that's what makes you a good leader," he said with soft affection. "You're willing to die for your people. You've given them everything without hesitation. You're stronger than anyone I know."

Priya stared into his eyes for a moment before nodding. "Thank you." A brief smile flitted across her lips before it was gone and replaced with a business-like expression. "Go make me proud."

He glanced away, hating to agree to a plan that would result in her death. Finally, he looked back at her, his heart full of determination. "I'll make sure you come back. I swear it."

"Okay." She moved forward, hesitated, and then pulled him into a tight hug. "You're a good man, Camden." With that, she pulled away and ran toward the doorway without even a backwards glance.

Camden heard the gunshots before she was even out of view. Though he'd known they would be coming, it was still sobering. As much as he wanted to, he didn't have time to worry for Priya. He had a job to do. Lives depended on it.

Moving on adrenaline and instinct, Camden started for the doorway, making sure to keep low to the ground as Priya had instructed.

As soon as he was in the doorway, he could see Priya forcing her way across the rooftop through a hail of gunfire. She ignored the bullets as they tore into her flesh. Instead, she seemed to be concentrating on getting to the men behind the weapons.

Camden looked away from her, searching for Stefan.

He'd never met the man, but Priya had described him in great detail. His eyes flicked over a beefy blond man who was shaped like a sausage. He dismissed him and moved on.

As his gaze swept the roof, they landed on Oakley and Kristie. They were huddled together against a small, raised wall that kept someone from tumbling over the side of the tower's roof. They looked battered and weary as they watched Priya with matching expressions of concern, but they were alive. Camden's heart skipped a beat, relief filling him at the sight of his fiancé. She was alive. Both of them were alive.

As much as he wanted to rush to Kristie's side, he held back. There would be time to check on her once this was finished. Right now, he had to deal with Stefan, or all this violence and death would be for nothing.

His eyes left the Taylor siblings to look at a man slightly to their left. The man was tall with dark hair slicked back from his forehead. Instead of looking concerned, the man was watching Priya with intense interest. His appearance was that of overconfidence and conceit. This man was definitely Stefan Demarco.

Unable to help themselves, Camden's eyes followed Stefan's to watch Priya. Despite her injuries, she was still pressing forward. She grabbed the barrel of a shotgun held by the closest person. She yanked the gun from the man's hands, swung her arm around, and elbowed him in the face.

The surprised man stumbled backwards.

Priya took this opportunity to elbow him in the back of the head as well.

At the jarring impact, the man's legs gave out and he collapsed unconscious to the ground.

Priya spared him a quick look as if to make sure he was staying down before spinning toward the next man.

Camden felt a rush of pride at her bravery as he turned his attention back to Stefan. Priya had proven to be an amazing woman and leader. He was honored to count her as his ally.

It was now his turn to help their people. As he slunk along the shadows toward Stefan, Camden blinked in surprise. His people? He didn't know when he'd started thinking of these dragons as "his people," but he liked it. He liked feeling as if he belonged somewhere. He liked having people think of him as something other than the gangly, awkward kid who lived in his best friend's shadow. He was appreciated and it felt good.

He was feeling so positive about their odds that the booming sound of a firing shotgun followed by Stefan's cruel laugh caught him by surprise. His gaze swung back to Priya to find her on the ground.

Her face was alarmingly pale, her body was riddled with bullet holes, and a large puddle of blood was forming around her. Her eyes were pinched closed, and her chest rose and fell in jarring movements as she struggled for each breath.

Camden turned back to Stefan with horror as the man spoke his next words with careless dismissal.

"The bitch is finally down." He waved toward the large blond man. "Carl, you can do as you wish with her."

As the blond man stepped forward with an eager expression, the familiar name clicked into place for Camden. This was the man who had raped Priya; he was the man who had tortured her for his own perverse pleasure.

Camden wasn't the only one to make the connection, because Oakley lunged away from Kristie and gave a roar of outrage. He rushed at Carl's back, yanking a sword out of the hands of a startled gunman on his march across the rooftop.

Camden wanted to assist him, to protect his human ally and help save his dying friend. Instead, he made the tough to decision to go after Stefan. Once she was herself again, Priya would kill him if he didn't.

Steeling his nerves, he stepped out of the protective covering of the darkness and approached the other man. He refused to cower in the shadows and go for a sneak attack. He was no coward. He had friends to avenge, and he would do it with his head held high. Stefan would know just who ended his reign of terror.

As he stepped out from his protective covering, Camden heard Kristie scream his name but tried not to look in her direction. It would only make him angry, and right now he needed to be in control of his emotions. "Stefan DeMarco?" he asked darkly as he approached.

The dark-haired man nodded in confirmation. "Camden Harrison," he stated in return. "You sure have become a thorn in my side."

Camden shrugged nonchalantly. "Well, you messed with the wrong college student."

Stefan smirked, his expression all arrogance. "Yes. I heard that. I had one of my men look into your brief history after Therius paid you a visit. Imagine my surprise when I discovered you've not even reached thirty years of age. My enemies are following an infant. Are they aware of that?"

Camden froze for only a second, then continued on his path for Stefan. "It doesn't matter how old I am. I can kill you all the same."

"Really?" Stefan asked with an amused laugh. "In your twenty-some odd years, did you learn to master the martial arts?" He tapped a finger against his chin, mocking a thoughtful expression. "How many kills do you have in dragon form? Do you know the best way to dig your talons into the back of someone's neck so that you can sever their spine? I do. I've become quite the expert at it." He glanced over at Kristie in a threatening manner. "I hear it's agony. The person suffers terribly. Would you like a first-hand demonstration? Describing it can only do so much. It's really better to watch with your own eyes."

"You lay a hand on her, and I will make you suffer worse than you can ever imagine," Camden growled through clenched teeth.

Stefan's eyebrows rose at the open hostility. Camden wasn't certain if his reaction was of amusement or shock. Either way, he didn't much care.

"Look at her," Stefan demanded in a barking tone as he waved a hand at Kristie.

Camden's eyes moved to his girlfriend as the other man had instructed. He finally looked to the woman he loved.

She was still huddled against the wall. Her entire body trembled, and Camden realized it was from shock. Her lower lip was busted and bloodied; her left eye was puffy and swollen half shut. Her once perfectly manicured nails were now broken and caked with blood, indicating she'd gone down fighting. They hadn't taken her easily.

As he surveyed her ripped shirt sleeve, Camden was a mix of emotions. He was proud that she'd not given in so easily, yet he was enraged at her injuries. Someone would pay for this. *Stefan DeMarco* would pay for this.

"Look at her," Stefan repeated. "Look at what I've done to her already, and you've been unable to stop it." His tone became even more arrogant as he added, "You aren't a killer, Camden. You and I both know that."

Camden's eyes never left Kristie, but his angry voice had

no trouble reaching Stefan. "I killed your Executioner, did I not?"

The sharp intake of air finally drew Camden's attention back to Stefan. For the first time, there was a glimmer of uncertainty in the other man's eyes.

"You lie," the oppressive leader said softly.

"I'm not lying," Camden said with conviction. "He's dead. I killed him with his own weapon. There aren't enough of the king's horses and men to put Humpty Dumpty together again." He smirked. The old nursery rhyme had never sounded so ominous before. "I ground his brains into your carpet. He is most decidedly dead." To add insult to injury, he couldn't help but add, "I killed your sorceress, too."

Stefan flinched and visibly swallowed. It took him a moment to find his voice, but when he did, he replied calmly, "I figured as much when I noticed your bitch had been poisoned. My sorceress did her job. She took out the main threat, leaving you open for the easy kill."

Camden moved forward, gripping his sword so tightly his knuckles ached. "You imply that Priya was the main target, that she was the biggest threat to your power structure. You say that, which makes me find it odd that all your dogs were gunning for me." Before Stefan could comment, he pressed on. "That poisoned dagger was meant for me. The Executioner was targeting *me*. I may be nothing more than a twenty-something college student, but I scare you. Your people were convinced to follow me without much persuasion because I've got charisma. That's what scares you. I think you've realized your people are tired of following a tyrant. They'd rather have someone like me, no matter the age. Getting away from you is worth that risk. It makes a very dangerous and scary predicament for you. If you can't stamp me out, you're completely finished."

"You don't scare me, boy," Stefan spat in disgust. "Your friends are all dead. You'll shortly follow. All you've been is a mere inconvenience. I'll have to clean your friend's brains off my balcony, and that will be the worst of this little revolution." He nodded in Priya's direction, as if daring Camden to see for himself.

Camden couldn't stop from turning to look where Priya had fallen. What he found surprised him. Priya was still down and deathly still, but Oakley was battling Carl and holding his own. The teen was fighting with a revenge-filled rage, his face red with exertion.

A split second before Kristie screamed his name, Camden realized he'd been baited into turning his back to Stefan. He had just enough time to dodge out of the way as a sword slashed downward at his skull.

Stefan had used so much force behind the strike that when his sword hit the ground, it gave a clang and shot up a shower of sparks.

Camden was on his back on the hard brick of the roof. He didn't have time to get up before Stefan was stabbing the sword downward at him. He scrambled backwards as quickly as he could. The sword hit the ground between his legs, dangerously close to his groin, and embedded itself between two bricks.

Stefan yanked violently at it, but instead of coming free, the handle snapped. With a snarl of disgust, he tossed the handle aside and stomped toward Camden. "I am going to enjoy watching you die."

Camden attempted to get to his feet, but the other man was on him before he could get upright. Stefan grabbed him by the shoulders and shoved him backwards onto the unforgiving brick.

Camden saw stars as the back of his head cracked against the ground. He was momentarily disoriented, giving his opponent an opening. Stefan dove on top of him. His hands transformed into claws and wrapped around Camden's throat. "Do you have any last words?"

Camden opened his mouth to say something sarcastic, but before he could even get anything out, Stefan let go with one hand and drove a fist into his face. He tasted blood, hot and tangy on his tongue. To be spiteful, he spit the blood into Stefan's face. "You're the one who should be worrying about last words."

Stefan growled and tightened his grip on Camden's throat. His free hand returned to its position, and he squeezed with all of his strength, cutting off any flow of oxygen to Camden's lungs.

Camden's bravado faltered when he felt the crushing pressure. He was already feeling dizzy from cracking his head against the bricks of the roof. Being choked was just adding to the damage.

His vision blurred and he feared he might pass out. If he passed out, everyone he cared about would die. Kristie would die. He knew that with a certainty that scared him. Priya was already unconscious, probably dead. It was up to him to do something. Everyone's lives depended on it.

Reaching up, he grabbed at Stefan's hands, attempting to pry the man's fingers loose. Though he tried, it was becoming a losing battle. He was feeling weak from lack of oxygen. It was an effort just to stay conscious.

In the background, he heard Kristie's screams but couldn't respond. He wanted to tell her to look away. He did not want her to witness his death. Not again.

"Get off of him!" Kristie's voice was closer now. "Leave him alone, you dick!"

Camden felt extra weight for only a moment. Then Stefan's hands released his throat. He sucked in a big, gasping mouthful of air and forced his eyes to focus.

Kristie was on Stefan's back, digging her nails into his face.

Stefan reared back with a snarl. Reaching over his shoulder, he grabbed Kristie by the hair. He then flipped her over his shoulder, dumping her into Camden's lap while he was still trying to recover from his near death experience.

She was there only momentarily before Stefan's hand wrapped around her throat. With inhuman strength, he yanked her up into the air. Holding her aloft, he marched purposefully toward the side of the building. "You've outworn your welcome," he snarled at her.

Kristie's eyes widened in fear, and she clawed at his fingers. Her feet kicked at the air as her face turned red with the exertion of trying to free herself from his grasp. "N-no," she pleaded. "Please. Don—"

Stefan shook her like a rag doll in an effort to silence her. "It's too late for pleading!" He lifted her up over the protective wall of the roof and held her out over the sonorous drop.

"Let go of her," Camden begged as he struggled to get to his feet. He felt panic well up inside of him at the knowing look on Kristie's face. She thought she was going to die. Stumbling over his own feet, Camden tried to get to them, tried to stop what would be the most devastating loss of his life. "Please!"

Stefan gave a brief, mocking smile over his shoulder at Camden before returning his gaze to Kristie. "You're of no more use to me," he said dismissively.

Before Camden could reach them, Stefan chucked Kristie over the side of the building and out into the open air beyond. She screamed in shrill terror as her body dropped from sight, plummeting over three stories to the cement patio below.

Camden gave a shout of horror as his girlfriend disappeared from view. A moment later, he heard the crunching sound of her body hitting the pavement. He felt sick to his stomach as her screams were abruptly cut off. Dread and grief filled him. There was no way Kristie could have survived that fall. He knew that deep down to his very core.

He'd known going in that people might die, but he'd never expected it to be the woman he loved. She was so beautiful and vibrant. She loved life and had a brilliant future ahead of her. She'd been planning on becoming his wife. Now, she was gone. "You're a monster," he choked out mournfully. "She was innocent in all of this."

Stefan dusted his hands off with a cruel smirk. "She was with you, wasn't she? I was able to get to you through her. That was her part in all of this. She was as guilty as poor dead Priya over there, and the guilty must die."

Yes. They should, Camden thought darkly. He felt hatred, hot and unforgiving, burn its way up his chest, racing through his veins. If Stefan had done this to get him to renounce his claim on the territory, the plan had backfired. He was not crippled with sorrow. In fact, he had never wanted to kill anyone as much as he did right now.

"Why don't you surrender, keep more of your followers from getting killed?" Stefan spoke the request as if it was actually an option, as if there was still a chance of a peaceful agreement. "I will spare some of your people if you do. I will give you a merciful execution so you can join your girlfriend in the afterlife. It will be better this way."

"No," Camden said darkly.

Stefan looked surprised at his hostile response. "What?"

"No," Camden repeated. "I will never surrender to you. Ever. Life will be better for everyone once you're dead." With that, he lunged forward and slashed his sword downward on Stefan's arm. The blade sliced clean through bone and meat. He was surprised when it traveled neatly through and slammed into the ground below. Stefan's arm severed, everything below his forearm dropping to the ground with a wet, bloody plop.

It took him a moment to react, to fully realize what had been done to him, but then Stefan was hollering in outrage and pain. He gripped at the bleeding stump, his eyes wide with disbelief. Then they lifted to Camden, and he gave a loud, inhuman howl. His holler transformed into something that would terrify any sane man. Before Camden's eyes, the other man's body began to change.

Stefan's skin rippled, transforming into scales as black as coal. He gave another roar as his figure molded itself into something different, this one loud enough to shake the floor.

Camden gulped and took a nervous step backwards. He'd thought he had an advantage, but that shrank away once Stefan entered dragon form. Even with one arm, the other man was more agile, more experienced.

Fearing all he'd managed to do was piss Stefan off, Camden's mind scurried for the best counter action to the man's sudden body modifications. Moving quickly with the decision that popped into his head, Camden followed Stefan's lead. He shifted into his dragon form. He felt his hands transform into talons; he felt his tail force its way through the seat of his pants.

Before Stefan, he'd never seen a dragon complete the transformation this closely. It was amazing, yet a little frightening to know his body was doing the exact same things, but instead of black scales, his back flowed with green.

Now that he'd embraced his other form, it came painlessly and easily, like he'd been doing this his entire life. One moment he was the human version of himself that his parents would recognize. The next, he was the beast within.

Despite the fact that Camden was bigger in this form, Stefan was still much larger and made an intimidating sight, red ridges trailing down the length of his spine in raised crests. It looked almost like protective plating, and Camden would just bet it was nearly impossible to break through. The other man had a built-in defense system.

Camden's only slight advantage was that Stefan was down an appendage. Since he'd changed shape, the severed flesh was no longer bleeding as a human's might. It was now leaking a green substance.

When the other man took a swipe at him, Camden lunged out of his reach. An involuntary snarl escaped his lips. The inhuman sound of it surprised him. He wasn't used to hearing a noise like that coming from himself, wasn't used to feeling it rumble up his chest.

"Trying to play with the big kids, I see," Stefan taunted him in a demonic voice as he took a cautious step to the side, looking for an opening in which to attack.

Camden ignored his comments. He was so angry, so full of bloodlust that he couldn't think about anything but ending the other man's life. What Stefan had done to Kristie could never be undone; it could never be forgiven. He'd taken the most important thing in Camden's life and stripped it away. He didn't want to exchange witty banter. He just wanted to be standing over Stefan's dead body.

With another snarl, he whipped his tail around, bringing the heavy weight and rough scales down against Stefan's elongated neck.

The other man gave an injured yelp before rearing back out of range.

Camden pressed forward while he was on the offensive. He whipped his tail back around, clubbing Stefan in the shoulder.

When he went for a third strike, Stefan blocked with his own tail. The more experienced man darted in toward him. Before it could be averted, he raked his claws down Camden's shoulder. Talons dug into meat as they easily pierced flesh.

Camden gave a shout at the sudden and unexpected pain. He attempted to yank his arm out of the way, but it was numb and unresponsive. Fear gripped him as he realized Stefan must have cut through muscle or tendons. Now they were both down a limb.

Stefan must have seen the fear in Camden's eyes, because he gave a cruel chuckle. "This is only the beginning of the pain I intend to inflict upon you. When I am done, your own mother won't even recognize your face."

Camden ignored this as well and instead brought a clawed hand up to gouge along the soft flesh of Stefan's abdomen, trying to slice him open enough to do serious damage. Along a dragon's back and tail, there were hard scales meant to protect, but the belly was more exposed, more delicate. This was where he aimed his attack.

Stefan hissed, but instead of jumping back, he moved in closer. "Your face will be unrecognizable, just like your girlfriend's is now." His expression was one of amusement as he asked, "Do you think her skull caved when she hit the pavement? Do you think she hit head first? I suppose it would have been quicker that way. If she landed feet first, she probably suffered a bit before dying. Her femurs would have snapped, and her organs would have been crushed." He smirked. "I think that might be one of the most agonizing ways to die. The pain must have been unimaginable."

Just as he'd been aiming for, Stefan's words made Camden freeze. He gaped in horror at the other man as he envisioned Kristie hitting the cement in great detail. He was unable to keep his mind from picturing her skull as it connected with the ground. For all he knew, she was still down there suffering, lingering. She might be wishing he was there to hold her hand while her life faded away.

While he was distracted with concern, Stefan jammed a sharp talon into Camden's gut. He dug it in as far as he could, forcing it through resisting flesh and tissue. "Are you ready to join her?" With that, he yanked his arm back in a squirt of blood.

The pain nearly dropped Camden to his knees. He gasped at the sting left by the vicious talons. His injured arm struggled to cradle his bleeding abdomen. It rose a few inches before falling uselessly to his side once again.

It would have been difficult enough had he been in human form, but as a dragon, his arm felt more awkward, short in proportion to the rest of him perhaps. It was a challenge for him to be in this form without having a messed up arm. Now, it felt nearly impossible to maneuver. He hadn't spent enough time in this form to be comfortable with it.

Breathing in through clenched teeth, Camden forced himself to think past the pain. He drew strength from somewhere deep inside that he didn't even know existed.

When Stefan went for the killing blow, his deadly claws aimed for the jugular, Camden clumsily spun out of his grasp. He broke free of Stefan's grip, spun behind him, and drove a foot into the other man's spine.

When he'd shifted form, Camden had torn through not only his clothing but his shoes as well. Now his feet were exposed, and there were matching claws to go with the ones on his hands. Those sharp nails sliced into Stefan's back, tearing at the scales that served as a protective layer.

Stefan snarled and kicked backwards at Camden, forcing some distance between the two of them. Then he immediately whirled around, his remaining arm rising defensively.

Camden swung his tail around in an attempt to bring it down on Stefan's forearm, but the other man managed to grab onto it with little effort.

Much like someone would a whip, Stefan wrapped the tail around his wrist. He continued to wrap it tighter and tighter, drawing Camden toward him. "I've had enough of you."

With his hand busy holding Camden's tail, Stefan used his only other available weapon. He leaned forward and sank his teeth into Camden's throat, aiming for the jugular.

The instant Stefan's fangs sank into his neck, Camden knew he was in trouble. He grabbed the other man by the shoulders, trying to hold him in place. If Stefan yanked backwards, it would tear his throat out.

He realized this was a losing situation. There was no way to pry Stefan off of him without doing irreparable damage to himself. The other man would have to let go, and Camden was almost certain that would only happen through a colossal act of violence. He would have to kill the other man to free himself. He didn't see any other way out of this.

With that grim realization, Camden forced his brain to work overtime. He struggled to find himself an offensive attack. He knew he wasn't a master at fighting in his dragon form, but he had grown pretty skilled with a sword.

Trying not to move too much, he glanced around the rooftop for his dropped weapon. He knew it couldn't be far. He'd had it only a few moments earlier. As luck would have it, he spotted the sword a mere few feet away.

Struggling to keep from injuring himself, Camden bent down and stretched out toward the sword. As he did, he returned his hand to its human form. His fingers felt along the ground, desperately seeking the weapon.

As if realizing what Camden was doing, Stefan gave a threatening growl and tightened his hold. He shook his head much like a dog would, doing as much damage as he could in an effort to stop his prey from defending itself.

Though he was in agony, Camden fought through the pain. He forced his hand to keep searching along the ground, and his persistence paid off. His fingers closed around the handle of his sword, and he yanked it upward.

Twisting his wrist around, he shoved the tip of the sword upward into Stefan's gut. With a howl of exertion, he leaned against the handle and forced the blade in all the way to the hilt. He felt the jarring impact as it sliced through everything and anything in its path.

Stefan gave a harsh gasp and released Camden as the point of the weapon punctured out his back to completely spear him.

Camden twisted the sword before ripping it back out of Stefan's body. He stepped back, watching the other man with wary eyes. Every inch of him ached, and he was exhausted. He wasn't sure he could hold himself upright much longer.

Luckily, the moment the sword was free, Stefan collapsed to his knees.

Camden lifted the sword up, his breath coming in shallow gasps. "It's over," he rasped with feeling. Before the other man could comment, Camden swung the sword around. He used all the force left in him as he brought the blade around into Stefan's throat.

When Stefan's severed head hit the ground, Camden's knees buckled, and he dropped to the bricks beneath him. His limbs were heavy and uncooperative. He couldn't stay upright any longer.

His vision swam, the sights before him blurring as time around him seemed to be moving in slow motion. Stefan's remaining gunmen threw down their weapons and raced back inside the building, but he had a hard time tracking their movements. Everything seemed off, funny. As he collapsed to his side, he shifted back into his human shape. He stared across the rooftop with glassy eyes and was almost certain he lost consciousness once or twice, but only for a few moments at a time.

Through heavy-lidded eyes, he saw something that made his heart give a dull thump of fear. Therius stood facing him, his eyes on Stefan's headless body. Camden had no idea how long the other man had been standing there, of how much he had seen. His unfocused eyes took in another figure, and he realized that Sage stood between him and the assassin, her attention all for Therius.

Therius's eyes left Stefan's dismembered head and slowly slid to Sage. For a moment, the two of them stared at one another as if frozen in place.

Camden struggled to lift himself up onto an elbow. Every last bit of energy and adrenaline had left him. He was defenseless. If things turned violent, he wouldn't even be able to help. Sage was tough as nails, but Therius was Stefan's assassin. He was born and bred to kill.

The two continued to stare at one another, the moment seemingly frozen in time.

Finally, Therius began taking slow, cautious steps backwards. His eyes never left Sage as he backed into the shadows and disappeared.

Sage stayed deathly still for a minute after he was out of sight. Her hands trembled with obvious terror, and her shoulders rose and fell with the nervous, shallow breaths she was sucking into her lungs. She eventually came back to her senses and surveyed her surroundings. When her eyes landed on Camden, she gasped. It was as if she'd been so terrified of Therius that she'd forgotten everything else around her, forgotten where she was. Once the situation came rushing back to her, she hurried to his side.

When she knelt in front of him, Camden teased her in a weak voice. "It's about time you showed up."

Sage brushed dark hair out of her eyes and surveyed him with concern. "Don't make me feel worse. You have no idea how badly I felt when I realized... I was in a meeting with my phone silenced. I left the office as soon as I got the message from Pius. I was in such a frantic state to get here that half-way here I sideswiped a parked car and popped a tire. I had to walk the rest of the way in heels."

Camden glanced at her feet and was surprised to find them bare and bloodied. "Where are your shoes?"

"I ended up ditching them and running barefoot." She shrugged carelessly. "I ran through some broken glass in a parking lot. It's not a big deal. The cuts are minor and will be healed almost instantly once I pick all the glass out. I'm more worried about you."

"I'm not dead," Camden groaned as she helped him to a sitting position. "Which means I'm fine. Help me over to Priya."

Sage nodded and hooked his arm over her shoulder. She helped him half crawl over to the spot where Priya lay.

Oakley had her body cradled in his lap. His eyes were wide, red-rimmed, and full of shock. Next to him lay Carl's headless body.

Camden blinked in astonishment. "You killed him? On your own?"

Oakley bobbed his head. "Yeah. He could have taken me out a dozen times, but he was toying with me because I was human. He underestimated me and paid for it."

Camden glanced at the headless body, still full of surprise. After a moment, he shook his head and turned his attention back to Oakley.

Kristie's brother had a painful-looking gash on his left arm, his lip was smeared with blood, and there was already an angry purple bruise forming on his cheek. "He deserved what he got," Camden reassured.

Oakley's hardened eyes lifted from Priya to lock onto Camden. "I know," he growled. "He was the one who...he hurt Priya." His expression became pained as he looked down at the woman in his lap. "I couldn't let him live. Especially after..."

Camden placed a sympathetic hand on his shoulder. "She'll come back. Just give her a little bit of time."

"I know," Oakley said quietly, relief finally touching his voice. He nodded toward Carl. "He won't, though."

Camden glanced at Carl's body, at the finality of the man's wounds. Such a blatant display of death made his stomach sink as another lost life pushed to the forefront of his mind. "Oakley," he said softly. "It's about your sister. Kristie... She..."

Oakley's eyes went to the section of building where Kristie had been thrown from the roof. "I saw," he said hoarsely. "I couldn't get away from Carl to do anything. I wasn't able to get to her." His eyes slid back to Camden's, and the two of them stared at each other in mournful silence.

It was only when Priya gave a pained moan that they drew out of their moment of mutual desolation. Both men looked down at her in concern.

With a soft sigh, Priya fluttered her lashes until her eyes opened. Her lips parted, and she reached a hand out to Camden. When he took it, she whispered, "We did it." Before he could respond, her back arched. She gave a cry of agony as her body convulsed in Oakley's arms. She was healing, but would pay the price for such a luxury.

Chapter 16

"For the last time," Priya said with annoyance, "I am perfectly fine. I'm a dragon. I'm immortal. I heal."

Oakley set her with a stern look and pulled her in against his chest, tucking her head under his jaw. "All the same, I'd like to keep you under my surveillance for the next couple hours."

"Stubborn human," she said with annoyance, but a pleased smile spread across her lips.

Camden watched them with amusement. When he'd first met Priya, he never would have guessed she'd be here now. She'd come a long way. They all had. He felt as if in the past week, he'd grown more than was humanly possibly...which made sense. He'd grown to be supernatural.

When he spoke, he tried to keep his tone authoritative, as many people were still looking to him for guidance. They would be until things were settled and he could officially pass leadership on to Priya. "Sage said all fighting has stopped below. She has been texting me with updates while you...healed. Word spread fairly quickly that Stefan fell. His remaining followers have either surrendered or fled. It looks like we've truly won this."

"Sage?" Priya asked in surprise. "She showed up?"

Camden nodded, checking another text as it came in. "Yeah. She had car trouble. She didn't make it here until the end, once most of the fighting had concluded. She's been very helpful while the two of us were healing, though." He noticed a grimace that flashed across Oakley's face. "What?"

he asked curiously.

"I'm just not so sure about Sage," Oakley said slowly.

Camden rolled his eyes in response. "You're just saying that because Priya does."

"No," Oakley argued. "Look. I hate to suspect the worst, but..." He shook his head. "She had a clean shot at Therius. She could have killed him. She didn't."

"I saw the two of them. It didn't look like she had an advantage to me," Camden argued.

"That was after you shifted back to human form and noticed them. Before that, she had him dead to rights, and she didn't take the shot."

"Therius was Stefan's assassin," Priya said with confusion. "He killed more of our own than almost any of them. Why would she even hesitate?"

"That's what I was wondering," Oakley added. "Her hesitation didn't make any sense. We need to keep an eye on her in the upcoming weeks. If she's planning to attempt to overthrow the power system, she'll probably want to do it while things are still chaotic."

"I was thinking the same exact thing." Priya gave him a bright smile and reached up to pat his cheek. "You're acting like the right-hand man to a leader already. Here I thought you'd just be like a trophy wife to me."

"A trophy wife?" Oakley asked with a laugh of amusement.

"I figured you were too pretty to be smart, let alone tactical."

Oakley sighed and hugged her closer. "Ah, I love this woman."

"You should. I'm amazing." Priya's gaze slid to Camden. "So what is Sage reporting? What are our casualties?"

"We have twelve confirmed dead from our side, eight still unaccounted for."

Priya cringed but nodded. "Okay." She took a deep breath and let it out slowly. "We'll have to facilitate a beautiful burial ceremony for them full of dragon rituals. They deserve nothing less for following us so faithfully."

"Hopefully some of the missing are going to be able to be revived," Camden said, trying to take the sting out of the high number of casualties. He went to say something else, but a familiar voice called out his name and made the words die in his throat. His entire body tingled with numb disbelief as he turned toward the doorway that led back into the building.

Kristie stood in the archway looking vibrant and so very much alive. "Camden!" She yelled his name and then was racing to his side.

Though his legs still felt wobbly, Camden moved toward her, feeling almost desperate to touch her, to make sure she wasn't just a wishful illusion. As soon as she was within arm's length, he swept her up into his arms and hugged her tightly against himself. "Kristie." He choked out her name, his voice thick and rough. He buried his nose in her hair and inhaled, drawing in her familiar scent.

A sob escaped him. It was ragged and full of emotion. "I thought you were dead." He loosened his grip only so he could pull back and look at her. He took her face in his hands and surveyed her with incredulity. "How are you not dead?"

She blinked up at him with her big blue eyes. "Well, Cammy—"

"She's your mate," Priya cut in as if this was something he should know. "You're immortal. By mating, you made her immortal as well."

Camden let out a noise of disbelief that melted into a laugh. "I didn't know! That is one of those 'minor details' you should have filled me in on."

Priya rewarded him with a guilty look. "I sometimes forget you weren't born one of us. You don't know the basics."

Camden rolled his eyes at her then returned his attention to Kristie. "I love you." Still cupping her face in his hands, he kissed her passionately, trying to put into that kiss all the emotion that was coursing through him. "I am so sorry I wasn't there for you when you came back. You must have been terrified."

Kristie shrugged. "I was only alone for a minute. Pius found me and walked me through it. Then Ward and his friend were there to help with moral support. It really wasn't that bad."

Camden looked over toward the doorway in curiosity. Pius was just disappearing back inside the building, presumably to help look for more survivors.

Ward was still present, standing just behind Priya and Oakley with his arm wrapped around the shoulders of a pretty brunette. He was battered and bruised. A large gash spread across his forehead, and blood trailed down into his right eye. He moved forward with a slight limp, but thankfully, his injuries weren't anything to worry over.

"What happened to follow us and stay hidden in the background?" Camden inquired.

Ward cringed apologetically. "I was doing that, but then I felt this tugging sensation...something was pulling me toward the locked basement. I know this is hard to believe, but I could feel Lila's terror. It was like she was calling to me through some sort of psychic connection. The guard down there was planning to execute hostages as punishment for the uprising. Once I realized what was happening, I couldn't let them kill unarmed allies."

The small brunette at Ward's side placed a hand on his chest just over his heart. "Ward saved me."

"It's a good thing Lila called me to them," Ward continued. "There were about a dozen kids locked up in the cellar. I took out the guard and helped escort them to safety." He looked down to Lila with an affectionate smile that was returned full force.

Camden recognized the love-struck look in the girl's eyes. He sent Priya a look of concern. "Um...how old is Lila?" It was weird enough that Oakley seemed to be in a relationship with a woman decades older than him. Ward was still in high school. It would be wrong in so many ways.

"Lila is sixteen," Priya assured. "She's one of the youngest of us, one of those kidnapped children I was telling you about." She smirked in amusement. "Lila is the daughter of Pius and his mate Elizabeth."

Camden cringed. He thought *his* girlfriend's parents were intimidating. Well, Ward knew what he was getting into. If he wished to date a girl whose parents breathed fire, then that was his decision.

Returning his attention to Kristie, Camden studied her with open amazement. "I can't believe you risked your life to help me." He ran a thumb over her bottom lip. "You're insane."

"I didn't just risk my life," she countered. "I died." A charming smile curved her lips. "I'd say this makes us even. You get no more special treatment for dying for me. We're even, pal."

Camden chuckled and pulled her in against his chest. "We're beyond even. No more dying. Okay?"

"Agreed."

Smiling, Camden lowered his mouth over hers, kissing her ever so gently. "I love you, Kristie Taylor."

"I love you, Camden Harrison," she whispered against his lips.

Camden deepened the kiss, his hands running suggestively along her hips. When he finally pulled back, he asked, "Will you marry me already?"

Kristie rewarded him with a bright smile. "You know I will."

Epilogue

Camden gazed at Kristie, awe welling up inside of him. She'd always been the most beautiful woman alive in his eyes, but she was even more stunning now. Now, she was a specimen of complete perfection. She was like an angel.

Her blonde hair was in a complicated updo of curls and braids. Her eyes sparkled with unadulterated happiness, and her cheeks were flushed with exhilaration. She wore a spaghetti strap wedding dress with a pale purple sash just under her breasts that left the rest of the gown flowing around her ankles. Her feet were bare, her toes curling into the warm Jamaican sand underfoot.

"You may now kiss the bride," the preacher said warmly, pulling Camden out of his reverie.

With an emotional smile, Camden pulled Kristie in against him and gave her a slow, passion-filled kiss. He tried to put into that kiss all the love and admiration he had for her.

When he tried to pull away, she wrapped her arms around his neck and pulled him closer, deepening the kiss. She opened her mouth under his and emitted a soft purr.

Groaning, he slipped his arms around her waist and tugged her against him again. A chorus of cheers erupted from behind them. As a united family, he and Kristie turned to face their guests.

Their immediate families stood before them. Dale and Alice had refused to be excluded from their daughter's wedding. Once they'd spoken to Camden's parents, there was no way it was going to stay a two person ceremony; eloping was no longer an option.

Camden and Kristie had decided to stick to the no frills ceremony on the beach they'd originally planned. Everything was kept quick and simple. There were no seats. Instead, the limited number of guests had stood in a semi-circle behind the bride and groom. Most of them were barefoot in the Jamaican sand as they soaked up the last dying rays of the sun.

Amongst the viewers were Ward and Lila, who was attached to him at the hip these days. Just behind them stood both sets of parents, the mothers each respectively wiping tears from their eyes.

To Ward's left were Oakley and Priya, two members of the small bridal party. Oakley looked confident and charming in his tux. His arm was wrapped possessively around Priya's hip, his hand dangerously low for public display. His fingertips grazed her backside, idly caressing.

Priya wore a backless, seafoam green dress that made her dark skin look even more exotic. Her dark hair was piled atop her head, loose tendrils cascading along her face.

On Oakley's other side stood Bradley, who was gazing at Camden with such open affection that he squirmed with embarrassment. Her hair and dress matched Priya's. Though Kristie hadn't instructed her two bridesmaids to coordinate their apparel, Priya and Bradley had insisted upon it.

A few feet away, there was a large covered tent where the bride and groom would be sharing their first meal as husband and wife. Beau watched from the shadows inside, looking more suave in his tux than any man in history to ever don formal wear. Beau could put James Bond to shame.

"This is so exciting," Bradley gushed, drawing Camden's attention away from Beau. "I can't believe you're married!" She pulled him into a big hug, squeezing him tightly. "You're all grown up now. I can't believe it."

With a laugh, Kristie took his arm and began leading him toward the tent. "Grown-ups don't have Batman sheets," she informed Bradley playfully. "It can get distracting when Robin is watching a girl do the nasty."

Bradley burst into surprised laughter. "I bet." She turned to Camden with a reproachful look. "Beau got you a ridiculous gift card to Bed Bath and Beyond. He figured you'd want girly towels and such to lighten up the former bachelor pad. Please buy some new sheets."

"That is a wise idea," Priya agreed as she ducked into the tent, dragging Oakley along with her. "You can't be making immortal dragon babies on Batman sheets. Besides, it's not becoming of a man who rules his own territory." She said all of this just as they were reaching the area where Beau was standing.

"Immortal dragon babies?" he asked with raised eyebrows.

Priya set him with a sharp look. "Yes, vampire. That's what dragons do, make dragon offspring. We are born immortal and superior to the humans. We don't cheat death through some silly virus as your kind does."

"Hey!" Bradley and Oakley cried in offended unison.

Priya waved them off. "You'll both be joining the supernatural community like little parasitic leeches before long. No sense getting all huffy over the truth."

Camden was too busy watching Beau's reaction to care much about Priya's insult to mortals. He watched the vampire with anxiety, awaiting the backlash from the information Priya had just divulged.

It was Bradley who reacted first as if just realizing what had been said. "Wait. What? Immortal dragon babies?" She gripped Camden's arms. "You're a *dragon*?"

"Yes," he answered nervously.

"Don't say it like that," Priya scolded with a slap to his chest. "You should be saying it proudly."

"You're a dragon with your own territory?" Beau asked. On Camden's confirming nod, he rolled his eyes. "It's going to be fun helping you defend that," he said sarcastically.

Camden's eyebrows rose in surprise. What Beau had meant as a jab, he took as the act of friendship it was. Beau would help him hold his territory. For the vampire, the extension of that help was downright gushy. "I thought you would kill me when you found out."

"Kill you?" Beau asked in surprise. "Why would I kill you for being a dragon?"

"I heard you and Bradley talking at the hospital." Camden saw his best friend flinch out of the corner of his eye. "You told Bradley when you found out what I was turning into, you'd 'take care of it'. What was I supposed to think?"

"That was only if you became something evil," Beau scoffed. "Not a dragon. Even then, I'd had other plans. If you became a murderous demon who went on a killing spree, I would have tried to have you exorcised or whatever. Killing whatever was inside of you wouldn't have necessarily meant killing you."

"Necessarily?" Camden squeaked.

Beau gave a careless shrug. "It all worked out, didn't it?"

Before Camden could respond, Bradley slapped him on the chest. "I can't believe you kept this a secret! Here I am worrying you were going to outgrow me. I thought you wouldn't want to hang out once Beau turned me and I stopped aging. I knew you hinted that something supernatural was going on with you, but this! This is...wow! Aunt Bradley and Uncle Beau won't seem so weird when your children are immortal themselves." A giddy grin spread across her lips and she pulled him into a hug. "You're immortal! This is amazing!"

"Uncle Beau?" Beau asked in horror.

Bradley rolled her eyes with a laugh. "You'll be cool Uncle Beau. I find that sexy."

"Really?" he asked in surprise.

She grinned up at him. "Definitely. Now let's go sit down. It looks like the DJ wants these two to have their first dance." She gave Camden another quick hug before darting away to one of the tables, dragging her boyfriend behind her.

Priya stepped up to take Bradley's place. "My leader," she greeted with a playful bow of her head.

"Don't call me that," Camden griped. "I'm deferring leadership to you, and you know it."

Priya smiled, her expression full of genuine affection. "You're a good man, Camden Harrison." She held a hand out for him to shake.

He looked at the hand in amusement. "Really? After everything we've been through together, you offer me a handshake?" He opened his arms to her. "I think I've earned a hug."

She glanced around as if to make sure no one was looking. "Oh all right, you silly man." She stepped forward and wrapped her tiny arms around his waist.

Camden enveloped her in his long arms, squeezing her shoulders tightly. "You'll be a good leader."

Priya pulled back and narrowed her eyes. "You just got married. You shouldn't be worrying about that crap." She patted his cheek a little roughly. "But thank you." She motioned toward the dance floor. "Now will you two go dance already? I'm starting to get hungry."

With a laugh, Camden took a step toward the dance floor, but Oakley grabbed his arm to halt him. The teen offered a teasing grin as he nodded at Kristie. "I suppose that's your cherry pie now. Take care of her. If you don't, I'll have to kick your ass."

"You can try, human."

"Like Priya said, I may be immortal sooner than you think. When that happens, I'll get super strength and will totally be able to kick your ass."

"Guess we'll have to wait and see." Camden grinned as he and Oakley bumped fists in an open display of camaraderie. It was something he hadn't thought possible only a few short months ago. As the couple ambled off arm in arm, he turned to Kristie. "Can I have this dance, Mrs. Harrison?"

"I thought you'd never ask." When he led her to the small dance floor, she wrapped her arms around his neck. "Mrs. Kristie Harrison. I like the sound of that."

"Me too," he agreed as the song they'd chosen for their first dance began floating through the speakers. "I never thought years ago when we met that we'd be here right now."

"I never thought when I was crying over your dead body that we'd ever get here," she chimed in agreement.

"Everything worked out." Camden pulled her in tighter against his chest. "Now we have an eternity to be together."

"I don't plan to waste a single minute of it," she informed him. "I am going to enjoy every moment we share." She ran a hand along his bicep, lovingly laying her head against his shoulder.

"Every moment?" he asked with a devilish smile that he pressed into her hair. "Even when I smash an entire piece of cake in your face?"

She pulled back with a gasp. "You wouldn't!"

"I have every intention, my dear." He tightened his grip on her and lowered his voice. "You know what else I have every intention of doing?"

She stared up at him with questioning blue eyes.

"I fully intend to have my way with you the moment all of our guests leave. First I'll drag you off to our honeymoon suite and cherish every inch of your skin." He punctuated this with a kiss to her bare shoulder. Or if I'm really impatient, maybe I'll keep you right here in our private slice of heaven. Now or later, I want to make love to you out in the surf. I don't even think I'm going to let you take that dress off if I decide to start celebrating here on the beach. I'll be too impatient. I've been waiting to have you all day."

Kristie shivered in delight. "I like the sound of that." Pressing her body suggestively to his, she said, "Designer dress be damned."

He gave a growl of desire. "When we're done fooling around in the waves, I'm going to bring you in and lay you down on the beach, just on the edge of the water. Then I'm going to make love to you in the sand."

Kristie closed her eyes for a moment, obviously envisioning such a scene. "After you do that, I'm taking you back upstairs to the hotel room our parents graciously shelled out for. First we'll share a shower, washing the sand from each other's bodies. Then I'm taking you back to the bedroom where I will ride you until the sun comes up."

When he lowered his mouth hungrily to hers, a few witnesses whistled in approval. Camden explored her mouth for a few precious moments, savoring her taste on his tongue. When they finally pulled back for air, he said, "Before any of that, I've got to smash cake on your face. That gets the whole ball rolling."

"Then smash away," she encouraged, giving him another slow, sensual kiss.

"I love you, Mrs. Harrison," he mumbled against her lips.

"I love you, Mr. Harrison," she said in return.

Camden gave her another quick kiss as their song ended. Then he spun to face the small group of assembled family and friends. "Who's ready for some cake?"

The End

About the Author

Melissa lives near Pittsburgh, Pennsylvania with her husband, Jeremy, and her son, Marshall Frost. Her favorite genre to write is Paranormal Romance.

Melissa attended London School of Journalism where she received her certificate in Novel Writing in 2011. She writes a monthly short story column titled *Frequent Flyer* for a government newsletter.

Make-believe is more than a child's game!